Saving Addy

Saving Addy

Hidden Series Book Two

LM Terry

Saving Addy

Copyright © 2019 LM Terry

Published by LM Terry

All rights Reserved

ISBN-13: 9781092843058

Dedication

To all the souls who have been hurt and still manage to see the magic in life.

Lovers and dreamers will always survive.

Table of Contents

Magic

And above all, watch with glittering eyes the whole world around you because the greatest secrets are always hidden in the most unlikely places. Those who don't believe in magic will never find it.

~Ronald Dahl

Preface

Addy

They are close on my heals as I run through dark alleys. The acrid smell of rotting food burns my nose as I dodge trash barrels. My sneakers and the bottom of my jeans are heavy, sodden with dank water from puddles I have splashed through. The devil is chasing me…he will make me pay for what I have done.

I tried making amends, but it didn't matter. My father warned me as a child that no one could escape their fate. I tried to be good, really I did. I guess I am destined to spend the rest of my days paying for my sins.

I shouldn't have returned to Mexico. But, I wanted to make a difference in this world. That is all I ever wished for, to follow in father's footsteps, to aid others. Eight years of hard work trying to turn my wrong into a right, but obviously it wasn't enough. Shit, I am so dumb, why, why did I come back? I know why. For the people who needed my help.

I round the corner trying to lose myself in a crowd outside a local bar and bump into a man bouncing off his large frame. He reaches out gripping both of my arms to steady me. I look up at the massive figure looming over, he smiles down at me. The tequila on his breath assaults me.

"Please let me go, I need to go!" I say to the guy with urgency looking over my shoulder.

The man does not relinquish his hold on me, instead he gazes over the top of my head. I study his face as he spots what has me running like a skitzy rabbit from a wolf. He will surely release me, let me run. Everyone here recognizes Javier's men, and they all fear them.

Evidently everyone but him.

He wraps me up in the protective cocoon of his chest. I'm mesmerized as I watch his eyes grow dark. I brace myself as I hear the men shouting behind me. I prepare myself to be plucked out of his arms at any moment. I take a few deep breaths and close my eyes.

Javier's lackeys skid to a stop behind me. The crowd hushes, whispers follow. I tremble and latch on to the man's shirt with my tiny fists willing my eyes to open. Everyone around has evaporated as if the magic of the moon has cast its glow down and transported them to the heavens.

I peek up at the burly man holding me tight to his chest. He stares the men down, his gaze flicks from man to man, like a hawk scoping out prey. I turn my face slightly to the side and peer behind me. Javier's men have halted and are now parting for him. Javier stalks out stopping a few feet in front. He cocks his head, narrowing his eyes at me with that trademark smirk and then lifts them to the man sheltering me.

"Well, well, what do we have here?" Javier hums with that voice that sends lightning bolts of fear shooting down my spine.

"What we have here, is *me* taking *her*." The big guy nods downward, shaking me slightly in his arms.

Saving Addy

Javier laughs loudly pivoting to look at his men, they all hesitantly laugh. Most appear like they don't find as much humor in the statement as he. "Oh really, and just where do you think *you* are taking *her*."

"Hmm, let's see. How about I take her to Oliver Wright and you all can fuck off?" he growls above me.

My heart stops for a long beat as I stare at the expression on Javier's face. I swallow watching him reach into his pocket to pull out a cigar. He lights it then offers it to the man holding me. The big guy leans forward to take the smoldering gift. I grab him around the waist tightly hoping that he doesn't dump me into Javier's arms.

He straightens and draws off it, inhaling deeply then lets the smoke roll out of his mouth. Like a thunderhead on the horizon I watch the transformation from innocent cloud to raging thunderstorm. My heart hammers in my chest, something is not right.

"Please give my regards to Mr. Oliver and let him know that I may be interested, after the training period of course. This one…" he pauses and shakes his cigar at me, "has cost me a great deal, but I would be happy to incur further expense for the proper obedience." Javier's words cut through the fog billowing over my head. What is he saying? His cryptic statement has sent my brain scrambling to decipher.

"And you are?" the large man inquires as plumes of smoke filter out of his nose and mouth.

"Javier, Javier Galindo." Javier flashes him a bright smile, bows and turns on a heel walking away. His men follow behind him.

My legs crumble beneath me with relief. The stranger's strong hands scoop me up and whisk me aside to a dark car parked across the road in the shadows. A man hops out of the driver's seat and quickly opens the back door for us. The big guy sets me on my feet gently pushing me into the car. As soon as I duck my head inside I come to my senses. What am I doing? I need to return to the others. How could I even consider getting into this vehicle?

I stop halfway and drag myself back out of the car.

"Thank you for your help, but really my friends are not that far away. I'll be fine now, thank you again for your help," I say struggling to control the tremor in my voice.

"In," my savior orders.

He is my savior right?

Right?

"Wh…who are you?" I ask struggling to speak.

"My name is Brian, but soon you will call me something much worse I am sure." He runs his thumb over my bottom lip and I quickly suck it between my teeth, denying him access.

Swallowing hard, I peer up at him, he smiles and places his hand on the top of my head gently pushing me down into the car. I slowly shrink myself into a ball and roll into the backseat.

Have I run from the flames only to jump into the fire? Time to pay up sweet Addy…time to pay up.

Chapter One

Addy

The first days of being Master Oliver's captive was all I needed to realize that fate had finally caught up. I accepted it. I knew I was being punished for what I had done all those years ago. Well, I guess I didn't accept it in the beginning. It didn't take long to break me, sometimes I think I should have fought harder, others I think I should've acquiesced sooner.

The man who kidnapped me was Master O's best slave trainer. He had saved me from one demon only to deliver me to another. But, the day I laid my sword down at his feet propelled me further into the bowls of hell. It didn't seem so. If I had known how things would end, I wouldn't have set that blade down, I would have struck that fucking thing into my chest.

He had been water boarding me because I refused to eat. At some point this little voice entered my head and told me that if I submitted he would save me. He would be my savior. That is how I've always seen him since bumping into him that first fateful day. I shouldn't have listened. Maybe in a different life he would have been. This life, my life, it isn't about being saved...it is only about being punished.

Brian fell in love with me that day, the day I submitted to him. I kept my eyes trained on his as he cut off my oxygen. The wet cloth over my face was barely rising and falling. I remained calm with my head in his lap staring up into his dark eyes. I didn't flinch. I didn't cry. I didn't fight. I laid perfectly still and allowed him to see into the depths of my soul as he held me on the edge of life and death. I saw something pass over his features and from that moment on he tried everything he could to keep me safe.

We spent our days and nights together. He trained me during the daytime, hoping that his boss wouldn't notice his feelings for me. He told me if Master O ever found out he would be angry. It was the nights I lived for. In the dark of my cell he would hold me, we would stay awake for hours just talking. We shared stories of our lives. I learned that he didn't deserve to be in hell. He was there because of the sins of others…I was there for my own.

Eventually, Master O discovered that Brian was coming to me and he sent me away. Master is the only person I've been allowed to speak to since then. He stripped me of everything, my name, my voice, my soul. No, that is not true. I kept my soul. I built a wall for it the day I came here. I spend my time making sure the bricks and mortar are secure. It's not as easy as it sounds, I must keep one foot on the outside of the barricade so I can function. You know the basics…eat, sleep and shower. I can't shut them out completely.

It is most hard when Master Oliver visits. Most of the days I can hide on my side of the wall. Usually, my captors only come three times a day to bring me meals and once a week I am allowed out of the room to shower. But, when he comes it is more difficult. It is the only time I'm able to speak. I don't want to communicate with him, he demands that I do so. It means I must listen to what he is saying so I maintain the proper responses. One foot in, one foot out. Kind of like when you sleep at night and keep one leg outside the covers…but only one. The rest of you remains covered to protect you from whatever lies awake in the dark.

Yesterday was one of those days. During his visit he told me that Brian made an arrangement with him the day he sent me away. That was almost thirteen months ago. The deal would have allowed me to be with Brian. Hearing his name made a slight crack in my wall, I stepped out a little further than I normally would, and it didn't end well for me. Unfortunately, Brian had betrayed him. Dread filled me as I realized that he was speaking as if he would end his life.

He told me he sold me. I had become useless to him. He introduced me to the man who had purchased me, no introductions were needed, I could smell his sweet tobacco scent before I even raised my eyes. I tried to retreat behind my wall, but I couldn't hide, that damn crack had formed so I was forced to endure, there was no hiding.

Anyhow, I have been working tirelessly since then laying more bricks fortifying my fortress. Oliver is taking me to my new owner soon. I'm not sure my wall will hold him out. I hadn't realized how many devils existed in this world. Hell must surely be empty.

Now, the real penance begins.

Chapter Two

Addy

The day is here. How do I know? Because they came for me right after lunch, it is not part of my normal routine. They made me shower and prepare myself. Master Oliver must be here. I thought maybe he had forgotten me. He was supposed to come eight weeks ago. I am ready; my wall is as secure as it's ever been. His delay gave me extra time to lay more bricks.

When I hear the keys clang, I place my forehead on the cold wooden floor and stretch my arms out in front of me, palms down. I quickly jump behind my barrier, leaving only one foot out. The door opens, more than one set of footsteps enter my room. Oh no, it is hard to deal with two devils at once.

"So, this was Wright's girl?" a rich voice says above me.

It's not him. It's not his voice. My pulse picks up a beat.

"Yes. I am glad you contacted me. Oliver had secured a buyer for her. He was supposed to pick the slave up several weeks ago, but he didn't show. I was just about to put her up on the next auction, I can't keep feeding and sheltering her without making a profit." This voice I recognize, he owns this place. He never speaks to me nor I to him…master doesn't allow me to speak to anyone. But, I've heard him outside my door talking to the other girls. I'm not sure what is going on. I need to see Master O. He will tell me what to do. Where is he?

"Hmm, what is her name?"

The owner laughs. "She doesn't have one, you can call her whatever you like."

"What do you mean she doesn't have one?"

"Oliver's rules, no one speaks to her, and she speaks to no one. Don't need a name for that type of relationship. Oliver had been paying me to care for her basic needs. My men bring her meals and take her down to shower, she knows what to do. But, I promise you she is a perfect slave, Oliver's best trained her. Would you like to spend the evening with her before you make the purchase? Sit up girl, let our customer see your pretty little face."

I slowly drag myself up to my kneeling position keeping my eyes lowered to the floor. The man crouches down and grabs my chin gently raising it, encouraging me to meet his gaze. I peek out from behind my wall. He is frightening, his dark eyes pierce me. It's as if he knows that I'm in here hiding. Where is Master O? What am I supposed to do? I haven't taken directions from anyone besides my master for over a year. He will be angry knowing that these men are here in my room…touching me.

"I don't need to spend the evening with her, I'll take her," the deep-voiced man says. He doesn't shift his eyes away from me and my heartbeat strums an uneven staccato.

"Are you sure? Usually customers want to taste the product first. We have many rooms set up here, you will find our accommodations are top-notch. You and your slave are both welcome to stay."

The man runs his thumb over my cheek then twists his head speaking over his shoulder. "Anna, come meet our new friend." He turns back keeping his hold on me, lulling me with the gentle strokes.

A girl crawls forward and kneels beside him. He shifts his focus to her. My eyes drift to hers. Large sapphires stare at me. "What do you think, pet, should we bring her home with us?"

"Yes, sir. She is lovely."

He grips my chin tightly forcing my gaze to his. Then he speaks to the owner as he stares deep into the world I have built for myself. "I will take her. We need to catch a plane so no need to entertain us this evening." He pauses as if deep in thought, then a smile slowly unfolds on his face as he adds, "I think I'll call her Addy."

My wall crumbles, I tear my gaze away from his, struggling desperately to repair the damage.

"Very well, shall we go down to my office and finalize the transaction?"

"Yes, but first I would like you to find something for Addy to wear. My girls are for my eyes only."

"Of course, why don't we leave them here while we have a drink. I will find someone to round her up something," the owner says as he ushers the scary guy from my room.

Saving Addy

When the door closes, and the lock clicks the girl they left behind reaches out slowly and places her hand over mine. It distracts me momentarily from my repairs. She whispers, "it's okay. He will not hurt you."

I tug my hand away and continue my work. I don't know who this man is, but he knows my name. Did Master O send him to test me? Or, did Javier hire him to collect me? It doesn't matter. I need to protect myself…whoever this is, he is just another vessel in which to deliver the punishment for my sins.

Chapter Three

Addy

The sky is beautiful, it's as if I stepped out from the gloom of inner earth into the garden of Eden. I pause absorbing the blue and fuchsia colors. The evening is chasing the sun away, turning it into a painting with brush strokes of an unworldly palette. I take in every spectrum. The breeze whispers along my skin, I shiver at the foreign feel. Why is God allowing me this glimpse? It is not meant for me. Is this just another form of punishment? A reminder of what life could have been.

A warm palm on my back drags me out of my thoughts to my current situation. I notice that the scary man and girl are gone. The hand belongs to a new guy, he is gently urging me towards a building. I glance at it. It is a hotel. I thought we were getting on an airplane. The scary man told the owner of the club we had a plane to catch. My gaze returns to the sunset. I don't want to go inside…each time I am taken into a building the outside world is stolen from me. It has been over a year since I have been allowed out.

The man by my side leans forward catching my eyes with his. "It is okay, Addy, you are safe now. Just come in, sweetheart. You will see the sky again soon, I promise."

Saving Addy

His eyes are blue like the heavens above. Or are they the color of the deepest parts of an ocean? For a minute I am lost, swimming in them, enjoying the moment of the weightlessness they provide.

The scary guy comes over to us. "Everything okay out here?" He reaches out and grips my hand pulling me along by his side as we make our way into the building. "I shouldn't have brought Anna, I can see it has drawn dark shit to the surface," he says.

Mr. Blue Eyes follows beside us. "She insisted that she come, she will work through it. Give her a minute to grasp the gravity of what just happened. She saved Addy, let her have a moment to wrap her head around it."

Quickly I try to get behind my wall before we cross the threshold to the hotel, but their conversation has me captivated. The girl, Anna, she saved me? I'm confused, she is a slave of the scary man…I am a slave of the scary man. I screech to a halt as my mind reels, I shouldn't have left, Master O will kill me. These people have been talking to me…no one is allowed to talk to me. Why did I fall into this trap, I don't know what to do? I need to go back to the club and wait for master's orders.

My new owner sighs and picks me up off my feet carrying me to a room at the far end of the hall. When we enter the room I see the girl, Anna, sitting on a bed weeping. Why is she crying? She said he wouldn't hurt me…she must recognize that he will. Maybe he'll punish her too for talking to me back at the club. He sets me down carefully on the other bed and then goes to her pulling her into his arms. She curls into him. He doesn't appear angry. He looks sad.

I allow myself to survey the room. There are several computers and another man typing furiously at a keyboard. He hasn't looked up once. He is fixated on the screen. I'm finding myself growing alarmed, I haven't been frightened in a long while. I've felt little of anything. I guess the day that Master Oliver brought Javier with him but that time I really didn't have time to be scared, I was focused on survival. I shudder thinking about him, Mr. Blue Eyes notices and pulls a blanket out of a closet. He hesitantly hands it to me. I'm not cold, in fact I'm rather hot. I'm not used to being in clothes, they are itchy, restricting and warm.

"Go ahead, Addy, take it. I saw you shiver, are you cold?"

Should I answer? Master O said I couldn't talk to anyone and that no one could speak to me. But, this man asked me a question, if I fail to respond I will be punished. What do I do? I don't understand what is going on. I want my master. I panic, this is awful. I need to know what he wants me to do. Why did everything change? I knew what was expected of me and I could hide behind my wall, but this is foreign.

I decide it best if I just ask for him. Master O can't get mad at me for that, can he?

"Sir, may I ask a question?" I squeak out.

Everyone in the room stops what they are doing and looks at me. Oh no, I did something wrong. You are such a dummy. I drop my gaze to my lap scrambling to pull both legs over to my side of the wall.

Mr. Blue Eyes sits down beside me placing the blanket aside. "Addy, you can ask us anything, you are free to say whatever you want. We are rescuing you. You are not a prisoner any longer."

Rescuing me? I don't understand, the scary man bought me. I need Master O.

"May I speak to Master Oliver...please?" I inquire struggling to keep the desperation out of my voice.

The girl across from me cries louder. Crud what have I done? I am in for a punishment for sure. The big scary guy stands, making me jump back on the bed. But he doesn't come to me, he pulls Anna to her feet and takes her out of the room. Deep breath, Addy, here it comes, get ready to hide....

"I'm sorry, sweetheart, but Oliver is dead," the man sitting next to me says.

No. That's not true. But, if it is what am I going to do? I stare at him. "Then who is my master?"

He sighs and reaches out pulling me into his arms. I want to pull away, but I can't, I can never defy them, not unless I wish to be punished. "You don't have a master anymore. I know this must be hard for you to grasp but you are free, Addy. Oliver will never hurt you again."

What? Oliver never hurt me. I'm scared, what if he is dead, who will take care of me? Could they be taking me taking me to Javier? "Are you delivering me to my new master then?"

He shifts to look at me. "No, we are not taking you to a new master, we will help get you back to your loved ones."

"So, the guy with the girl...is he?"

Mr. Blue Eyes closes them drawing a deep breath. "No."

"Are you?" I peek up at him shyly. I need to know who I should listen to.

He looks over his shoulder to the guy at the computer nodding for him to join us. The man gets up and kneels on a knee in front of me. "Addy, my name is Anthony, and this is Liam. The couple that left, their names are Dylan and Anna. We run a security business that saves young women who've been kidnapped by traffickers. We only bought you to bring you out of there, we are not one of them. It's okay to be confused but, you need to understand that you do not have a master anymore. You are free to do as you wish. But, don't worry we are not abandoning you. We will help get you to your family and friends."

I stare at the man he called Liam. My head is hurting, I can't do this. Everything is falling apart. I want my room at the club. "Take me back," I say on the verge of hysteria.

He exchanges a glance with Anthony then stands retrieving a bag setting on the desk. He pulls out a syringe. "Addy, I am going to give you something to help you relax for a bit."

"No, please, I want to go back. You don't understand, I need to go back." I try to stand but Anthony draws me down into his lap and then Liam sticks the needle into my arm. There is no time to retreat behind my wall as the heaviness of sleep tugs at my eyelids and darkness envelopes me.

Chapter Four

Liam

Addy thinks we are the bad guys. She is confused and who can blame her. From what Dylan told me Oliver had kept her at the club keeping her isolated from basically everyone but him. Eventually, I sedated her.

The whole situation just sucks. Anna and Addy are both distraught. Both tug at my heartstrings. Anna has become like a sister to me. Anthony, Dylan, Anna and I all work together. We locate women that end up in the sex trafficking industry. Anna's father started the business many years ago.

I'm worried that Addy may be lost. She panicked when she caught on to what was happening. You would assume that rescued girls would be happy to be found. But, that is not always the case. It depends on how long they have been captive…or how badly they've been broken.

Time…time is a bitch. Sometimes we are just too late.

"Hey man the plane is about to land. How is she doing?" Dylan whispers, both girls are sleeping.

"Fine, I've kept her sedated the whole time. I'm not looking forward to waking her. We have a lot to explain."

"Yes, we do. But at least she is out of there. You should have seen it Liam. She had nothing in her room but a thin mattress and a blanket."

"That's fucked up. I text my dad, he is at the estate. Hopefully, he will be able help. I don't know Dylan. She may be lost for good."

"No, don't say that. I watched her closely when I called her by her name at the club. She is in there. She is smart I can tell. She has sheltered herself. I see why that asshole Brian held a liking to both Addy and Anna...they are cut from the same cloth."

"I'm glad you took Anna out of the room when you did. Addy didn't seem too upset when I told her Oliver was dead. She was more agitated with her not having a master anymore. She asked if you were and when I said no, she asked if I was. Thankfully Anthony stepped in, I was so frustrated."

"It's okay, Liam, there is no right or wrong here. We will just take one day at a time with her. We have to be patient," Dylan says patting my leg as he gets up going back to his spot by Anna.

I'm so glad they have each other. They are perfect together. I glance at Addy, sleeping in the seat next to mine. He could be correct. She might be hiding inside herself. She looked so beautiful when she got out of the car. I don't think she even noticed that Dylan and Anna had gone into the hotel.

Her big brown doe eyes scanned the sky, I could almost see her cataloging every image, every color and tucking it away within herself.

Without thought my hand reaches out to her and runs over her hair, it is so soft, I brush a strand that has fallen over her face back and tuck it behind her ear.

I wonder what her story is. Maybe I will stick around for a while. Dylan could use an extra hand couldn't he? I should return to the states and clean out my apartment. I had been working for the FBI, but I recently quit. I've joined the team full time again. This is where I belong.

Where do you belong, Addy? She wiggles in her seat, the drug I gave her is wearing off. I pull her into my arms and signal Anthony over to give her a little more to keep her asleep…at least until we are home.

Chapter Five

Addy

S omething isn't right. Where am I? I open my eyes to see that I am in a beautiful room laying on a wonderfully soft bed. Shit, I jump off and quickly lower myself to the floor. Someone walks over to me. I brace myself for the punishment that is to follow.

It is the scary man, Dylan. "Don't be afraid. Anna will be back in a second, she is gathering clothing and personal items for you."

For the first time in many, many months I feel like crying. The knot in my throat is getting tighter by the minute. I don't know what is expected of me here. I miss the club...it was easy there.

"Is she awake?" Anna says from the doorway.

Dylan sighs. "Yes. Look, Anna is back. Shower and then we can get dinner and discuss things okay?"

He reaches down and gently pulls me to my feet. "Go with her, she will help you. You are safe here." He walks out of the room, stopping to give Anna a kiss on the cheek.

"Come on, the bathroom is right in here." She steps towards a door. She opens it wide so I can see in.

I follow Master Dylan's orders and hesitantly walk in keeping my eyes trained to the floor. She follows me. "I'm not sure what things you might need but this is a start." I watch as she sets a pile of clothing and other toiletry items on the counter. "There is shampoo and conditioner in the shower already. Also, there is an electric razor down here under the sink if you would like to use it. This will be your room while you are here. If there is anything else you want, please let me know." Then she leaves me...alone.

I catch my reflection. It has been almost two years since I've seen myself. I crumble to the floor. I don't recognize the girl in the mirror. I sit there for a long time, unsure of what to do. Someone knocks lightly. "Are you okay Addy, I don't hear the water?" Anna says. She is talking quietly on the other side. The door opens and I right myself to kneel before them.

Anna crouches down in front of me gently cupping my face with her small petite hand. It is so soft and warm. I haven't felt the touch of another woman in so long. The lump in my throat grips me again. Dylan walks in behind her.

"Tell us what's going on, sweetheart," he says.

He frightens me, Anna doesn't seem scared of him.

"Addy?" he questions with more authority in his tone.

"I'm sorry Master Dylan, this is all new. I...I am just not sure what to do...how to please you. I...could you provide me with some direction." I peek up, oh no, he looks angry now. I crawl back a few steps, intimidated by his presence.

Anna looks up at him and reaches out taking his big hand giving it a squeeze. He pauses for a moment and then walks out.

"Here, why don't I help you?" She stands and turns the shower on. She pulls me to my feet and undresses me then pushes me gently in under the spray of the warm water. "Go ahead and wash yourself. I'll sift through the clothing and find you something to wear."

She turns away busying herself and I do as she asks. When I am finished, I wait for her. She stares at me through the glass, suddenly she realizes that I am waiting for her next direction. She opens the door and shuts off the water. I step out to dry myself then she hands me a bra and underwear. I stare at the items in my hand.

I whisper to her so that master cannot hear if he is outside, "will Master Dylan always let us wear clothes?"

She lets out a long breath as I put them on. "Addy, he is not my master, he is not yours either. He is my fiancé." She lifts her hand to show me the dainty ring on her finger. I glance up meeting her eyes, I cover my mouth with my fist, suddenly flustered. I'm embarrassed.

Embarrassment is something I could not afford. They stripped me of everything, there was nowhere to hide. Men looked at me, touched me, I had no choice, none. It left no room for things such as embarrassment. It was an emotion they didn't allow or tolerate.

I want to be alone now. I need to repair my wall, too much is getting in. I am thinking too much.

"It's okay, no one is judging you, Addy. We all understand what you have been through."

Saving Addy

I peek over her shoulder as she hands me a t-shirt. I stare at my reflection. She swivels meeting my eyes in the mirror. "I can't do this, Anna."

"You can. You only need to focus on taking care of yourself right now. Nothing else matters." She turns back and holds out a pair of leggings. Once I am dressed she pulls me into her arms hugging me tightly. "It will just take time, but everything will be okay."

When we come out Dylan is sitting on the bed waiting for us. I stop outside the bathroom door.

"Anna, Mrs. Cortez is putting a tray together for Addy, I think she would be more comfortable eating in here for tonight. Could you please find Luis and ask him to join us?" She gives me a small smile of encouragement and leaves us alone.

He pats the bed beside him. I move closer to him and slip to the floor. I haven't been allowed to sit on anything but the floor, surely he doesn't want me to sit on the bed. "Addy, no, you do not need to kneel at my feet." He points to the spot again. I slowly rise and with great caution sit. "I apologize if I appeared angry earlier. I'm not mad at you, sweetheart."

"I'm confused Mast...um, Dylan. Those other men told me that Master Oliver is dead. Are you sure? I don't understand he was supposed to come for me and take me to my new master." I watch his face and the darkness that swirls in his eyes, but he quickly tucks it away.

"Addy, I'm not saying this to frighten you but yes he is gone. I am certain. He died at my hands." He holds himself perfectly still, afraid that I will bolt for the door at his bold admission.

Oliver is dead. He is really dead. I don't know how I feel about this. He has been my only companion, my master, the man that takes care of me, provides me with food and shelter. I stare at my hands, slowly retreating towards my wall, I have been out from behind it for too long.

He grips my chin forcing me to look at him. "Don't, Addy, I recognize what you are doing. You need to stay with us. We will help you, but you can't hide. Anna is getting Luis. He is Liam's father. He is a psychiatrist. I want you to try to talk to him. He can help, he helped Anna. She was a victim of Oliver too."

I swallow hard. He killed Oliver maybe he knows what happened to Brian. He would come get me.

"You look like you have something you want to ask me, go ahead." He releases my chin and puts his arm around me.

I freeze.

He slowly pulls away and raises his hands in front of him. "I'm sorry, I don't want you to be afraid of me. I will never hurt you. I promise."

He is being nice, but I don't deserve it, I can't forget that I am being punished. I can't stay here. I need to see if he will call Brian to come for me.

"Do you know Oliver's men? Well, no…I mean do you know Brian? He worked for Oliver. He would come get me, then I won't be a bother to you and Anna. He will, if you contact him."

Dylan's face falls as a knock interrupts us. Liam opens the door and strolls in with a tray of something that smells delicious. My stomach grumbles.

"Sorry to interrupt, Mrs. Cortez insisted that I bring this now." He chuckles as he sets it down on a small table near the windows. "You must be hungry, Addy." He waves his hand urging me to him. "She is the best cook around, you won't be disappointed, I promise."

I turn and stare at Dylan, waiting for him to tell me I can go. He runs his palm over his face. "Eat, we will talk more when you are finished."

Liam pulls out a chair for me at the table. I walk over to him and hesitantly sit. He pushes it in slightly then takes the seat across from me. I stare down at the plate in front of me. It looks amazing, my stomach growls again. Then I notice that there are utensils and a napkin. A napkin!

This is too much.

My throat constricts so tightly that I don't think I could swallow the food if I tried. I am used to eating on the floor, not at a nice table with a fork...and a spoon.

I shift in my seat to glance back at Dylan. "Mast...sorry, Dylan. Do you know Brian? I would like him to come for me." I lower my head. I can't believe how stupid I am being, I shouldn't be asking for anything, but I cannot stay here. This is not for me.

Liam speaks up, "Addy, we can talk after you eat. You need to get some food in you."

I turn back to my plate, continuing the stare down with the meal.

"Addy?" Liam says scooting his chair around, so he is beside me. "What is it, are you not feeling well?

I notice over his shoulder that Anna has returned with an older gentleman, he must be the psychiatrist that Dylan told me about. They are quietly speaking with him by the door. My gaze roams to Liam's, I whisper to him, "I'm sorry but I have to go." Then I quickly attempt to step behind my wall.

He reaches out and grasps the side of my neck, his fingers pressing on the back of my head while his thumb caresses my cheek. "Addy, no, don't leave."

I hesitate, his eyes capture mine and the weightlessness I experienced at the hotel returns. He has me, he won't let me fall. He is throwing me a safety net if only I would reach out and grab it. He leans forward and kisses me on the forehead. The moment his warm lips touch something unexpected happens...a tear slips down my cheek dragging me with it. I claw at the ground trying to avoid it pulling me over the cliff, but I'm not strong enough to stop the force. My dad used to call them my big crocodile tears, he always gave into me when he saw them.

Liam leans back, gazing into my eyes. They are quickly filling with more tears; the dam has been breached. I panic and try to stand but he doesn't release me. "It's okay, I have you. You can let go. I won't abandon you."

"Please make them go away," I whisper.

He immediately looks over his shoulder. "Hey, why don't you guys head down and eat. I will stay with Addy."

Liam turns back, I can't see if they leave, he is providing a barrier. I hear the door close and it becomes quiet. He holds my eyes captive. The only movement is his thumb slowly running over my cheek. The tear drop meanders its way down and then plops to my lap.

The dam breaks.

Chapter Six

Liam

I can't imagine how overwhelmed she must be. One thing I've learned is there are no answers for how to help someone. Sometimes all you can do is be there. Become a port in their storm. I wanted to be there for my girlfriend, Sophia. It was what I lived and breathed for the better part of my adult existence. Then that world came crashing down when she took her own life. But, time goes on and here I am, still trying to serve those that I am able. That is what I live for now.

Her tiny body shakes in my arms, her sobs are silent. I'm not sure if she is used to grieving in quiet for worry of retribution or if this is the real her. It is hard to say. Reality is that I'll never get to know the girl she was. Those that wronged her forever changed her footprint. Only time will tell what side of the scale will tip when all is said and done. Will she come out stronger or will she struggle the rest of her life in fear and shame?

She pushes off my chest, trying to pull away from me. I release her from my arms.

"I am sorry…Liam," she mumbles as I hand her a napkin to wipe away the tears from her face.

"Don't apologize, Addy, you can cry on my shoulder any time you need."
I tap her under the chin lightly encouraging her to meet my eyes.

She daintily dabs at her cheeks drying up the flood that was released when
I kissed her forehead. I'm not sure why I did that, I rarely get so involved
with the girls we save. This girl is different, I guess we all feel like we know
her. We have been specifically looking for her. It's natural to reach out to
her.

"So, how about we try this meal thing again? If I take this tray back to
Mrs. Cortez full of food she will scold me," I say giving her a smile letting
her see I am only teasing.

She looks down at the plate and I notice she moves her hand to her
stomach. She is hungry I can tell, but something is preventing her from
eating. Then it dawns on me, Dylan told me she had nothing in her room
besides a thin mattress and a blanket. I draw a deep breath to control the
anger that rolls through me at the humiliation that this girl suffered. I
reach out and pick up her fork, loading it with a bite of pasta and then
hold it out for her to take.

Hesitantly she takes it from me and leans slightly over her plate popping
it into her mouth. As she pulls it away, she closes her eyes. When she
opens them again, she peeks at me through her long, wet eyelashes, tears
still clinging to them for dear life. She looks down at the plate as she rolls
the fork around in between her fingers. I see the emotions playing across
her face. Then she stabs at another bite and brings it back up to her lips.

I let out a slow breath. She is eating. Small victories are what add up to a
successful finish. It is promising to see that she is speaking and eating.
She asked about Brian, I'm not sure how distraught she will be when she
learns that he is dead. He took a bullet for Anna, so this might be a touchy
subject when the time comes. We know that Brian had feelings for her,

but we do not know if the road went both ways. Did she have feelings for him or was it one sided? That she asked us to contact him tells me there is something there.

As I ponder over these thoughts in my head I suddenly sense her eyes upon me. I glance up to see that she has finished her supper and is watching me intently. She has a questioning expression on her face, almost as if she was trying to read my mind.

"Is he dead?" she asks void of any emotion.

"Yes, Oliver is dead."

"You said that...Dylan told me he killed him." She takes in a shaky breath and continues, "I'm asking about Brian. He is gone isn't he?"

I peek over my shoulder for backup that is not there. Man, I shouldn't have sent the others out of the room, but I could tell she was overwhelmed. Sighing, I turn back to face her, I must be honest with her. If we start this thing with dishonesty or we try to hide things from her, she will never trust us.

Her hands are folded in her lap as she stares at me patiently for my response, she doesn't push me. She sits there politely...waiting. I place my hand over hers. "Yes, Brian is gone."

She nods her head once and turns back to her plate. And, then she fled. Just like that. I couldn't have stopped her if I wanted to. Anna used to do this too, I don't understand where they go but the mind is a powerful tool. She is somewhere safely tucked inside herself. Self-preservation is sometimes a lifesaver, but it can also be a lonely place.

Addy

When I get back to my side of the wall I crumble. Oliver and Brian…they are both dead. Where does that leave me? Here with a bunch of strangers that is where. These people will not allow me to be alone like at the club. They must think I am an absolute idiot. Everything here is so foreign, even down to the damn napkin on the table. When Liam handed it to me, so I could wipe my tears, I wasn't sure what I was supposed to do with it at first. I'm used to them drying on my face.

Have I gotten so far gone, I've forgotten basic everyday items? Yes, Addy, you have. You deserve none of this. You don't deserve nice things or gentle touch. You are being punished.

Is it possible that God is finally satisfied? I shouldn't allow myself to believe such a thing. But, Anna's tender caress and then Liam kissing me on the forehead, it felt nice. I don't want to jinx myself. What I did was terrible, I know I may pay for what I've done the rest of my life.

I'm so tired, the meal was delicious though. Whoever this Mrs. Cortez is she must be a master chef. I stand up and peek over my wall. He is still here. He is handing my tray to a chubby, jovial looking lady and I see the older man is back. Dylan said he is Liam's father. They look alike. What am I going to do?

Crud, they are watching me. I need to decide what to do. They aren't the bad guys. They are *good* guys. Is that possible? Yes, Addy, you are such a dummy, your dad was a good guy. My throat constricts, no I cannot cry again. I'm too tired to be thinking about these things but it's been so long since I have allowed my mind to wander to my life before.

"Addy, this is my father, Luis," Liam says introducing us.

Should I step out? I guess I will risk it. I could use direction. Just for a bit. But if the scary guy comes back, then I'm out of here. I tiptoe out and force my hand out to shake his. It is warm and comforting.

"Hello, Addison, I have been waiting a long time to meet you. Our Anna has been searching for you for quite some while," he says not releasing his grasp.

He takes the seat Liam just vacated keeping a gentle but firm grip on me. Liam pulls up a chair across from us.

"I realize you are tired, but I would hate for you to go to bed with questions. We want you to feel protected here. You are safe, do you understand that?" he asks.

I nod my head yes as I try to pull away from him, but he doesn't allow it.

"Would you like us to call you Addy or Addison?"

My programming doesn't grant me the option of not answering him, I am surprised I only answered with a nod to his first question. I whisper, "either is fine...but, I guess people used to call me Addy."

"Okay, Addy, do you have a last name?"

I stare down at my hands watching his thumb rub back and forth over the top of my hand. I don't want to tell him my last name, what if he knows Javier? This all could be a trap. I glance around the room, is this Javier's home? Everything looks expensive. It is possible and maybe all these folks work for him. He could be toying with me.

"Is there anyone we may call for you? Family or a friend?" he inquires.

I don't answer. I should ask him a question and then he will forget his. Something that would help me determine who these people are.

"Addy, we want to get you back to where you belong. Can you help us out? What is your name, dear?"

"Sir, um, Luis, where are we at? Are we in the United States?" I ask nervously.

"We are at Anna and Dylan's estate in Mexico. Are you from the states then?"

Oh, Addy, you said too much. You cannot trust these people you are in Mexico! Mexico! Everything is coming full circle, time to pay the piper. These people must know Javier. Why else would they have been looking for me? How else would they have known about me? I need to protect myself. He is probably here now. I cannot let myself become lax. Face the punishment, shelter myself the best I can, that is what I must do.

"Addy?" Luis coaxes attempting to bring me back out, but I am done. I need to get to work. Javier is here. If I thought Oliver was good at delivering my punishments, I am sure it will be nothing compared to the man who has every right to delve them out.

Chapter Seven

Liam

"Liam?" Mrs. Cortez comes up behind me. "Honey, here is a glass of warm milk, perhaps it will help you rest." She leans over setting the mug down in front of me. "You need to get some sleep. Your papa is worried about you."

"Thank you." I smile at her and pat the side of her plump face as she kisses my cheek. "You are too good to us."

"Miho, this is what I love." She smiles again before turning to leave the dining room.

I reflect to the conversation my dad and I just had. He is a smart man. He asked me to think about something before I went to bed tonight. He told me to consider whether I was prepared for the relationship I was about to jump into. I scoffed at him. What the fuck? I'm not about to get into anything. But, what came out of his mouth next made sense.

He didn't necessarily mean a romantic relationship, but he said if I help this young woman, if I truly want to help her, I will come out of it with something. There is no way to help someone as broken as Addy without becoming emotionally invested.

Is he right? He is a psychiatrist for fucks sake, he should know. I've sat here since we left her so she could get some sleep. She wasn't talking anyway, something frightened her. She ducked out of there like the devil was on her heels. And, maybe he is, there are many demons lurking in the shadows of her eyes.

I should just leave this to Dylan and Anna. My dad will be here, they really don't need me. He scared me with his conversation. Does he see something I'm not? I know I'm drawn to her. Could it be that I am wanting to fill the void Sophia left? Could be and that would not be fair to Addy. She doesn't deserve to be some charity case to heal my broken heart. I should take off. It is decided then, I will talk to Dylan tomorrow and make my plans to head out.

I gulp down the rest of my warm milk before it cools and drag myself up from the dining room table. As I walk down the hall and pass by her room, I feel the tug again. I'll peek in one last time. Anna said she would check on her through the night, but it wouldn't hurt to take a quick second.

I pull the door open slowly so I don't wake her. She isn't in her bed. I tiptoe into the room, the pale moon shines in from the window casting a heavenly glow over everything. Not in the bathroom either. Then I spy her, sleeping on the floor, curled up into a little ball.

My heart stops and my breath catches in my lungs. My logical brain tells me to wake her and make her get into bed but, this thing in my chest overrides that. It has cracked open and is bleeding out all over the damn carpet. Bathing it in rich burgundy red.

Saving Addy

I can't leave her. I can never leave her.

She needs me.

I grab a blanket and lay down beside her pulling it up over her and I. She makes a cute little mewling sound, but she doesn't wake. I rake my fingers through her hair. The moonlight frosts it with silver luminosity. She looks like an angel.

Is it possible she had tumbled from Heaven and landed in Hell?

I have no choice now. I must help my fallen angel find her way in the dark.

Help her discover the light.

Before her wings wilt and she is trapped in the darkness forever.

Addy

I'm frozen unable to move. Someone is beside me, the faint murmur of their breath whispers over the back of my neck. I pull myself up slowly and twist to see that it is Liam. I scoot away and tug my knees up to my chest. Why is he here?

My eyes dart around. There is a soft light coming from the window allowing me to study the room. My gaze settles back on the man sleeping beside me. He has blond hair and a short, well-groomed beard. When he is awake, he is very in control, calm but a little intimidating. Not as much as Dylan but they both are used to being in charge I can tell. But, sleeping he looks like a cute, cuddly teddy bear. He stirs and the blanket falls giving me a glimpse of his chest. Okay, add to that a cute, cuddly teddy bear with rock hard abs.

I drag my eyes away from him returning to the windows. I didn't have a window in my room at the club or at Oliver's. The moon must be full as brightly as it is illuminating the space. Quietly I crawl over to the bench seat, I hesitate in front. Willing myself to shut the voices off that tell me I don't belong on the furniture I climb up on it. I glance behind me to make sure that Liam is still sleeping.

The windows are wide and covered in white chiffon curtains except for the large arc window above. I kneel on the bench and raise my face to it. I am at just the right angle to see the moon. It is full tonight, the shadows of craters visible on its surface. I close my eyes soaking up the radiance.

My father and I used to cherish the night. We would sit out in the garden behind our small modest home almost every evening. Sometimes we had company but most nights it was just him and I. I loved it there. He indulged my love of the outdoors. He was always buying me new things for our garden. Gifts of pixies, fairies, and gnomes. He would hide the whimsical trinkets to surprise me.

He was a humanitarian, and the events we encountered during his efforts to make a difference in the world unfortunately caused us to see great darkness. To counter act that he let me create a nook in our yard where the dark didn't exist. I wish I could go there now, but it is gone.

Liam clears his throat behind me making me open my eyes with a start and jump off the seat cowering back down on the floor.

"Hey, Addy, sorry I didn't mean to scare you." He crawls over and lifts my chin with his knuckle forcing my gaze to his.

Saving Addy

"I wanted to see the moon," I whisper with a trembling voice.

"Would you like to go outside and look at it?"

I'm sure my eyes look like saucers at the thought of his suggestion. Outside, he will take me outside…at night? I can't find any words, but I nod my head in response.

He smiles, my heart trips on a beat. I watch him grab the blanket off the floor. He wraps it around my shoulders and then holds out his hand for me to take. I accept and let him tug me up. Is he really taking me outside? As we get to the door of my room, I stop. "Are you sure?" I ask nervously.

"Yes, Addy. I am sure."

We quietly pad through long halls and finally reach several large glass doors that open to a patio. When they open the warm sultry air slides over me. He leads me to a bench and sits down patting the seat beside him. I wrap the blanket around me tightly, it's not cold, but it provides me some safety as I venture outside my wall for the moment.

I lift my face to giant ball of light above us. Closing my eyes, I drift back to thoughts of my childhood home. For the first time in so long I allow myself to wander through my memories, running my hand over them, touching them. The breeze tickles across my skin. The scent of flowers and dirt wafts through the air, filling my senses. It smells like home here. A thawing begins in my chest, a cozy warm tingle glides along my veins transporting the warmth through my entire system.

My eyes fall open to find Liam staring at me. I stare back into his, floating in them. They appear almost translucent in the moon's light. "Thank you," I breathe out. Could I be dreaming? This is such a stark contrast from my reality a mere few days ago that it doesn't seem real.

"Can I put my arm around you?" he asks.

He asked to touch me. It is such a foreign concept I am sure I am in a dream now. "Yes," I reply in a voice I haven't heard in a long time, my confident tone. The one that knows what she wants and isn't afraid to take it.

He unhurriedly slides his arm along my shoulders and then tugs me closer to him. He pauses a moment; his eyes watch mine and then he gently draws my head into his chest. When my cheek brushes against his warm skin I melt into him with a slow drawn-out sigh.

"You are safe, Addy," he says. The rumble of his voice vibrates into my ear.

Could it be over? Dare I allow myself to think it is over? Am I done paying? I don't know but I haven't felt this…this comfortable in a long time. I'm not hungry, not cold, not…. lonely. I peek up at him. He is staring up at the moon as if deep in thought himself. I close my eyes documenting every feeling, every smell, every sound. My body has been depleted for so long, even if this is not the end I will store this all aside, fill myself up as much as I can. Like storing away provisions for an expected long winter.

Chapter Eight

Liam

Ugh, what the fuck? I open my eyes to Dylan towering over me with a thick finger stuck in my chest. He puts another one over his mouth instructing me to keep quiet. I glance over at Addy sleeping. He pulls the finger out of my ribcage and nods to the door. Fuck, I rub my chest, literally what the hell has him so pissed off?

I slide out of bed grabbing my shirt off the floor and follow him out. Shit, I should have stayed in Addy's room, the whole posse is waiting for me out in the hall. I peek in one last time to ensure she is still sleeping then quietly close the door.

"Office now," Dylan roars.

Everyone except me quickly retreats down the hallway heading for his office. He glares at me.

"What?" I ask.

When he doesn't respond, I give in. "Fine, fuck, you're not even going to let me get a cup of coffee first?"

He turns and stalks down to his office. I follow along behind him. Jesus what did I do to deserve all the sunshine and rainbows this morning.

The atmosphere in the room is all doom and gloom as I enter. I take my usual spot off to the side of Dylan's desk by the window and cross my arms over my chest. Something tells me I am about to be on the receiving end of a shit storm.

My father leans forward and rests his arms on his knees. "What are you doing, Liam?"

"What do you mean what am I doing? Looks like I'm being bombarded by a hive of angry bees at the ass crack of dawn," I snip back.

"You know what I mean," he says in his stern dad voice, one I don't hear often, not since I was a boy.

I sigh and stare up at the ceiling. I realize why they are mad. They think I overstepped with Addy. Finding me in her bed this morning must have caused quite the ruckus. I don't care, I've always played things the safe way, followed the rules and done what's been expected of me. Dylan even calls me his voice of reason. But, this I'm not budging on, I can't. Do I really have to explain this to them? Dylan of all people should understand.

"I'm doing what I think is best for Addy," I say.

"For Addy or for you?" Dylan asks.

I glance over at him. "For her, I shouldn't have to spell this out to you Dylan. You fucking took Anna and shoved her in a trunk, so don't go preaching to me."

He flinches but continues. "This isn't the same thing and you know it."

40

"No?" I cock my head to the side. "Fuck if it ain't. I'm not going to sit here and defend myself to all of you, I didn't do anything wrong."

Anna's voice cuts through the room, "Liam, explain it to us. We all know you. We realize this is out of character for you. No one is accusing you of doing anything improper. Please," she pleads.

I run my fingers through my hair and straighten in the chair. "I went to check on her before going to bed and found her sleeping on the floor. I covered her up and remained with her. She looked so small in there. She woke up in the middle of the night and I took her outside, she wanted to look at the moon. She fell asleep out there and I carried her to bed. She...she wouldn't let go of me, so I stayed. Okay? No big deal now can I please go back down there to see if she is awake? She will be hungry."

Everyone's eyes dart to one another, great, they think I'm crazy. And, maybe I am.

"She is very vulnerable, Liam. You understand this. If you keep this up she may latch on to you for no other reason than her need to replace the loss of Oliver and Brian. She needs to learn that she is in charge of her own life again," Dylan states.

"She needs me," I say with a tremendous amount of authority.

Anna settles herself on the edge of my chair. "Is this about Sophia?" she asks hesitantly.

"No." I hug her around the waist. "It's about Addy, I need to be there for her, I can't explain it."

She runs her hand over my head soothing me. She understands. I knew she would.

"I think we should let Liam take the lead on this," she says.

I peek up at her, her gaze drops to mine, and she smiles continuing her case for me. "She is frightened of you Dylan. And, since you rarely allow me out of your sight she will always be nervous around me too. This might be good. I mean really, do any of you think Liam has any bad intentions?"

"No, but we all recognize she is looking for someone to accept direction from," Dylan pleads for the opposition.

"And, if I remember right it was Liam who suggested you take a firmer road with me when I was healing. He knows what he is doing," she says.

"No, no, I don't, Anna." I lean back in the chair pulling away from her. "Look, I realize seeing me in her bed shocked you all but it's not like that. I don't understand what it is, I can't explain but I need to be with her…for now anyhow. If it becomes a problem, then I will leave and go to D.C. until she is gone. I promise."

An empty promise is what it is. Something has sprouted between Addy and me. She senses it too. It doesn't matter what the others expect. I could just tell them the truth…that she is my angel. She was sent here for me. I believe this as surely as I know my name. She is my angel. She has come to me so I can help her to the light and in return she is going to breathe life back into me.

"I'll go get her for breakfast and meet you all in the dining room. Is Mark around? I think she should have a physical."

Anna glides over to sit in Dylan's lap, I notice that my mention of Addy getting a physical has triggered her. When Oliver had her captive, he allowed someone to hurt her. Any reference of exam rooms takes her to a dark place.

42

"He is here," my dad says. "I'll go with you to the infirmary after breakfast," he adds as I stand.

"Great. Well, I'll see you all in about thirty." I stalk out of the room. They will not make this easy for me. Fuck them.

Addy

Was last night a dream? I stare at the crumbled sheets beside me, was it real? Man, I really have to pee, I hope someone comes soon. Wait…I stare at the bathroom door. The rules aren't the same here. Are there rules? I should ask. No, I shouldn't. I don't know what to do. I assumed this was Javier's house, but I could have overreacted. I didn't detect any cigar smoke when we walked through the halls.

Normal, you need to act normal. Quit calling people master, quit acting like you can't eat without help. First things first, bathroom. I don't need to wait to be hauled to the toilet only to have someone watch me relieve myself. Hopefully, I will be able to perform without an audience, ughh, okay here goes nothing.

I tip-toe to the bathroom and shut the door behind me. Ohhh, god thank you for allowing me this bit of relief. When I stand up, I catch my reflection. I turn away from the mirror, forcing myself not to look. Not yet, I'm not ready. I fumble around washing my hands in the sink keeping my eyes averted from the glass that would give me a glimpse of the broken pixie trapped there.

When I get back to the bedroom Liam is sitting at the foot of the bed. He grins at me, looking proud that I went to the bathroom by myself. Heat brushes my cheeks. God, I'm such a ninny. How did I go from being an independent woman to someone who thinks going to the toilet by herself is a major accomplishment?

But, it is.

Should I stay on the outside of my wall?

"Good morning," he says still grinning at me. The cutest little dimple breaks out over his left cheek when his smile deepens. My own cheeks tighten, no, Addy, stop, don't do it…you will crack.

"Morning s…Liam," I say struggling to prevent the sir from falling from my lips. Normal, act normal.

"Are you hungry? Mrs. Cortez has a buffet this morning. Every Friday is a breakfast buffet, and it is an absolute must. But, I warn you we may have to roll back down here because we'll be so stuffed."

"Sure, I will just change." I search around hesitantly, uncertain where Anna put the clothes she brought me yesterday.

Liam stands going to a large bureau tugging out several pieces and handing them to me. "Here this should do. I'll be right outside the door waiting for you." He places the items in my arms. When his hand brushes over mine a prickle of electricity skates through my system. When I glance at him I see he is holding a brick.

One of my carefully laid bricks.

I study my wall. Shit, I really need to get that thing back up to snuff. It is in terrible disrepair. When he opens the door the aroma of breakfast assaults my senses. I guess it can wait until after I eat.

Saving Addy

Clothes, such a luxury. At one time I thought I would go to my deathbed naked. When I first got to Oliver's, and they took my clothes away I tried to pretend I was a little naked nymph exploring the woods. That didn't last long. Torture has a way of snuffing out fantasies. It was just too dark there for the whimsy to exist.

The fabric is so soft against my skin, caressing it gently. I take a moment to catalog everything about it, this might not last. I need to fill myself up while I'm here. This might simply be a pit stop on the road of my punishment.

Liam is leaning up against the hall outside my room when I open the door. He stands to attention as I step out. Suddenly I am unsure again. Is it just going to be him and I? That I can do but something tells me it won't be a private buffet for our enjoyment only. This place is big, an estate Luis said…in Mexico. I gulp sidestepping back towards my wall.

"Hey, I will not leave your side I promise." Liam reaches out and brushes a stray hair out of my eyes.

My fingers still rest on the doorknob to my room. What if I freeze up down there? I don't want to sound stupid. Oliver told me all the time how foolish I was.

"Okay, let's come up with a plan. If at any point it becomes too much for you squeeze my hand and we will come back. The others will never know, just our little secret." He dips his head trying to capture my eyes.

He is a magic mind reader. I nod in agreement.

Chapter Nine

Addy

When we walk into the dining room, a silence falls over the space. I hesitate in the doorway, but Liam gently tugs my hand forcing me to follow along behind him. He pulls out a chair for me and I timidly perch myself on it. Anna is across from me smiling.

"Good morning, Addy," she says cheerfully.

My eyes dart between her and Dylan. "Good morning," I say attempting to control the pitch of my voice.

The jovial looking woman I saw last night comes to stand behind me placing her hands on my shoulders. "Oh, mija, it is so nice you joined us. I am Mrs. Cortez." She leans over kissing my cheek. She is warm and soft. I love the sparkle in her eye. She reminds me of my abuela.

Liam grabs the plate in front of me. "I will load you up, anything you don't like?" he asks.

"No, anything is fine," I say peeking up at him.

Nervously I glance around. Everyone seems to be watching me. No, not me…us. Liam doesn't seem to notice. He casually strides over to the breakfast buffet spread out on a long table on the back of the wall.

"Did you sleep well?" Dylan directs the question towards me.

"Uh, yes. Thank you." Does he know Liam took me outside last night? He has a skeptical expression masking his scary face.

Anna pats his large hand. "Liam said you went out to look at the moon. It was beautiful wasn't it?"

I let the breath out I had been holding. They know, but she doesn't seem to act like it was a big deal. "Yes, it was. Getting to go outside and see it was even more amazing," I reply.

"How long had you been captive, Addy?" Luis, Liam's father asks.

One of my legs slips back over the wall, I need to tread cautiously. Questions are a tricky, dangerous thing. Liam reappears with my plate setting it down in front of me. A mountain of food covers the entire thing. He places his hand on the table beside me, offering me an out. All I need to do is reach out give it a squeeze and he will take me away. I stare at it for a moment. It is there if I need but for now I am okay.

"I'm not sure but almost two years I am guessing," I reply to Luis, glancing at him.

Liam takes my fork from the napkin it is carefully tucked in and spears a piece of watermelon. He offers it to me. He nods pleased that I am functioning at an acceptable level. I accept it and shove it into my mouth. Fuck, I close my eyes. The burst of refreshing flavor erupts releasing little happy endorphins to swim through my veins.

47

When I open my eyes, I notice everyone is staring at me. Heat surges to my face. I tap my fork lightly on the plate, poop, so much for acting normal. "Sorry, I uh…I haven't had fresh fruit in…well I can't really remember when." I cringe at my admission.

Dylan's voice rumbles through the room, "Addy, rule number one…don't apologize for grabbing life by the balls and enjoying it."

I peek up at him. He is smiling at me. Hmm, he's not so scary when he smiles. I pull my shoulder up to my cheek, feeling shy. I nod my understanding towards him.

My fork finds its way to the next delicious thing on my plate. Sausage, greasy wonderful, ball grabbing worthy sausage. When I shove it in my mouth the natural reaction to close my eyes and grab my antique, old school library card cataloging system, takes over. I file it away for another day. I open my eyes. Again, all gazes are on me.

Dylan chuckles. "You like food don't you? Girl after my own heart."

"If I was blessed to have Mrs. Cortez as my personal chef, I would be in Heaven," I reply.

Liam slides his arm on the back of my chair. I glance at him, and he gives me a nod of encouragement.

"Do you enjoy cooking? I suck at it but these two," Anna says nodding towards Dylan and Liam, "they are amazing at it."

I peek at Liam and he smiles. Ohh, there is that little dimple again, my lashes flutter against my skin and I almost forget to reply to Anna. I clear my throat and take a drink of water before answering. "Yes, I do, well, I did. I don't know is it a skill one can forget?"

Mrs. Cortez comes out from the kitchen hearing my statement. "Oh, of course not, mija, you come down and find me once you settle in and we will cook together. You will discover you have not forgotten. Just like riding a bike."

Everyone is so nice, has the curse has lifted? "Thank you, I would appreciate that."

Liam brushes his hand across my back as I'm finishing up. Anna and Anthony both excuse themselves from the table and Mrs. Cortez retreats to the kitchen. Dylan, Luis and Liam seem to tense as things quiet down and my nerves signal I will not like what happens next.

One more bite and then I'm out of here. But my greediness for that last morsel stalls my retreat and I don't make it over. Liam grabs my hand, holding me hostage on the edge of the wall.

"Addy, I think you should get a physical. Just to be certain you are okay. We probably should have done this yesterday, but we didn't want to bombard you on your first day here."

"Okay," I say hesitantly. Is that it? That is not so bad. I'm not understanding why they seem so nervous about it.

"Okay?" he asks.

"Yeah, sure." I shrug my shoulders at him.

He lets out a sigh of relief. "Good, Luis will go with us. We have an infirmary here on the estate so it's within walking distance. Mark our medic will meet us. He'll do the physical, you can trust him."

49

Liam

Addy is a breath of fresh air. This was not what I was expecting, especially after we first found her. She is like a small child finding the beauty and awe in everything she encounters. It took us forever to walk the short distance to the infirmary. She stopped to look at everything…and I mean everything. The flowers, the plants, the little statues of cherubs outside of the house, the estate pets and the children. When her nose wasn't to the landscape, it was pointed towards the sky, starring at the puffy clouds. You can see in her eyes she is storing every color, shape, smell…well everything…she is locking it all away.

Refreshing but slightly sad at the same time. Was she like this before or is she like this because she had been captive for so long? She didn't seem scared when I told her about the physical. I asked if she would like me to stay with her, but she declined and said she would be fine. Even here in this cold medical building she seemed fascinated by everything. Her eyes flitted over each item. I hope she is okay in there.

"She is fine, Liam," my dad says beside me, placing his hand on my knee to stop the insistent shaking of my leg.

When I remain quiet he continues. "I would like to speak to her today, in private."

"Listen dad, I am sorry I snapped at you this morning. I was feeling a little ganged up on if you know what I mean."

"I understand son, you are a decent man, Liam. I don't doubt that, and to be honest my worry is not just for the girl but you. I would hate to see you get hurt. She has been through a lot and while she might seem to be doing well now, you realize that she will have dark days."

Should I tell him? He may have me committed. "Something tells me I am meant to be here for her. I recognize how crazy this sounds. It sounds crazy to me too. But, something deep down screams at me that this is the path I need to walk down."

"Then we will go down it together, just promise me you will talk to someone if you need. You are not in this alone and I don't want you getting so wrapped up you forget that. Okay?" He pats my leg giving me a warm smile.

"Thanks dad, I will I promise."

Mark comes out of the room closing the door behind him. My dad and I both stand but he motions to remain sitting and he takes the chair beside us. My stomach is full of butterflies all trying to escape waiting for what he is about to say. His face looks grim. "How bad is it?" I ask not sure if I really wish to hear what he is about to say. Maybe she didn't let him get very far.

"Her overall health is actually very good. I see nothing we should be concerned with. However, I want you to be aware of a few things," he says looking more at my father than me. Shit.

"Did she tell you something? You are making me nervous. Just spit it out."

My dad places his hand on my bouncing knee again. "Go ahead, Mark, what is it?"

"She has been severely scarred. She has no open wounds and I would guess that the most recent ones were from a few months ago. No broken bones only the scarring." He lets out a long breath before continuing. "She allowed me to do whatever I needed to do, she retreated somewhere in her mind. I tried to ask her about the scars I saw but she did not respond."

"Where?" I say my voice dripping with anger. Someone scarred my angel. Only a demon could harm that beautiful creature. I hope that everyone who hurt her are all rotting with maggots infesting their dead corpses.

"Mostly her backside a little over her stomach but that looks like it might fade. All probably caused by whips or rope burns. But, the inside of her thighs are covered in scars that appear to have been made with a blade. They are in perfect symmetrical lines."

Someone cut her? Somebody actually fucking cut her. I stand up and rush to the room she is in. My angel needs me.

"Liam," my father calls after me but I don't stop.

When I open the door, she is standing by the table waiting. She jumps, looking at me nervously.

"Are you okay?" I ask taking a step towards her hesitantly.

"I'm fine, I would like to go back if Mark is finished," she says with a shaky voice.

"Anything you want, angel."

She drops her head. "I'm not an angel, Liam."

Did I say that out loud? Now it's time for my cheeks to heat. "I'm sorry, Addy. I...shit I shouldn't have said that. But, you look like an angel. Sorry, I, fuck, I should just shut up. I will take you to your room, you must be tired."

Saving Addy

She nods keeping her arms wrapped around her tightly and follows me. We stop briefly to say goodbye to Mark. He informs us he will come up to the house later with the results of her blood work.

On the way back, she is quiet and keeps her eyes on the path, not looking up once to explore the surrounding. Is it because of the physical or because of my stupid mouth? I don't know and I sure as hell can't ask her with my dad tagging along.

When we get to her room, she steps inside and then turns to us. "I'll be fine, I'm just going to take a nap...if that is okay?"

"Absolutely, Addy," my father answers. "Rest and I will come back and check on you in an hour." He brushes his hand over her arm and then takes his leave.

I linger by her open room. I should say something, ask her something, fuck I don't know. As if sensing my internal struggle, she reaches out and touches my chest lightly with her fingers. "Thank you, Liam, you have been too good to me." Then, she turns and closes the door behind her.

I stare at it for a long time and rub my hand over where she touched me as I slide down the wall. I can't leave, not after what Mark said. My ass is planted here, I need to be right here if she needs me. My broken angel doesn't even know where she came from. She has forgotten her decent from Heaven. Fucking assholes.

Chapter Ten

Addy

Addison Lane Davis are you the most stupid person on this giant spinning ball of dirt? What the hell are you thinking you crook? You just got done paying for one sin and you steal again! Why did I do that? My hand just reached out and took it. Maybe they will not miss it. Once a thief always a thief, my heart whispers. My dad would be so disappointed in me.

Liam called me an angel, an angel! When he finds out what I really am won't he be disheartened. Angels aren't thieves. I reach up under my shirt and tug the book out. But, I have it now, it wouldn't hurt to study it, to read it. I've already fucked up might as well enjoy it. No, don't do it, Addy. You can't go through any more punishments fess up now...right now!

But...I run my finger over the shiny cover, but nothing, Addy. Do it now before you coward out and you jinx what you have going here. What if they get mad and send me away? Master O would have had me whipped for this. My body trembles at the thought. I guess I'll take my punishment if that is what it is. It could end there and not be months and months of suffering like the first time. Well, the first time I thieved more, much more. Go do it, the moral clock is ticking. Tick. Tick. Tick.

Saving Addy

I shove the book under my shirt and throw the door open wide. Tick. Tick. When I step out Liam looks up at me from the floor, he hasn't left. He quickly stands and places his hands on my shoulders. "Are you okay, Addy? You don't look well," he says rubbing my arms up and down trying to stroke heat back into my limbs.

I can't confess to him. No, I need to go to Dylan. I need to be punished. I swallow hard. Tick. Tick. Tick. "I need to talk to Dylan about something," I squeak out.

"Dylan?" He drops his hands to his side a puzzled expression on his face. Confused or hurt?

"Yes, please."

"Okaaay," he draws out. "He is in his office. Would you like me to go with you?"

It would be good to have someone with me. Liam seems nice. Oh, I don't know, then he will realize how bad I am. I guess he'll find out, eventually. Dylan would tell him anyhow. I shake my head yes.

He takes my hand gently in his and leads me to Dylan's office. Tick. Tick. Can I do this? Tick. Tick. You should have done it the first-time dummy. But, you were just trying to make a different life for yourself. God evidently didn't see it that way. A sin is a sin. Tick. Tick. Tick.

Liam stops in front of a door. Poop, we are here already. Tick. Tick. He reaches out and cups my cheek. "Addy, I don't know what is going on, but I can tell that you are terrified. You don't have to be frightened here. No one will hurt you. No one."

My wall is in shambles and I am about to get punished. I didn't think this out. I should have done some repairs. No going back. You just have to suffer through. Liam realizes that I am not listening to him and knocks.

My teeth chatter together. A muffled "come in" rumbles on the other side. Oh god. Tick. Tick. Stupid moral compass why work now? Liam pushes the door open and pulls me inside. Dylan looks up from his desk surprised to see me tagging along with him.

He leans back in his chair, his eyes going from my deer in the headlight ones to Liam's. "Is everything okay?" he asks.

"Addy asked to speak to you."

"The physical went well?" he questions as he rises coming around to us.

The moment he is in front of me I drop to my knees and stare at his boots. "I am so sorry. I…I…took something that belongs to you and…I am so very sorry. It won't happen again. Please punish me I deserve to be punished." I shake my head back and forth still focusing solely on his boots. "I'm bad. I'm bad." Tears plunge into my lap as I pull out the book I stole from the infirmary and place it on the floor at his feet.

Quickly I suck in a few deep breaths halting my tears. Tears mean harsher punishment. Stop them now, Addy.

The silence above me is deafening.

Dylan takes a step forward and my entire body shakes as I try to remain still. Accept it, you are a sinner. Sinners deserve to be punished.

"Fuck. Addy. No, sweetheart. You are not in trouble." He sits down cross-legged in front of me and pulls me into his lap. Liam crouches down taking my palm in his as Dylan cradles me. "You are safe, no one is punishing you," Dylan whispers above me and I hear his voice catch with emotion.

My body trembles but I force myself to peek over at Liam, his grip on my hand is warm and gentle. He doesn't appear angry, no not angry, not even disappointed. I close my eyes, shaking as Dylan rocks me back and forth in his arms.

What is this? I steal from them and this is how they treat me? With...with kindness? The moral clock stopped ticking. No punishment awaits? Have you ever stood at the beach bracing yourself for a giant wave? As it gets close it somehow loses momentum and when it finally arrives it barely nudges you? That is what this feels like. I need release. I need pain.

My emotions will boil over with no place to go, I need to be punished to make these feelings leave.

My body convulses, and a voice erupts from me I have never heard before. The sound of a wounded animal in the forest. Haunting, howling, loud and with it a tsunami that hits the beach with furious intensity. Dylan holds on tight and tucks my head under his chin. His beard tickles my cheek. I weep into him. He takes the brunt of the wave.

Liam's warm hands glide back and forth over my legs. "Let it all out, Addy. You are doing so good, angel. Let all that shit out. You are safe. You are safe with us."

Liam

Now I understand why she asked for Dylan. At first I was almost jealous. But, now I realize, she wanted him to punish her. The waves of emotion rolling off of her are terrifying. She has been crying for so long her voice is becoming hoarse. Dylan glances at me with concern.

"Liam, we need to get your dad," he says.

He sees my struggle to leave her.

"Here, I will go find him." He gently places her in my arms. I'm not sure she even notices, she is so consumed by the torrent surging through her. I tuck her tightly into me.

"Shh, it's okay, Addy. You are safe, you are safe." I'm scared, really scared. I have seen no one like this before. I thought she would cry it out and everything would be fine. All this over a book? Something is going on. Something so deep it has split her in two.

Dylan comes back with Luis and Mark. My dad sits down beside me. He doesn't even glance at me, his focus solely on the little crying ball in my lap. "Addy? Addy, can you look at me?" She doesn't respond.

"How long has she been like this?" Mark says.

"Over an hour," Dylan replies.

"I think we should sedate her. We can't let this continue. I'll be right back." Mark jogs from the room.

I glance up at my dad. "I'm scared," I whisper to him.

He places his forehead to mine grabbing me. "She will be okay son. Have faith that God will lead her through this."

She stops crying, little hiccupping sobs survive for a few seconds and she peeks at us. Her eyes are puffy and red. But, she is present. She has returned.

Saving Addy

"Sweetheart, you are good. Don't worry we are all here for you," my dad says cupping her cheek. He takes a handkerchief out of his pocket and gently pats at her face.

"He is the one who demanded they hurt me," she whispers hoarsely.

"Who, Addy? I'm not sure I know what you mean dear."

"God…he has been punishing me." She turns and burrows into my chest, along with the knife that was just impaled there by her words. Fuck, she thinks she has deserved everything that has happened to her.

Mark comes back and my dad moves aside so he can give her the sedative. "She sounds a little better. This should help her rest though; poor thing looks wore out."

She doesn't even flinch as he administers the drug.

Chapter Eleven

Addy

I woke up several times in the night. Each time someone was with me sitting in the chair by the bed. I couldn't keep my eyes open. Exhaustion has taken up permanent residency. My mind would wander to Dylan and Liam. Why didn't either of them punish me? Before I could conjure up an answer, the night would steal me back into the darkness.

Unfortunately, the sun has risen. The dark has released me and now it's time to face the music. When I open my eyes, they meet Luis's and Anna's kind ones.

Anna rises from the bench seat by the window and perches on the side of the bed. Luis remains in the chair close by.

"Addy, I am glad you are finally awake. We've all been worried about you. I will run you a bath. Okay?" Anna says.

I nod my head at her slightly. A bath? I stole from them and she is offering me a bath?

She hops up and heads into the bathroom. Luis comes over as I try to sit myself up. He reaches out and helps me to a sitting position. "How are you feeling today, Addy?"

"Tired," I reply. My voice cracks prompting him to grab a glass of water off the nightstand and hand it to me.

"You had quite a day yesterday."

"I'm sorry."

"Addison, you have nothing to be sorry for," he scolds, reminding me of my father.

Anna bops out grabbing a few things from the wardrobe and heads back into the bathroom.

"After breakfast there is someone I would like you to meet."

Standing in the middle of my world I glance at all the rubble. How did I let this happen? I had everything so neatly tucked away behind my wall and now it is a mess. Memories strewn around, bad ones mixed with the good ones, past life mingled with the current. I grab a few bricks trying to stack them up as fast as I can, but they are so heavy, heavier than I remember.

"Addison, did you hear me? After breakfast you and I will take a little walk, I have a friend I would like you to talk to. His name is Father Landon he'll meet us at the chapel here."

Father? As in a priest? My mind swirls, I had wanted to see one when I was first abducted. I should have before I went to Mexico, but I had been so busy with life I didn't make time. Then it was too late, and everything caught up with me. Maybe Luis is right, I could confess this new sin, taking the book, I could confess that. Surely, I'm done paying for the other stuff.

My heart falls to my stomach as images of what has happened to me run around my brain. How can I step foot in a church after all of that? I am too filthy.

"I can't go there," I whisper.

"May I ask why?"

"Umm, I don't think I should go to the chapel," I answer, wringing my hands together.

"Why not?"

"I don't belong there." I pull the covers up over my nose so that only my eyes are peeking out. There it is again, embarrassment. If he knew what had happened to me he would understand.

"Everyone belongs there if they choose. Addy what you said yesterday has been weighing heavy on me. I think Father Landon will help you better than I can right now. Don't get me wrong, I'm not abandoning you, I'm just getting us both a little extra guidance. Okay?"

Hesitantly I give him the slightest of nods as Anna comes back out.

"Good, after breakfast then." He pats my knee and then leaves Anna and I alone.

"Ready?" She asks standing by the bathroom door.

When I crawl out of bed I realize how tired I am. I feel like I've just run a marathon. My achy limbs protest as I make my way over to her. Once inside, she points to the garden tub. I rip off my clothes without her assistance this time. I notice that she is looking at my back. "It's okay, it's not as bad as it looks." I tell her.

She winces and perches on the step beside me. She drapes her fingers through the bubbles deep in thought. "Oliver took me too," she admits.

"I know, Dylan told me," I whisper.

"Who did that to you?" She nods her head towards my backside.

"Several people I guess. Most of them were made by someone Master Oliver brought with him to the club a lot. We weren't allowed to speak but one time I heard Master O call him Derrick."

Anna pales and sways looking as if she might pass out. My hand darts out to steady her. "Anna, Anna, are you okay? Take a deep breath, Anna." I climb out of the tub, naked and dripping. Perching in front of her I tell her to breathe in through her nose and out through her mouth. I place my palm on her stomach, "Anna, breathe from your tummy. Yes, that is it, everything is alright."

She gazes at me as she focusses on my instructions. After a few minutes her symptoms subside. "Addy, I am supposed to be helping you not the other way around." She laughs.

My head is clear, my alertness is sharp and focused. "Uh, I think you did."

She looks confused but doesn't ask what I meant by that. "I'm sorry you are freezing, get in the water."

I step back in and she tilts her head to one side looking at me quizzically. "Addy, I need to tell you something. I'm not sure if now is the right time but since we are alone." She pauses taking a deep breath before continuing.

"I knew Brian."

My face whips to her. "Brian? Oliver's Brian?"

"Yes, he is the one who took me to Oliver. He told me about you."

That is how they know about me. Brian. Did he send them to save me?

When I make no response other than the shocked expression upon my face, she starts again. "Hmm, I don't know how to say all this. Oliver and Brian had a deal, me for you. If Brian found me, then Oliver would give you back to him. Oliver reneged on the arrangement."

"Oliver told me that Brian betrayed him," I tell her.

"I think he thought Brian had grown soft, become a liability to him," she says.

She curls herself into a little ball and continues her story. "Brian said he should have taken you away. He sounded regretful that he didn't get you away from Oliver. I told him we would help him find you. I asked him to call Dylan and Liam, to tell them where they could locate me. He called them, but they didn't get there in time. Oliver would have killed me, but Brian dodged in front of me and…he took the bullet." Anna crumbles and once again I discover myself kneeling beside her comforting her through her panic attack.

"Shit, I suck at this. I think you are helping me more than I am you," she says.

Saving Addy

"Anna, are you telling me that because of Brian, you all came for me?" He saved me. Brian saved me. I always knew he would why did I doubt it. That little voice was right.

"Yes, when he died helping me I realized he wasn't the monster I thought he was."

"No, no, he was no monster," I say. "He was a victim just like you. His mother sold him to Oliver's boss. They taught him the tricks of the trade, he did what he had to so he could survive. When the big boss retired Oliver started him on training the girls."

Anna stares at me, she swallows hard. "Did you love him?" she asks.

Hmm, love. The only person I ever loved was my dad. I didn't love Brian. I didn't hate him either. He was just a port in the storm for me. The only comfort I could find in the dark. I shake my head at her. "No, I wouldn't call it love but I did care for him."

A tear runs down her cheek. "I want to show you something."

We forget the bath and instead I get dressed and follow her down the long halls of her home. She stops outside of a door and gives me a serious look. "Addy, Dylan will never hurt you. I promise."

"I know."

"He wants to help you, we all do."

I nod my head at her as she opens the door wide. She steps aside. I peek in around the corner. It is a huge library. I turn and stare at her.

"I love books too," she says smiling widely. "You are welcome to take anything you like while you are here."

I spin in the spacious room. There are books everywhere in every nook and cranny. Shelves run high into the ceiling. But, what really catches my attention lies beyond the large windows. A garden, a big beautiful flower garden. I rush to them, pressing my palms against the glass. She giggles behind me and I turn, my cheeks flushing with warmth.

"Your enthusiasm is wonderful, Addy."

I flush to a full bloom rose. "I'm sorry, I love gardens. My father and I used to have one."

"This evening we should have dinner out there."

"Yes, I would like that, Anna. Thank you."

"Do you want to grab a novel before we head down to breakfast?" She asks.

I bite my bottom lip. Do I dare ask? "Could I have the book I took? I mean if that is okay. I kinda wanted to read that one."

She looks puzzled. "Sure, I will get it from Dylan."

"Thank you, Anna," I say as I take a final peek at the garden beyond the glass.

Liam

My dad insisted that I get some sleep. I haven't seen her since her breakdown. My eyes focus on the spot that Dylan and I sat with her on the floor. Holding that broken angel in my arms was heartbreaking and frightening at the same time. Would this have been how it would have been with Sophia? Oliver had my girlfriend Sophia for eight years. I'm not sure how long Addy endured that asshole but yesterday she finally succumbed to the pain. It was the scariest thing I've ever encountered and believe me I have witnessed my fair share of suffering.

"A little anxious at seeing her today?" Dylan asks, ripping me from my dark thoughts.

"I guess, I hope she is feeling better."

"Me too."

"Hey, before I forget. I got a call from Javier Galindo."

"Why the fuck is a drug trafficker calling you?"

"Well, he says one of his employees has been looking for his niece. He hoped we might be able to help. They heard Oliver Wright abducted her and they recently learned of our takedown and wanted to know if we had found her or if we could help them locate her."

"Fuck, since when do we help people like Galindo?"

"I know, I thought about it, but the girl isn't to blame for who her uncle works for. We can't judge who we serve, can we?"

"No, I guess you're right. We should help find her."

"He is coming Monday morning at nine. Will you join us?"

"Yep, sure thing. She could be someone we already rescued, and this will be a happy reunion."

A knock on the door interrupts our conversation. Anna comes in with a smile on her face. I breathe a sigh of relief. Addy must be better today. Anna and my dad took the early shift, so she more than likely just came from her. Everyone decided to take turns through the night not wanting to leave her alone. We are all a little nervous after Sophia. No need to risk her hurting herself with so many of us to watch over her.

She plops down in Dylan's lap. "Well, she is up and seems to be much better today." She leans her head back into his chest, staring up at the ceiling. Helping Addy is taking its toll on her, she has dark circles under her eyes. "We talked about Brian."

I sit up straighter in my chair. Jealousy should not be an issue, but the thing is like a living, breathing beast inside of me stalking around. It huffs at hearing Brian's name, rutting the ground ready to tear into someone or something at the mere mention that anyone else might have Addy's attention.

"How did it go, baby?" Dylan asks, stroking his hands over her stomach.

"Good, however, she also mentioned Derrick, and it threw me into a panic attack, but Addy talked me out of it. How she was able to remain so calm and in control I really don't understand. I felt bad. I'm supposed to be helping her not the other way around. She has these scars on her back, she told me Derrick made most of them."

We all sit in silence for a moment. Derrick raped Anna when she was held captive by Oliver. Dylan put a bullet in Derrick's head. He should have had a much slower, more painful death. My mind wanders to Brian, I'm curious about Addy's and Brian's relationship.

"You told her about Brian taking a bullet for you?" I ask. He saved Anna's life. If he hadn't jumped in front of her at just the right moment she wouldn't be sitting here now. That is the only fact that has tempered Dylan's and I's perception of him. Brian was a slave trainer, and it's hard for me to forget that he tortured girls, Anna included. I blame him as much as Oliver for the evil that so many young women experienced.

"Yes," she replies in barely a whisper. "She didn't seem upset. I just flat out asked her if she loved him."

My heart stops, I want to know her response and yet I don't. What the hell is wrong with me? Why am I becoming so enraptured with Addy? I should not be so possessive of her. She is not mine. But, I can't help but feel she is.

Anna leans forward and picks up the book that started the whole debacle yesterday. She continues relaying her story as she thumbs through the pages. "She said no, she didn't love him. Brian wasn't a monster. He was a victim. His mother sold him to the organization. Oliver started him training girls when he took over the business. Brian was as much a victim as Addy and I." She slams the book shut, anger radiating through her.

Dylan pulls her in tight, rocking her back and forth. "Shh, it's okay, baby. Brian is in a better place, he may have been a victim, but he made some pretty bad decisions along the way that hurt a lot of people. Maybe saving you was his way of making amends for those choices. Just like you felt the need to make amends to him for taking that bullet that was meant for you. You found Addy for him. It's all coming full-circle Anna."

"I guess," she says wiping at her eyes. "I suppose we should get down to breakfast. I walked her down there, she is with Luis and Anthony. I showed her the library and told her she was welcome to read anything she wanted but she wants this one." She holds up the medical journal in her hands.

"Hmm, that would not be my choice for reading enjoyment," Dylan chuckles.

"It's what she wants, so it is what she will get. She was more interested in the flower garden outside than the books, her face lit up when she saw it. She shared with me that her and her father had a garden. I told her we would have supper out there this evening so both of you can put that on your agenda for today." She gives us both a look, letting us know we both better be there.

When we get down to the dining room, I see that Anthony and my dad have each taken up residency on either side of Addy. The beast huffs again, pacing back and forth. Mine, she is mine. I stalk to the seat across from her. She was listening intently to Anthony's wild tale but as soon as I sit down her gaze is drawn to mine. She doesn't say anything we both just drink each other in, a silent acknowledgement passes between us.

Mrs. Cortez bustles in placing platters upon platters of savory morsels on the table. Our eyes don't leave each other. Then she speaks as if no one else was in the room. "Liam, Luis is taking me to the chapel after breakfast. Would you be able to accompany us?"

She asked me to go with her. My dad and the others bristle, but I do not take my eyes off her. "Absolutely, yes." I say reaching across squeezing her hand lightly. And then...my...heart...stops. She smiles...just a hint of one but none the less it is a smile. If I thought she was an angel before, her smile literally sealed the idea. She may be the prettiest thing I have ever seen. She glows, she radiates an aura of gold. A beautiful golden angel, sitting at a table of mere mortals.

She blushes and gazes down at her plate before raising her eyes back up to mine. "Thank you, Liam, I am nervous about going to speak with Father Landon."

Anna breaks the awkward silence that follows. "Addy, here is the book you wanted."

Her smile turns into a frown. "I'm sorry for yesterday. I should have just asked to borrow it."

Dylan speaks up, "Remember my rule? Grab life by the balls, that is all you were doing. It's okay, it's just a book. I doubt anyone would have missed it. So, no more thinking about it."

"Yes s...Dylan," she says, stopping herself from saying sir at the last minute. That must be hard for her. Actually, all of this must be tough for her.

Chapter Twelve

Addy

I was a bucket of nerves at breakfast. The fear of being punished for taking that book yesterday almost kept me from going down to the dining room but, Anna insisted. Everyone has been so understanding. I wish I could just get back to being me again, not this awkward, stumbling around in the dark presence that I currently am.

Asking Liam to go with Luis and I was hard for me. I was worried he would say no. He makes me feel safe. I'm still clinging to that safety net he threw me. Someday I will have to let loose but for now he seems willing to keep it extended.

Breakfast passed by entirely too fast and I find myself stalling the closer we get to the chapel. The level of patience these folks have is incredible. I've stopped to smell every flower, kick every rock and sigh dreamily at every puff of cloud that has floated by. Somehow, we still managed to make it to the steps of the steepled structure.

I pause at the first step and gaze up at the building stretching to the sky. The last time I was in a chapel was the day I said goodbye to my dad. Then I went to live with my uncle in Mexico and church became a luxury

I didn't get. He wasn't much of a religion guy. He was more of a bottom of a bottle type. A whisper brushes against my ear... *he may be a cold in the ground type now, all because of you, Addy.*

I shake my head at the notion and shove my uncle out of my mind, I try to focus on climbing the stairs. Liam has taken my hand in his. Only the warmth of him is keeping me grounded. Then Luis opens the door. As I peek in I watch a priest stand from the pew he was nestled in. He makes his way towards us. Liam tries to coax me inside, but I can't. I just can't.

Father Landon reaches us. "Good morning, please come in. It is a beautiful day."

Luis responds, "Yes, it is lovely. Addy, this is Father Landon. Father, this is Addison."

He extends his hand out to me. "It is nice to meet you."

My eyes glide over his shoulder taking in the charming little church.

"Would you like to come inside?" he asks.

I shake my head no. I don't want to taint the place. The devil has had me...none of that can seep out here. This place is good.

"Why don't you both wait for us here. Addison and I will take a walk," he says.

Liam releases his grip on my hand, giving me a quick peck on the forehead. He isn't going with...I don't want to do this. Luis and Liam both disappear as the door slowly falls to a close behind them. This is how it should be. I should be left outside. Only good people should be inside those walls.

My eyes gradually drift to Father Landon. He looks too young to be a priest, late twenties I would guess. So young he probably hasn't even had time to encounter a sinner like me in his few years. He smiles and studies my face as if he is working on reading my mind. Quick, Addy, mix up some mortar. You cannot let him see what's in here. I chuck the bad memories behind part of the broken wall. He takes my hand and leads me to a shady spot under a tree. He plops down to the ground. I'm busy struggling to get everything tucked away, all the dark, ugly things I don't want him to notice. He tugs my arm forcing me down beside him.

"You have a lot going on in there," he taps my forehead lightly.

I'm trying to tidy up like you do when an unexpected house guest arrives, shoving shit under a bed or in a closet. But, the knock on my head gives me pause. I take a deep breath looking around behind me. I guess I will have to let him in. Just for a bit, perhaps he won't notice the mess.

I exhale slowly and beg my heart to keep my secrets.

"Breathe, Addison. I'm not here to pry. I'm here to listen if you would like to talk. If we are lucky, I can help you interpret some of the things you are questioning right now."

When I don't say anything he continues, "Why did you not want to go into the church?" he asks.

"I don't belong there."

"Hmm, do you belong out here?" he waves his hand out to encompass everything around.

"I…I guess so," I whisper, wringing my hands together.

"There is no difference. Inside or out it all belongs to him."

Saving Addy

My throat tightens as I ponder what he said.

"So, why do you really not want to go in?"

I think about it for a minute, this is not something I thought I would ever have to do. Talk to a priest about…well about this!

"Addison, why?"

Tears plop into my lap. "I am bad, I don't deserve to be in there. I'm bad and so, I needed to be punished and…and…the discipline was…it was dirty. I'm dirty now."

He remains calm. "So, you consider what happened to you a punishment?"

"Yes, it was, I'm certain it was." I sob louder, looking back at the church. Please let Liam come out, I want to go to the house. This man will pull the demons to the surface, I don't want to encounter them today.

He places his hands over my wringing ones. "Addison, God doesn't work that way. He was not punishing you. We all have already been forgiven for our sins."

"No, no, I am being punished. I did something terrible and that is why they took me, why they hurt me, why they humiliated me," I spit out.

He pauses gazing deep into my eyes. I try to look away, but I can't. He is searching for an answer. Doesn't he realize I am right? Why won't he listen? Then what he says next leaves me in a sobbing mess in his arms.

"Those men hurt you because they were broken souls, Addison. They didn't punish you because you deserved it. You didn't deserve it. You didn't. You. Did. Not. Deserve. It." He shakes my shoulders gently.

He tucks me under his chin, letting me cry into his chest. The black cloth caressing my face becomes darker, soaking up my sorrow. "You didn't deserve it, Addison. No matter what you did, you didn't deserve it."

"Then why?" I wail.

"I don't have the answer to that. Like I said they were broken men. I understand you have been telling yourself you deserved it to make sense of it all. It may have been what kept you going, kept you alive. But, you are safe now. You don't have to hide anymore. You don't have to sit back thinking you deserved what happened to you. You can allow yourself to be angry. It wasn't right, it wasn't fair, and it sure wasn't what God wanted to have happen to you."

"But, I stole something that wasn't mine. I took it and…and I shouldn't have."

He tips my chin up to look at him. "Stop, Addison. You could have stolen the ring off the Pope's finger, and you would not have deserved what happened to you. Listen, this is what is going to take place. You will go inside that building and confess to me whatever you think you need to. Then you are going to let him back in. After that you can begin to tear down that wall."

He knows about my wall. How does he know? He pulls me up with him and leads me to the chapel. Liam and Luis are now sitting on the steps chatting. They both pause when we pass by them but neither say anything. Why aren't they stopping him? They'll understand when I burst into flames the minute I… Stepping over the threshold I stop in my tracks…nothing happened, no sparks, no heat, nothing.

The doors close behind us. The sun is shining through the stained-glass. Beams of light cast dust rays over the pews. The windows are beautiful, from the outside they were dark almost ominous looking but inside is where their true elegance lies. Only with the light does it illuminate, breathing life to each artistic pane.

Is that why? The *why* of what happened to me. Could it be that the men who hurt me didn't have any light and without it they couldn't see the beauty of the world? I crumble to ground. I cry and cry and cry. Father Landon crouches beside me placing a firm hand on my shoulder, he doesn't stop me. My sobs echo around us.

Finally, I cry myself out and I rise leaving a pile of broken bricks. He ushers me to the confessional and there I leave my sins behind. When we emerge from the tiny room, he tells me that he will wait for me with the others. He instructs me to take my time, time to rest, to listen, to forgive myself.

Warmth slowly saturates into me. I repeat over and over the words Father Landon said. I didn't deserve it. I didn't deserve it. I didn't deserve it. But, what do I deserve? That is the question now. What am I going to do? Sit and wallow in the hurt or take back what they stole from me?

They stole from me.

Yes, yes, they did. I had been so caught up in trying to make sense of it all, blaming myself for what I had done. I never once considered what they took from me.

My uncle, Javier, Oliver, Derrick and even Brian. They all took something from me. I want it back. I want it back!

That little voice calls out, the one I stopped listening to when it whispered to me that Brian was my savior. It was right after all. Brian did save me.

He told Anna about me, she saved me because of him. Anna, Dylan…Liam, they all saved me.

Listen, Addison, listen. It is quiet here. You will hear him.

I close my eyes. There it is. My dad's voice…*It's okay, you can let them in. I love you little pixie.*

Liam

When Addy comes out of the church, she looks different. She is calm. She found something here. Something she couldn't find anywhere else. Her eyes are all red and she is tired but peaceful none the less. Father Landon gives her a hug, invites her to Sunday service and then we all make our way to the house.

She stops as we get inside turning to my dad. "Thank you, Luis, you were right. I needed that more than I've ever needed anything."

He blushes and hugs her gently. She pulls back and stares into his eyes for a second. "Are you feeling well?" she asks.

Her question puzzles me, he doesn't seem surprised but answers, "I'm fine, dear, I just need a nap and I'm sure you could use one too." He squeezes her once more and then excuses himself. Her gaze follows him as he walks down the hall, an expression of concern dancing over her features.

She turns back to me. "Thank you for going with me today, Liam."

Saving Addy

"Of course, I will walk you to your room." We continue on in silence until we reach her door. Before she steps inside, I take her hand. "Addy, I need to talk to you?"

She glances up at me with those big brown eyes. "Yes?"

"The others…well I don't know how to put this. The others seem to think I may be overstepping with you. I don't want to overstep. But, shit, I'm sorry I called you an angel the other day. There is just something about you. Fuck, you probably think I am crazy too."

She giggles prompting me to stop my rambling. The sound of her laugh reminds me of little jingle bells. She tugs my arm pulling me inside her room closing the door behind us. She whispers in my ear, "it's okay, Liam, I'm not an angel, I'm a pixie."

What did she say?

Giggling again she continues. "Ahh, now you think I'm crazy. Maybe we both are? It's the wings. You can see my wings. That is why you assumed I was an angel." She is laughing hard, doubling over trying to catch her breath.

God, she is beautiful. I can't help but smile, even though I have no fucking clue what she is talking about.

"No, seriously," she says slumping to the floor resting her back against the door. "I'm sorry, I am just messing with you." A somber disposition replaces her enthusiasm. "My dad used to call me his little pixie. I hadn't thought about it for a long time until today. When you brought up the angel thing again, I don't know it struck me funny."

I slide down beside her on the floor. "Hmm, maybe we are both crazy," I say nudging her gently so that she knows I'm only teasing. "So, your dad nicknamed you his pixie. I can see that." I wink at her and she blushes.

"My father was a humanitarian. We traveled a lot, going wherever he felt he needed to be. It wasn't always a nice place, so he let me create a garden in our backyard. We filled it with flowers and fantasy. I've constantly had one foot in reality and the other in a whimsical world. So, he called me his little pixie. I miss it…I miss him."

"Is he gone?" I ask placing her tiny hand in mine.

"He died when I was sixteen. I went to live with my uncle after that." A shadow passes over her features. Something tells me her time with him was not good, I make a mental note to question her about it some other time. She has shared more with me in the last five minutes than I expected. I had wondered if she was lost after the breakdown she had yesterday. Her resiliency is amazing.

"You know, I do see them, your wings, I see them right here." I place my hand over her heart.

She gazes down at her chest and places her palm over the top of mine. A tear slides down her cheek. "Please don't listen to them," she whispers.

"Listen to who?" I ask, her heart strumming evenly beneath our hands.

"To the others, you aren't overstepping. You are my light." She leans over and lays her head in my lap.

Fuck, I don't know what is happening. I am the voice of reason, but Addy brings out something different in me, she reminds me of life before. Before I realized how ugly the world could be. She reminds me of simpler days when things were not so serious. She reminds me of laughter, sunshine, fireflies, campfires and shooting stars.

We are both crazy. I gaze down to find her asleep in my lap. As I rake my fingers through her soft hair, I can't help but think of Addy as Alice and me the Mad Hatter. *Have I gone mad? Alice replies: I'm afraid so, You're entirely bonkers. But I'll tell you a secret. All the best people are.*

Yep, I've gone bonkers for sure.

Chapter Thirteen

Addy

When I wake up, I realize I fell asleep in Liam's lap. He smiles at me when I sit up. "Oh my gosh, I'm sorry, Liam. You should have woken me. How long was I out?"

"All day, I was about to wake you for supper but, you are just too cute when you sleep. I couldn't bring myself to do it." He tucks a lock of hair behind my ear.

Blushing, I draw my legs up to my chest. "You all must think I am a complete loon."

"No, you know what I think you are," he says winking at me.

I pull my shoulder up to my cheek. "An angel, yes, how could I forget?"

"We should get down to supper. Anna has been texting me like crazy. She has it all set up out in the flower garden."

Instantly I hop up. Yes, the garden. Outside where I can breathe in the fresh air, hear the birds and smell the dirt. Liam laughs, I watch as he rises to his feet. I feel bad. He looks stiff, he really should have woken me. He places his arms above his head stretching. His shirt rides up over his abdomen allowing me a glimpse of his rock-hard abs. My heart trips over itself trying to find a normal rhythm. I chew on my bottom lip.

He is extremely handsome. Calvin Cline underwear model kind of good looking. My mind runs away to a place it hasn't visited in a long time. The place that signals a hot tingly sensation to my crotch. I excuse myself to the restroom.

What is happening? I told myself that if I ever got away, I would never look at another man, never let one touch me. But, just now, just now I wanted nothing more than to run my hands over Liam's firm stomach. To feel his warm lips on my mouth, on my....

"Are you okay, Addy?" his voice rumbles through the door and straight to…fuck. Stop.

"Yes, just freshening up. I'll meet you outside." I brave a peek in the mirror. Addison is staring at me. She is back that is why this is happening. It is perfectly normal to be attracted to a good-looking man. Right? Yes, totally normal. It doesn't have to go beyond that. It can't continue beyond that. That part of me is dead so, it was a weak moment.

When I get outside to the flower garden it steals my breath away. It is so beautiful, there is a tiny little pond filled with koi fish. I was wrong, I can't smell the dirt, all I can breathe is Mrs. Cortez's sinfully amazing meal. Anthony comes up behind me. "Are you hungry, Addy?"

I don't turn to him as my attention goes from one delightful thing to another. "Yes, yes, I am but there is so much to see."

He laughs which makes me finally shift to face him. "I like your enthusiasm young lady." He taps the end of my nose. "Come, Mrs. Cortez's food is best when it's warm." He tips his elbow out allowing me to slide my arm through his and he escorts me to the table.

Liam rushes forward and pulls out a chair for me, giving Anthony a not so friendly scowl. Anthony just laughs and sits down in the seat beside me. "Don't worry, he is not always so grumpy," he says sticking his thumb out towards Liam.

I giggle. Liam doesn't appear as amused, but I find it endearing how possessive he has become over me. He slides his arm over the back of my chair and gently jerks it closer to him and farther away from Anthony.

I smile at him and pat his leg under the table. He gifts me with that cute little dimple. You can barely see it with his beard but it's there, peeking out just above the hairline. He leans over and whispers, "he is trying to move in on my angel, but he will fail."

His warm breath brushes over my ear and my neck. Goose bumps tickle over my skin, sending a slight shiver through my entire body. When he pulls away he winks at me. Then I notice everyone's attention is on us. Crap, we need to remember we are not alone. When he is with me it's like we are in a bubble floating on a breeze, the rainbow glazed bubble lifts us high where nothing bad can reach us.

"Addy, how did this morning go?" Dylan's gruff voice pops the bubble and I drop back down into my seat.

"Great. Good. Very well," I ramble trying to tame the flames dancing on my cheeks.

He grunts in response. Liam was right they seem a little tense with how him and I are getting along. I force myself not to glance at him the rest of the meal, even though he brushes against me the entire time. His touch sends ripples of pleasure tiptoeing across my skin.

I'm sad and glad when supper ends. Luis excused himself earlier, he doesn't look well. Tomorrow I will speak with him about it, maybe he is tired. Me being here has probably been taxing on everyone. I should figure out a way to get home. Home, and just where would that be? I guess I'll go back to Utah. No, I can't go there, my colleagues know I was abducted, they will look at me differently. I don't want that. I'll start up somewhere new. Fuck, where do I begin?

Anthony again holds out his arm for me, I glance around nervously. If I don't accept his offer they will be mad at Liam. "I'll walk you back to your room," he says winking at Liam over my shoulder. I turn my head slightly to see him scowl.

"Thank you," I reply as I allow him to lead me back through the house.

When we get to my door Anthony releases me. "I am the resident fashion expert around here. Tomorrow I am going into town, would you like to join me? We could go shopping." He tweaks a strand of my hair between his finger and thumb.

"Oh, I don't know. Thank you but I should probably work on getting home."

He looks surprised but continues without missing a beat. "Of course. I will pick you up a few things. Let's see, I would guess you are into the colorful? Bright and cheerful?" he asks.

I giggle. He is adorable. I think he is flirting with me but I'm not sure. Or is he always like this? "Yes, but really you don't need to."

He takes my hand and places a light kiss on the top before releasing it. "Until tomorrow," he drawls as he bows and turns heading down the hall.

I shut the door and lean my back against it. These folks are all so nice. It's hard to consider leaving but I can't stay here forever. I've been a burden long enough. In the morning I'll speak with Dylan and Anna. Mexico is not a safe place for me to be. If any of Javier's men spot me he will come, of that I have no doubt.

Well, what now? I'm so used to doing nothing, sitting, waiting but now I can do whatever I want. I pull out a pair of sweats and a t-shirt and head to the bathroom to shower. The prospect of showering whenever I wish is wonderful. Little things seem so much better. That is what I will take away from this, from what happened to me. I'm going to enjoy everything I can.

When I come out, Liam is sitting on the window seat, he startles me. I place my hand over my chest. "Shit, you scared me," I squeak.

He laughs. "That was the first time I've heard you curse," he says. "I like it." He cocks an eyebrow at me.

I shift my weight from foot to foot, slightly nervous at the way he is looking at me. "Mmm, I try not to, but you know, even the devil was once an angel," I say.

He stands coming towards me, I back up until my butt hits the dresser behind me. "I have a surprise for you, Addy." He reaches out and tugs me in closer to him. I stare at his chest as he holds me captive in his arms. Something has definitely changed in him. I search through the mess in my head looking for what it could be, ah, here it is. Oh, poop, I know what it is. He is jealous. That's what this is. He is jealous of Anthony walking me to my room and now he is…

His breath whispers over my neck as he dips his lips close to my shoulder. "You do like surprises don't you, Addy?"

I shiver in his arms. "Um, yeah. I guess," I say in a voice that sounds way too raspy to be mine.

"Do you trust me?" His whiskers brush across my cheek sending a bolt of energy through my veins.

"Yes," I whisper turning my face towards him, lightly grazing his ear with my lips.

My head is swimming, no one has touched me in this way for so long. I was sure I would never get this ever again. I assumed they had killed that part of me. My breath is coming out in little pants. Now that I think about it, I don't know if I've experienced anything like this. Boyfriends, yes a few. It never led to more than kissing and light petting. My career consumed me. There was no time for much more than studying and work. I always had the need to make amends for what I had done, it drove me to obsession.

But, this…. this is…new.

He leans back gazing into my eyes, drowning me in their deep blue depths. "I've read that pixies like to dance under the light of the moon," he whispers.

He pulls me down the dark hallway to the glass doors leading to the patio. When we step out, I see a stereo perched on a table close to the house. He walks over to it and flips a switch. I'm mesmerized by him as I stand in the middle of the red stone tiles, the pale moonlight washing over me. Then the notes from the black box skip towards me. I almost drop to my knees when I realize how long it has been since I heard music. It is foreign to my ears.

My eyes fill with tears, so many things I have missed. Liam hesitantly moves close and then holds out his palm. I place my hand in his and he wraps his fingers around mine tightly then quickly spins me into his chest. "You are beautiful," he whispers into my ear before spinning me away from him.

Our arms are outstretched, paused in the moment, drinking each other in. The music takes me back to a time when life was good. I smile at him and a happy crocodile tear slips down my cheek. "Thank you."

He whirls me into to his chest and brushes his lips across my forehead. "I don't think I can ever let you go, Addy."

I'm at a loss for words. It frightens me but yet it doesn't. He is my light. He is illuminating the space behind my wall. He is chasing away the dark. I couldn't stop him even if I wanted to. I rest my head on his chest as we sway over the patio. Notes dancing over our heads. The magic is returning, it's been gone so long. I've missed it. It vanished when my father died. But, Liam might be someone who can bring it back.

Chapter Fourteen

Addy

Liam and I dance for hours, no words passing between us. None were needed, I absorbed every moment. The longer I am in his arms the safer I feel. He feels like...home. Since my father passed away, I have not had this feeling. After he died, I went to live with my mom's brother in Mexico. He was the only person I had left.

My mom and dad met on one of his mission trips to Mexico. She was a drug mule for Javier Galindo. My dad fell in love with her and tried to help her but, unfortunately she was not only a drug runner she was a drug user. The combination was deadly. When I was seven she left us and ran back to Mexico. We never saw her again. It wasn't long after that we learned that she had died from an overdose.

I have dual citizenship, so I crossed the border regularly to visit my uncle and my abuela. He tried to stay out of the drug business, and he did to a point. Unfortunately, he had a gambling problem and got himself in trouble with a few loan sharks. Not knowing where to turn he turned to Javier. But, it didn't take long and soon his debts to him became an issue as well.

When I moved in with him at the age of sixteen he was so far in debt with Javier that we were seeing daily visits from his thugs. They frightened me and so I decided to give my Uncle Leo all of my inheritance. I knew my dad had intended the money to be used for my college education, but I had to do it. Javier's men beat him so severely one night that I had no choice.

My uncle promised me he would stop his gambling, but I soon learned addiction is something that cannot be curbed with a simple good intention. I recognized he wanted to quit, he couldn't. Javier agreed to pay off the loan sharks once again. But, this time he made a special request for me to be the one to pick up the money. I should have known better.

Going to Javier's was the most frightening thing I have ever done. The way he looked at me was terrifying, but it was what he said when I left that day that spurred me to run and never look back. He told me that if Leo did not repay the hundred-grand, he would expect something more than my uncles hide….he would demand mine. The exchanged glance between him and I was palpable, we both knew that my uncle could never repay him. We also both knew that the minute I walked out that door I was as good as his. I would belong to him, to do with whatever he chose.

That was the day I committed my sin. I went back to my uncles packed a few belongings and crossed the border with Javier Galindo's hundred-grand in the bottom of my bag. I'm not sure if he killed my uncle, if he did then that is another notch in my old sinner belt. I just couldn't be his…. not his…. anything but that.

Life was good, I worked hard to counteract my thievery and to follow in my father's footsteps but then I made the mistake of going back to Mexico. It was the most foolish thing I have ever done, well besides stealing from Javier Galindo that is.

Saving Addy

"You are being awfully quiet. What are you thinking about?" Liam asks.

"Nothing, just how nice it is to be outside." I can't tell him what is on my mind. I have told no one except Father Landon.

"It's getting late, why don't you head to bed. I will come check on you in a minute. I need to pack up the stereo." He holds my face in both of his hands kissing me lightly on the forehead.

"I am tired. Thank you Liam. It was a nice way to end the day." He releases me and I turn to walk inside.

Walking down the halls by myself is surreal. Not having an escort is both comforting and discomforting at the same time. A sound howls down the hall and causes me to pause. Now you are just spooking yourself, Addy. Then I hear it again. Someone is in trouble. I rush down the hallway and stop in front of a door that the noise seems to come from.

"Anna, you have been a very bad girl haven't you?"

Shit, it is Dylan. No! This can't be.

"Yes, sir," she replies.

Smack! I jump, he hit her! I glance back and forth down the corridor. I should get help. But as I turn to run something else catches my attention. I place my ear up to the wood listening intently.

"Ahh fuck yes, Dylan. That feels so fucking amazing," Anna moans out.

I cover my mouth, ummm, shoot. I'm confused, she doesn't sound like she is hurting. She sounds...

Another loud moan echoes from behind the door.

As I am about to turn away and make my escape something warm presses against my back. Before I realize what is happening I am pushed up against the cold wood. A seductive rumble vibrates over my neck. "What are you doing, Addison?"

The moaning inside the room intensifies coming to a crescendo and I try to slide out from between Liam and door, but he pins me between his arms.

"Nothing, I…I thought he was hurting her. I heard him…um…I heard him hit her and I…shit Liam I don't know. Please let me go." The commotion behind the door is getting more intense, and it's making me feel something I am pretty sure I should NOT be feeling.

"Shh, it's okay, Addy. He isn't harming her." He doesn't move, he keeps me trapped. His mouth is so close I can almost…oh shit. A little gasp escapes my lips as he brings his down on the side of my neck. So warm, so intoxicating. He slides his arm away from the frame and brushes it over my chest lightly, resting it over the base of my throat. His thumb strums back and forth over the rapid beating of my pulse.

His hand slips down between my breasts and rests at the waistband of my sweatpants. His finger dips just below the band, gliding across my sensitive skin. A tease or a threat, I am not sure I recognize the difference anymore. I can't, I want to, I really, really want to but…his teeth gently trap my earlobe.

"Liam," I say my voice trembling. "I'm sorry, I can't do this."

My words break the trance and before I can even turn around he is gone.

I fumble my way back to my room like a drunk person bumping down the hall. I finally find the door and collapse inside. Nooo, why did I stop him? I bury my hands in my face, sobbing. I wanted to but yet…I can't. Anger builds as my tears spill. Not at Liam but at them. Them…those fuckers took everything from me. Everything! I will never be normal…never! I sob until eventually I fall asleep in a pitiful little ball on the floor, just like they always demanded. Stupid, pathetic Addy, their voices haunt me the rest of night.

Liam

I've been up all night. There is only one choice for me now. I've booked my flight for D.C. and I leave first thing Tuesday morning. Today and tomorrow is all I have to make it through. Surely I can keep my grubby paws off of her for that long. Today is Sunday so shit this should be easy, I'll go to church with my dad and then I'll hide in my room until Tuesday arrives. Yes, that I can do. Simple.

My heart is bleeding out, will I survive until then? I have no choice. I'm bad for her, what the fuck was I thinking pinning her up against the door? I forced her to listen to Anna and Dylan.

Dylan is going to fucking kill me.

Stupid, Liam, you are so, so damn dumb. I grab a drink and plop down in the chair in front of his desk. I will just tell him, that way I won't be tempted to stay, he will make sure of that.

"Liam, I'm surprised to see you up and at em' so early on a Sunday morning," he says from behind me. I jump like a damn teenager caught looking at porn.

His laugh rumbles through the room. Fucker always gets enjoyment from scaring me, I guess I deserve it today.

"What's up?"

"I'm flying out on Tuesday at 3:00 a.m."

"What? Why? I thought you were going to stay and help Addy. She is comfortable with you. I think you should stick around," he states, kicking his feet up to his desk.

"She won't be after last night," I say, burying my head in my hands.

Dylan's boots thud to the floor and his chair creaks as his weight shifts. "What did you do?" he hisses. I detect the threat in his tone.

"I fucked up is what I did. We were outside, listening to music. She came back in while I put the stereo away and when she passed your room, she overheard you and Anna. She thought you were hurting her, so she paused outside your door. I...I fucking pushed her up against it and...and...shit I kissed her neck and was about to take it a step farther and she stopped me. I ran like the damn coward I am and well...I'm leaving. I'm sorry, Dylan."

His fist comes crashing down on the desk as Anna steps in.

"What is going on..." she cries.

Dylan roars, "What is going on? What is going on is that this idiot just fucked up royally."

"I know, I know, I'm sorry I'll be gone soon." I jump out of my chair and rush by her stopping long enough to give her a quick peck on the cheek.

Church with my dad and then I'll hibernate in my room. Shit, Dylan is right what an idiot. My thoughts are so jumbled that I bump into him in the hallway. "Son? What is it? What is wrong? Is it Addy?" he says grabbing hold of my arms to look me directly in the eye.

Saving Addy

"Can we talk about it after church?"

"Yes, just, Liam, you are worrying me."

"It's nothing. I wanted to tell you I'm flying to D.C. Tuesday morning. I really need to get my place packed up. I'll be back as soon as I can. I just need to get it done."

"Okay," he says with a skeptical expression on his face. "We will discuss this later. I'm going to see if Addy would like to go down to breakfast with me. Do you want to join?"

"No, I'm going to skip breakfast this morning. I'll meet you at the chapel." I take off down the hall before he can stop me. I can't see her. I don't want to see the disappointment on her face. I'm sure she thought I was a much better person than the one she saw last night. How could I have done that after all that she has been through?

The minutes tick by at lightning speed and before I know it people are pouring into the church. I purposely sat on the end of the very back row. Hopefully it fills fast, and my dad will have to sit with her away from me. I doubt she even shows up, who could blame her. I probably set her back to the day we found her with all my stupidity.

Families filter in and I was correct the pew fills up till there is no more room around me. But, the minute she steps in the building I sense it. I force my gaze to remain in my lap, I can't look at her. I don't want to see the hurt in her eyes, the damage I caused.

When the service starts I risk a glance. They are four rows in front of me. My dad on one side of her and Dylan on the other. Anna peeks over her shoulder at me at mouths the words, "I'm sorry."

I point to myself. I am the one who is sorry, the one who should be apologetic. Father Landon begins his sermon and I stare into my lap. I cannot lose my resolve. I need to make sure I am on that plane on Tuesday. Liam the voice of reason everyone always says, well evidently not this time. Suddenly I notice others whispering and then a commotion breaks out. I glance up to see my dad slumped over in the pew and Addison standing over him. What the hell?

I stand up, people are backing out of the way, some members of the church are stepping outside. Rushing over to my father I realize he is unconscious. "What happened? What is wrong with him?" I yell out to no one in particular.

Addison gently pushes me away from my father. "Anna, can you please take care of Liam." She leans over my dad checking him over to determine his condition. "He is breathing, and his pulse is weak but there. Dylan, I will need you to carry him to the infirmary." She keeps her fingers over his neck and her other hand grabs Dylan's forearm watching the tick of his wristwatch. "Okay, let's go now."

Anna is holding me back, I stare as the angel takes charge, it's as if she has done this a hundred times. No hesitation. My dad....I can't lose my dad. What is wrong with him?

Dylan scoops up my father as I stand by helplessly. "Is Mark here?" he barks out.

"No, he left last evening to visit his family," Anna replies.

"Shit!" Dylan says as he rushes out of the church with my fathers' limbs dangling lifelessly by his sides.

Saving Addy

Addy grabs my arm and pulls me along beside her as we follow Dylan. "Liam, does your father have a heart condition or any other medical conditions I should know about?"

I stare at her confused. "No, no, he is healthy as a horse. Well, until now!" I shout as I pull at my hair.

"Any medications?" she asks.

"No, shit, what the hell is wrong with him?"

Dylan hauls my dad into a room and Addison stops me outside placing her hand on my chest. "Liam, it will be okay. I will figure out what is going on, wait out here with Anna. I promise I will treat him as if he was my own father."

I nod, she is so confident. She turns and closes the door behind her. Who is this girl?

Anna comes over and wraps her arms around me. "He will be okay, Liam. He just has to be." I return her hug, not saying anything.

About thirty minutes later, Dylan returns to the sitting area. "He is okay, he is awake."

Anna and I both breathe a sigh of relief. Tears stream down her cheeks. "I told you."

"What happened?" I ask Dylan.

"Addison will explain everything to you. She is more qualified than I am." He pulls me into his arms giving me one of his giant bear hugs. "I'm sorry, Liam. I am sorry I have been so hard on you. You are my best friend. I shouldn't have said those things to you this morning."

I pull away looking at him. "My dad isn't dying is he?" Dylan never talks like this.

He chuckles. "No, he will be fine, Liam. It is just that this reminded me of how important you and your dad are to me. You are my brother. Now get in there, he wants to see you."

Dylan wraps Anna up in his arms as I head down to the room they took my dad to. I hesitantly open the door peeking in. He is laying down and Addison is getting ready to insert an IV into his arm.

She turns to face me and smiles. "It's okay come in. He is doing much better."

He looks pale but alert. "Sorry to scare you kid," he says sucking air through his teeth as Addy's needle pokes him.

"I'm just giving him some fluids. He is a little dehydrated. I've told him, he should visit his regular doctor. I'm afraid that he may have developed diabetes. He hasn't been eating and his blood sugar dropped to a dangerous level. I've given him some glucose and it has come back up to normal, but he will need to monitor it." She pats his arm as she finishes with the IV. "Give me the name of your physician. I will call and fill him in as to what is going on. I'll also get an appointment scheduled."

"She is a bossy little nurse practitioner isn't she?" he jokes.

Nurse practitioner?

"Okay, what's his name and I will go make the call. Also, if you let me in on what your favorite meal is, I'll leave a tiny hint with Mrs. Cortez," she says winking at him.

Saving Addy

My dad spills the goods on his doctor information and Addison jots it all down on a small tablet. "Got it. Don't let him up. I want to make sure his levels stay up and that we get the fluid in him before we have him up and moving."

I numbly shake my head at her. The gold aurora is glowing brightly now, I wonder if my dad can see it. She *is* an angel, dropped here at just the right time. She throws us a wave and then she is gone.

I pull up a chair by my dad's hospital bed. He reaches out and takes my hand. "It's okay, Liam, I'm good. Thank god she was here." He nods towards the door.

I stare at it. "She was sent here for us wasn't she?" I ask him.

"Well son, it is however you want to look at it. But, yes, I think she was and maybe the road goes both ways and you are here for her too."

My head jerks back to gawk at him. "I have to leave dad. I am no good for her."

"Why don't you let her decide that."

Anna comes barging in before I can tell him what happened last night. "Luis," she cries rushing to him throwing herself over the top of him.

My dad laughs wrapping his arms around her. "Shh, it's okay. I'm fine."

His laugh is music to my ears.

Chapter Fifteen

Addy

My spark is back with clarity. I should have trusted my instincts with Luis. He hasn't looked well for several days and all of his symptoms pointed to diabetes. Overall he is a healthy guy, he may even get by without needing to take insulin. Proper diet and exercise and he should be fine. At least he is aware of the situation. It broke my heart when I saw how scared Liam was.

It took me right back to the day my dad dropped over, except his was from a heart attack. That was the day I decided I would go into medicine. I've always loved science and helping people. The two go hand in hand. Javier's money all went to my education. Somehow I thought the good that I would do would negate the fact that it was stolen drug money.

Even though I feel bad that Luis is not well, it helped remind me of who I am. My focus is back. When I was held captive, I would sit for hours and write down everything I could remember from school, but when Oliver found out about Brian and I that ended. I was left in that room at the club with nothing but me, myself and I. Anxiety overwhelmed in the beginning, I was so worried I would lose my skills, that I would forget everything I learned. But, today I found out it is still here. I've still got it.

Saving Addy

"How is my patient this evening?" I say upon entering Luis's room. He is all settled back in his own room, nice and cozy.

As I approach the bed Liam stands and excuses himself. "I'll leave you two to take care of business. Goodnight, I'll see you in the morning dad." Then he rushes out.

My heart sinks, he hasn't really spoke to me since last night. Crazy as it sounds, I miss him. He is avoiding me. I turn my attention to Luis forcing a smile to my face. "Let's check that blood sugar, shall we?"

"Yes, and then let's talk about you and Liam," he says shoving himself up higher on the pillows behind him.

My mouth falls open. Did he tell his dad? An inferno rushes to my face. "I...oh, Luis, there really is nothing to talk about."

"Tsk, tsk. Addison, this is not my first rodeo with that boy. He has fallen head over heels for you. What I am wondering is how you feel about him."

I plop down in the chair that Liam just vacated, it is still warm...I can still sense him, I can still smell him. My eyes slowly rise to meet Luis's wise ones. "He has been my light. He has given me the magic back and he...he feels like home."

Those damn big crocodile tears plop, plop, plop into my lap.

"He is leaving Tuesday morning." He states and I can hear the sadness in his voice.

"No, he can't leave you now. I will go and find him. It's time I should be going anyhow. I should go...home," my words drift off, losing momentum as they fall out. Where do I start? Where do I go?

"Addison, that is not what I want, and you know it. You need to be here right now. Maybe we should let him go. What's meant to be will be. Now, let's get this over with, I hate being poked."

Well, conversation over. Why did he tell me if he didn't want me to leave? Leaning over in the chair I poke his finger testing the tiny little drop of blood. My mind races trying to figure out a way to stop Liam. He can't go, he can't leave me.

"Thank you, Addison. You saved my life this morning, none of these other people would have known how to help me. You are an angel." My eyes dart to his. Liam told him. "You know everyone has always called Liam the voice of reason. It is true and I have never been surer of that statement than I am right now." He pats my hand. "Now, find your bed, Addison, you need to rest, it has been a long day."

"Are you the patient or am I?" I scold. Then I smile at him as I walk out and close the door behind me.

Instead of finding my bed I make my way down to Dylan and Anna's room. I hesitate outside the door making sure I don't interrupt anything. Oh, Addy, can your life get any crazier. I knock and step back to wait patiently for them to answer. Dylan swings the door open when he sees it is me he steps out. "Is everything okay, is it Luis?" he asks, fear crossing over his scary features.

"No, I'm sorry I don't mean to interrupt your evening. I just wondered if I could talk to you and Anna?" My trembling voice betrays my aura of calm.

"Anna is asleep, I will wake her," he says.

I reach out and stop him. "No, please don't wake her. It was a long day. It can wait until tomorrow."

He peeks in to check on her then closes the door and takes my hand in his. "No, it's okay. Let's go down to my office, if you are okay with just talking to me?"

I stare up at him. "Umm, yes I suppose that would be okay."

When we get to the office, he pours us both a drink. "Thank you for everything you did today for Luis. That was pretty scary."

"Of course, It was nice to be needed again." I take a sip of the whiskey, choking a little as it burns my throat.

He sits across from me gazing deep into my eyes, searching, trying to figure out who I am. They deserve to know. They came for me, they saved me, the least I can do is tell them who I am.

"My name is Addison Lane Davis. I am a nurse practitioner from the United States. Utah to be exact, that is where I got my bachelors and masters. Originally from Arizona, that is where I was born and raised. Brian abducted me while I was in Mexico. An organization that I was a part of was there providing free immunizations along the border. My passion has always been helping children." My voice trails off as I remember the day I bumped into Brian. Taking a deep breath, I continue. "I should go home, but, I don't know where to start. Luis told me that Liam is leaving. I know it is because of me. His dad needs him. I will leave so that he doesn't have to."

"Thank you for sharing that with me, Addy. Of course, we will help you get home, do you have someone you would like to call?"

My eyes fall to my lap. I have no one…absolutely no one. "I don't really have anyone. It's okay, I just need to get my identification and then I can cross the border. I am a dual citizen."

Dylan looks surprised. "So, no family? How is that you are a dual citizen, if you don't mind my asking?"

Chewing on my bottom lip I try to decide if I can trust him with a small bit of the truth. "No, no family maybe some extended but no one I could call. Um, my mother was from Mexico and my father a United States citizen. I mainly resided in the states with my father. I crossed often to visit family, but they are all gone."

Dylan stares at me, he is taking his time, gathering his thoughts before responding. "Addy, if you don't have anyone I don't feel comfortable sending you off on your own. You have been through something traumatic and while I recognize how strong you are I know from experience that you will need help. Anna and I would love to have you stay with us for a while. At least until you work through some things, Luis will help you. We will all help you."

"I can't stay. Liam…"

Dylan cuts me off. "Liam is a big boy. While I think he should stay he has made his decision." He pauses and sighs before continuing. "I am sorry for the other night with Anna and I, I am sorry it frightened you."

My cheeks are burning, I turn to look at the door. Hmm, this was not what I wanted to talk about.

"Addy, what Liam did was wrong. He knows this and he feels terrible about it. Liam is the most admirable man I know, and he knows his limits.

He is worried that he will go too far with you. He knows that you are not ready for something like that and that is okay."

A knock at the door interrupts us. Thank god, this is not a conversation I want to have with Dylan. He rises to answer the door and I hear Anthony's voice.

"Hey man, I heard a lot went down today. How is Luis?" Anthony asks.

"He is fine now, resting in his room if you would like to see him."

"Sounded pretty scary, glad to hear that he is okay. I will visit him tomorrow. I was actually looking for Addy. Have you seen her?" he asks.

Dylan opens the door wide so that Anthony can see me.

"Ah, here she is." Anthony glides into the room coming to me taking my hand in his and placing a kiss on the top. "Addison, I had an excellent day shopping and I hear that you saved our dear Luis's life so I will have no arguments and you will accept everything I bought you. Do you understand?" He pulls me to stand.

"Ah, really today was nothing. I probably got more out of it than Luis did." I say, blushing at his compliments.

"His heart is still beating so I would say he gained quite a bit," he replies.

"Well, he reminded me of who I am so I would argue that he has kept mine beating as well."

Dylan chuckles. "You may have met your match, Anthony. This girl is much smarter than the ones you usually communicate with."

Anthony places his hand over his chest as if Dylan just stabbed him. "Ouch," he says.

When I giggle they both turn to me. "Anthony, thank you. Anna told me that you are a master shopper. Show me what treasures you have brought me." Whew at least this gives me a getaway from the deep conversation I was just having. Although I realize as we walk out that I did not get my way. I am pretty sure Dylan has no intention of helping me get back to the states, not yet anyhow.

When Anthony and I get back to my room there are shopping bags everywhere. He starts dumping them out on the bed. I watch every item fall out, a complete wardrobe for a lucky girl. Lucky girl…I don't deserve this. I don't deserve any of this. I take a step back away from the bed. If someone were to walk in the room and see the look on my face they would think that I had a bed full of serpents not beautiful articles of clothing laid out.

Anthony notices my reaction. He sits down and pulls me into his lap. "Stop. You will accept this from me, it is my gift to you."

"I don't deserve a gift from you, Anthony. I don't deserve anything. You barely know me. Actually, you don't know me at all," I say trying to rise from his lap.

"Shh, Addy. I need you to listen to me. This is my way of helping you. I'm not like the others, I'm not good at deep conversation, or feelings. So, this is my way of helping. You need these things please accept them."

Peeking up at him, I see the sincerity on his face. He is being serious which I think might be a rarity for him. "Okay."

"Good, now on to the next thing. Let's go." He pushes me off his lap and grabs my hand dragging me out the door.

"Wait, where are we going?" I dig my heels into the carpet, but he continues pulling me along.

I stumble along behind him as he continues down the hallway and then he opens a door, pushes me inside and shuts it abruptly behind me. I turn and try to open it shaking the handle. It's locked! He locked me in! Then I hear a sound behind me and freeze.

"Fucking Anthony," Liam's voice rumbles over my shoulder.

He nudges me aside shaking the handle to the door himself. I watch him and then glance around. This must be Liam's room. He bangs on the door and I jump. "Anthony, unlock this fucking door!"

Anthony's muffled chuckle comes from the other side. "I will unlock it in an hour. Talk to her you dumbass."

I back away slowly from Liam, he looks angry. He sighs then turns to me. "I'm not mad at you, Addy. This fucker is always a pain in my ass." He points to the door.

This is not good, I am locked in. Locked in. Locked in. Locked in. The words repeat over and over in my head. Bricks need more bricks. Tears start to slide down my cheeks.

"Angel, hey, it's okay. Don't be scared. He will unlock it in an hour." Liam wraps his arms around me brushing his lips over my forehead. "Hey, you know what I can just call Dylan and he will come unlock it. I'm sorry I don't know what the fuck is wrong with Anthony."

"No, wait. I need to talk to you. You can't leave me…um I mean you can't leave your dad." I push off his chest talking a small step back.

His eyes swirl as he processes what I said, he caught my slip. "*You* want me to stay?"

I kick an imaginary rock around with my toe. Staring at the ground. "Yes."

"Addy, I am so sorry for what happened the other night. That shouldn't have happened. I think it best if I distance myself from you, before I hurt you."

"It's dark behind my wall, Liam. I need your light."

He stares up at the ceiling. He is going to say no. He is going to take the magic and the light with him.

Chapter Sixteen

Liam

One final day, I just need to make it today then I can hop on the plane and Addy will be safe from me. The expression on her face last night when I told her I had to go broke my heart. I shouldn't have started anything with her, it was a stupid, foolish thing to do. Better I leave and then the others will get her back on the right track. She doesn't need me. She said I was her light, but that is not true. The things I want to do to her would send her running out the door screaming.

I skipped breakfast again and now I am just waiting to get this damn meeting with Javier Galindo over. Blah, I wish I wasn't here. Men like Javier make my blood boil. But, I am here for the innocent girl he is helping his employee find.

"Please take a seat," Dylan says as he ushers the devil himself into the office. I straighten in my chair, the hairs on the back of my neck bristle. "This is my partner Liam Sharp."

I rise and shake the man's hand. Dylan pours us all a drink. I notice a man come in and stand guard by the door. Fuckers. Scum of the earth right here.

"Thank you for agreeing to meet with me," Javier says.

"Of course, tell us a little about the girl you are looking for," Dylan inquires leaning back in his chair.

"It is my employee's niece she was abducted by one of Oliver Wright's men almost two years ago. We've been trying to locate her to no avail. But, I heard a rumor you brought his empire down. So, here I am, is the story correct?"

"Yes, we have been successful at dismantling Oliver's organization," I reply giving him a smug face. I don't like this fucker.

He smiles. "Good, then I'm sure you can help me. He pulls a photo out of his pocket running his finger over it. Her name is Addison Davis." He reluctantly relinquishes his hold on it and hands it to Dylan.

My. Fucking. Heart. Stops. It literally takes several minutes for it to contract and beat again. The beast inside me huffs with an intensity that could rip this man's throat out with a mere flick of a claw. But, my training allows me to mask everything and before Dylan can speak I answer Javier. "Hmmm, I don't recall any of the young women telling us their name was Addison. You do realize that most of Oliver's girls are sold within several months of being abducted. If it was almost two years ago, I am confident she was not in Oliver's clutches when we ripped his shit apart," I grit out. As I talk I imagine my hands wrapping around this man's neck.

Dylan gives me a sidelong glance. He knows me well enough I am sure he can sense the violence rolling off me. "I am sorry, my partner is right. But, we will go through the records we have of Oliver's. If we find anything we'll let you know."

Saving Addy

Javier leans back in his chair draining the last drop of liquor from his glass. "My employee will be so very disappointed," he says. "We were positive you all would be able to help us. You see, we had word that Oliver had taken a liking to her. I am sure that if you search through your records, you will come up with something." The man's threat reels off of him with a stench that makes me want to vomit.

"We will do our best to locate the girl. May we keep the photo?" Dylan responds calmly.

"Yes, of course, whatever helps to get her back where she belongs."

"Allow me to escort you out," Dylan says giving me a glance of concern as they walk out.

The minute they are gone I run down to Addy's room. She isn't here. Fuck I hope she is not outside. I don't want Javier to spot her. Something is wrong…. very wrong. Javier is a dangerous man.

I rush out the back door and turn to slide down the side of the house scanning the area as I do. Where is she? Please let her be inside somewhere. Then I spy her. She is crouched down behind a bush. The color has bled from her face and I can see that she is watching the driveway. She knows he is here, and the sheer terror etched in her expression rips my soul out.

I want to go to her, but I can't draw any attention to where she is hiding. She is hiding…this is so messed up. A motor starts and the sound of gravel crunching under the weight of a car sends her running like the devil himself is behind her.

She runs never once looking back. Where is she going? Why didn't she run towards the safety of the house? When I get close enough, and I think that she can hear I yell out to her. "Addy, stop. It's okay he is gone."

She doesn't even pause; in fact, she picks up speed. Shit, this girl is fast. We run all the way to the outer edge of the property before I finally catch up and launch myself at her knocking us down. I land on top of her with a thud, stealing both of our breath away.

"No, no," she screams once she is finally able to suck in a gulp of air. "Let me go." She scratches at the ground, her fingers digging into the dirt.

"Calm down. It's okay he is gone."

"I shouldn't have trusted you all. I'm so stupid, so stupid," she says.

I roll her over, but she claws at my face, blood trickles down my cheek. "Addy, listen. You are safe he won't hurt you."

Dylan runs up to us as I pull her hands together trapping them against the ground.

When she spots him, her face contorts to one of terror and rage. "Fuck you. Fuck you. Let me go, let me go," she shouts bucking wildly under me.

Dylan squats down as I struggle to control the hellcat beneath me. He reaches in his pocket pulls out a syringe bites the cap off and jabs it into her neck.

"I hate you. I hate you both," she cries as the fight slowly leaves. Her head lolls to the side before her eyes close, the hellcat vanishes, and the angel returns.

Saving Addy

"What in the fuck?" Dylan says.

"I don't know man, but this is not good." I stare down at my angel, the ache in my chest burns as I calmly stand drawing her limp body into my arms.

Once she is settled back in her suite, we gather the others to the dining room. Dylan explains the situation to everyone. "I'm not sure what is going on, but we need to get her talking and sooner rather than later. Javier is not a man to be messed with," he says, fear evident in his expression.

"Could it be what Galindo says is true, and that she is just overwhelmed and scared to return to her family?" my dad asks.

"She mentioned that she went to live with her uncle after her father passed. But, she is frightened for a reason and I don't think it is coming from a place of shame," I reply running my hand over my face. I'm still in shock over the whole ordeal.

"I think we need to ask her. We must be straightforward," my dad says.

"It won't be as easy as that," Dylan replies drumming his fingers on the table. "We had to drug her to get her to calm down. She is restrained at the moment."

"What! No!" Anna wails. "We have to release her before she wakes up." She rises knocking her chair over in a rush to see Addy. Dylan leans over grabbing her around the waist and pulls her into his lap.

"Shh, it's okay. We had no choice. Look at Liam's face. She did that to him, she wanted away from us Anna. We can't release her until we are sure she won't run or hurt herself. She was very frightened. If she runs and Galindo is a threat, she will not be safe out there on her own. We need to figure out if she is in danger or if Luis's theory is correct and she is afraid of facing her family." Dylan rocks her back and forth as she quietly listens.

"She will be terrified being tied down," Anna pleads.

"I know, baby but, we have no choice. Just for a little while until we figure this out. I think it would be best if you let the rest of us handle this. I don't want you getting upset. When she has calmed down, then you can see her again," Dylan orders.

"I'll talk to her," Luis declares. "Wait here and I will return, hopefully with some answers."

Addy

Why does my mouth feel like the Sahara Desert? Slowly everything comes back to me. Javier, Javier was here! My eyes fly open to meet Luis's. I try to sit but I can't, they've restrained me. Oh, Addy, you are a stupid, stupid girl. Why didn't you escape the minute you found out you were in Mexico? My ears ring and my entire body trembles.

"Addison, you need not be afraid. Everything is okay," Luis says in a soothing voice.

I shake my head back and forth. No, no, everything is definitely not okay. Javier was here. I'm not sure why he didn't take me with him, but he will return. I was stupid to trust anyone. Just worry about your wall and when you get a chance, you will run…. you will run and never look back.

"Breathe, Addy. You are in no danger here with us. You understand this, you need to breathe and take a minute to think about it. We all care deeply about you. As soon as you are calm, we will release the restraints." Luis reaches over to hold my hand in his. I don't want him to touch me, but I can't pull away.

I turn my face from him. The smell of Javier's tobacco still lingers over my senses. No, I'm not going to him. Being here has reminded me of everything I lost. I can't go back to that life. I would rather die than return to being someone's slave. I tug at the restraints and curse out loud, "Fuck you, let me go if I have nothing to fear."

"Addison, I need to ask you something and I want an honest answer."

I laugh, crazy, as if I were a witch who has been tied to a stake about to be set alight. It's not over, it was never over. I turn to Luis and spit right in his face. "Fuck you." I don't understand where this is coming from. I'm sure I resemble a woman possessed but, I can't take it anymore. I can't take it!

He pulls a handkerchief out of his pocket and calmly wipes his face. "Addison, I can see how frightened you are. We want to help you. Javier Galindo came here because he is looking for his employee's niece, he gave us your name. Is this correct, Addy? Does your uncle work for Javier?"

My laughter continues. It will never end.

Wall. Hide. Run when I get a chance…if I get a chance.

"Addison? Is it true?" Luis tries to pry the information from me.

I will never trust anyone again. Never. I dust myself off and start the tedious task of laying my brick.

Luis sighs and walks out leaving me alone. Good, I have much to do.

I work for what seems like hours. Just as my eyes are about to drift closed Liam and Dylan enter my room. I tremble at the sight. Something is not right…they've changed…or have they? Maybe they have always been like this, they are wolves in sheep's clothing. I see it now. I should've known.

Willing my body to stop it's incessant shaking I close my eyes. They tug at the restraints releasing me.

"Up," Dylan's deep voice rumbles over me. The familiar command makes me scramble to obey. Before I register my body's reaction I realize I am on the floor kneeling before him.

His hand runs over my hair soothing me. "Addison, look at me." Immediately my eyes are drawn to his. "Does your uncle work for Javier Galindo?" No beating around the bush, a direct question. One I cannot answer.

What is this? Is it a trick? He is a bad guy. I always knew he was. "I do not know, sir."

"What do you mean you do not know? Do not play games with me, Addison," he warns.

I try to crawl away from him, but he crouches down grabbing a fist full of my hair stopping my retreat. "Answer my question."

"I have no idea. He didn't work for Javier when I lived with him. My mom worked for him," I respond in a trembling voice, trying to scramble over my wall.

"Where is your mother now?"

"Dead."

"And your uncle?"

"I don't know, sir."

Dylan releases the grip on my hair and glances at Liam. Liam looks like he wants to rip Dylan's throat out for a minute, but he quickly masks the expression.

"Are you afraid to see your uncle?" Dylan asks a bit nicer than his previous tone.

"No, sir." Fuck, I don't like this. Master O was right. I have no brain. I respond like a damn robot.

"Then why did you run?"

I shrug my shoulders.

"Addison," Dylan warns offering me another opportunity to answer him.

These men are no different, how could I have ever trusted them? "I ran because I hate him, sir."

"Your uncle or Javier?"

I think about it for a second. "Javier, sir."

Dylan stands to his full height. I peek up at him seeing the look he is giving to Liam. Is it possible I could alter the current course? I can't go to Javier. I can't.

I reach out and grasp the bottom of Dylan's pants. "Please, sir, please don't make me go to him." Not looking up I cling to that scrap of material, hoping that he will accept my submission. These two are the only ones I know who could stand up to Javier…but wait they probably work for him. Javier will get a good chuckle out of my begging his men to save me.

He runs his fingers through my hair gently massaging the back of my head. "Addy, I want to understand why you are so frightened of him."

Again, I answer just like the little programmed slave I am. "He…he is a bad man."

His hand stops for a brief second before continuing. "Good girl, now I need you tell Liam and I everything."

I sit up and blink at him. "Everything?" My eyes roam to Liam, he nods his encouragement to me.

My brain is clearing or maybe it is clouding. Have they tricked me? I don't know what to do anymore. What is up? What is down? Shaking my head, I try to figure this all out. Why are they acting like this? What is real?

My mind flits to the day I laid my sword at Brian's feet. What am I doing? I have to fight. I will not submit any longer.

"No," I say in an act of defiance that could get me punished.

"Addy?" he warns, deathly calm.

"No."

He sighs above me. "Liam?"

Liam crouches down and tips my face up to his. "Addy, it is important that you tell us what is going on, we need to know everything."

His eyes try to drown me in their ocean of blue offering me that weightless peace, but I let go of the safety net he threw me the first day. I watch the net sink as I slowly drift back to my wall. "No."

"Get on the bed," Liam orders.

"No."

He grabs me and shoves me onto the bed. Soon enough I find myself restrained once again.

"You will either talk or you will remain tied up. Your choice," Liam says as both of them leave my room.

I smile and tuck myself behind my wall.

Chapter Seventeen

Liam

Well shit, that didn't work. Dylan and I thought we could use domination to get her to tell us what is going on. It may have worked but neither of us wanted to take it further than what we did. The others think she is just fearful of returning to her family, afraid to face them and to deal with what happened to her.

I argued with them. They insisted that I go ahead with my plan of traveling to D.C. They said there is nothing I can do for her. She is lost. But, is she? My gut tells me she is frightened for a reason. She said Javier is a bad man. She is right he is an evil bastard.

Dylan and my dad want to continue trying to get her to talk. But, I hear a clock ticking, a time bomb perhaps. I'm about to do the most stupid thing I have ever done. God help me.

I've called in a few favors from my friends still with the bureau, my bag is packed and now all that is left is to wait for Anthony. He is the only one in agreement with me. Dylan thinks she is safe on the estate. He could be right, or he could be wrong. I'm not willing to risk it. My angel was so scared that she clawed my face, spit at my dad and defied the person she feared most in this house, Dylan. From what I have learned about her in our short time together, I know that this is not her. She is just afraid.

"Hey man, you sure about this?" Anthony says jogging up to me.

"No, but I can't leave her here. Let's go before Dylan gets up and rips our heads off."

He tosses his bag in the back of my car and we head inside. The house is dark and quiet. We have one chance, if she screams it is over, they will force me to walk away from her. He pulls a key out of his pocket smiling at me. I don't know how he got it, but it doesn't matter. Slowly he inserts it into the lock turning it. Anna ordered Dylan to untie her, but he insisted that she be locked in.

She isn't in the bed. Crap she is wide awake, sitting on the floor in the middle of her room curled into a little ball rocking herself. With great stealth Anthony and I move in. He grabs her from behind covering her mouth. She bucks wildly against him. I jump in front of her. "Shhh, it's okay, angel. I'm getting you out of here. I'm taking you far away from Javier."

I hate to drug her again, but we have no choice. She quiets but stares at me with wide-eyed horror. I place my forehead to hers, whispering sweet nothings to her as I plunge the syringe into her neck.

No looking back now.

Addy

Again, I wake up to the worst cotton mouth of my life. How many times are these fuckers going to drug me? It's quiet, I try to control my breathing so that if anyone is with me they do not detect that I am awake. Just a few minutes, I need time to process what Liam told me. He said he was taking me far away from Javier. Someone was behind me when he came into my room last night. He didn't act alone. I could be in Javier's bed right now for all I know.

"Addy, you are safe. Don't pretend to be asleep. I sense that you are awake," Liam's voice glides over me.

The sound makes me jerk, fuck. How did he know? Tears try to force their way out of my closed eyes. My throat and chest burn. This is too much. I am scared. I wanted it to be over. I wanted to live. A life as a slave is not living, it is death…no it is worse.

Liam moves closer but I still don't open my eyes. I don't want to interact with anyone right now. The bed shifts under his weight and he pulls me into his arms. His smell, his warmth takes me back to our first night under the moon, when he felt like home. Is he bad or good? Will I ever be able to tell who is safe or dangerous? It doesn't matter Javier will soon have me and then I won't have to think about such things. Tears leak out from beneath my lashes and a hiccupping sob escapes before I can bite it back.

"Addy, we are not in Mexico, you don't have to be frightened. We are in the states," he whispers, his lips drifting over the top of my head lightly.

His words prompt me to sit upright, I search his face for the truth of his statement.

"I brought you to D.C. with me. Whatever Javier did to frighten you, I feel it. I couldn't leave you behind," he says brushing hair away from my forehead.

Cautiously I slide off his lap and glance around the room. It is a small bedroom, masculine with dark blue and brown colors. It smells like him. I pull the blanket up to my nose, inhaling his scent. This isn't his suite at the estate. I breathe a sigh of relief. If what he is saying is true, then maybe I can hide here, I will never return to Mexico. Never.

"Is it just you and I?" I ask.

"And Anthony, but he is staying at a hotel nearby. He is planning on going home in a few days, he wanted to make sure you were okay before he leaves."

"I need to use the restroom," I whisper. It's not a lie, I do. But, I also want a few minutes alone. Liam is lulling me again. I'm not confident that I can trust him.

"It's right here," he stands going to a door. He reaches in and turns the light on for me. He goes to stand on the far side of the room watching me anxiously.

Slowly I back off the bed keeping my eyes on him and then rush in locking the door behind me. My pulse beats fast, am I really in the states? Dare I hope?

"Addy, if you would like to shower there are towels in the cupboard. Anthony packed a bag for you, it's here when you are ready. I will make us something to eat."

He didn't tie me up and he let me lock the door. I haven't locked a door myself in...well in two years. I glance in the mirror, the broken pixie stares back at me. Man, I look like shit. Nothing like the girl I was. The confident, brave young woman who stole a hundred grand and then used it for her education. Nothing like the girl who traveled to third world countries to help those in need. No, I'm just a shell, consumed with ugly dirty things.

They poisoned me. Literally filled me with poison and now I don't recognize good from bad, right from wrong. I spit at Luis, oh god, I spit at him. Why, Addy? What if I was mistaken, what if these people don't work for Javier? He said Javier was looking for me. He was helping my uncle. I know this isn't true but is it Javier's lie or theirs?

Okay, first off I need to shower. Then I'll go out and see where I am at. If we are in D.C. it should be obvious. Will he let me outside?

After I finish showering I peek out and just like Liam said there is a suitcase right beside the frame. I reach for it and drag it into the bathroom locking the door as quickly as I can once the treasure is secure in my hands. It's not the clothing Anthony bought for me at the estate. No, these things are for a different climate. Sweaters, leggings, fuzzy warm socks, flannel pajamas. My fingers glide over the items, they are so soft. Maybe Liam isn't lying, and we aren't in Mexico, what time of the year is it? Fall, winter? I smile to myself. The thought of seasons changing hasn't entered my mind in a long time.

I only had one season while captive. It was a constant state of uncomfortable. Cold, hungry, lonely and more often than not full of pain. All year long, always the same horrible existence. After I dress, I dig in the suitcase finding a brush and other girly items. Liam doesn't come to the door once, he isn't rushing or yelling at me to hurry. He is allowing me to take as much time as I need. After I finish I peek in the mirror. There she is, I look a little more myself. Besides the dark circles and my thinner state, I almost resemble the girl I used to be.

I take a deep breath and exit the room. The bed is now made, at least he doesn't expect me to stay tied up all day. I don't want to be restrained

124

again. Fighting claustrophobia is becoming a challenge for me. You would think one would get accustomed to it, but the mind always fights, always. My stomach grumbles as I detect a wonderful aroma coming from the other room.

When I exit the bedroom, I am greeted to a small residence that is open and airy. The living space is filled with black leather furniture. A long counter separates it from the pale blue kitchen. Liam is standing in front of the stove. The apartment is warm and inviting. He glances up at me smiling. He gestures to the table with the large spoon in his hands. "Have a seat, it's almost done."

I notice that there is a bench seat on one side in front of long old windows. There are dark blue and yellow pillows settled along the sill. The space is cozy, a place where you could curl up and watch life pass by. I slide into the seat turning so I can see out. We are in what looks like a quiet neighborhood. Brick steps leading up to the building. A fresh blanket of snow covers the ground. Beautiful white, pure, clean snow. As I glance around at the outside world, the sun makes an appearance from between the clouds and suddenly the ground turns to glitter.

"I'm not a big fan of the cold, but the snow is pretty," Liam says behind me causing me to spin abruptly and stare at him. He smiles and everything that happened in Mexico comes rushing back. He saved me. He took me away from the one thing that frightens me more than anything. He is my light why did I doubt? I notice the gash I made over his handsome cheek. No!

"I can read your mind, Addison. Stop, you had no reason to trust us. Don't feel bad about any of it. It's just a scratch," he says setting a skillet down in the middle of the table in front of me.

My eyes never leave his. "I'm…I'm so sorry."

125

"Don't worry about it, Addy, you were scared." He sits down across from me and reaches over taking my plate filling it. "Eat, you have to be starving."

No need to tell me twice, I am starving. A knock makes me jump. I quickly swivel to look out the window to the front of the building searching, scanning for a team of Javier's men. Only one set of footprints leads up the steps.

"It's an old colleague of mine. He is just dropping something off," Liam says rising from the table. He opens the door, I can't see the visitor, but he hands Liam a large envelope and then he is gone. Liam holds it up in front of him shaking it. "I have something for you."

He walks back and slides the envelope to me. "What is it?" I whisper.

"Open it," he says grinning ear to ear.

Hesitantly I fold the clasps up releasing the flap and peek in. I pull it to my chest, could it be! My eyes well with tears. "Liam." I can't speak I am so overwhelmed with emotion. He is giving me my life back. I hop up and round the table. I throw myself at him almost tipping us both over in the chair.

Liam laughs pushing me back slightly so he can look in my eyes. "I've never seen someone get so excited to see their driver's license," he says.

"It's more than that, you have everything. I saw my social security card, my passport!" I exclaim. "You are returning me to myself." Tears stream down my cheeks, he tries to brush them away, but they don't stop so he pulls me into the warmth of his arms.

"Shh, it's okay, angel. It's all going to work out." He rocks me back and forth like an infant.

"I spit at your dad," I say guiltily.

He snorts. "He will do much worse to me I'm sure. By now he and Dylan have probably realized that I took you. I haven't looked at my phone, I shut it off like the petulant child I am." He laughs harder. "You are getting me into trouble young lady," he scolds but I know he is teasing.

I think about what he just said. He defied his dad and his friend. "Why?"

"Why?" He stares at the ceiling struggling to find the right words. "I couldn't leave you, Addy. The little hellcat you had morphed into wasn't you and I knew that. You were so scared it broke my heart." He stops deep in thought tracing my bottom lip with his thumb. "Something told me I needed to get you away from there."

Anthony bursts into the room. He pauses taking us in. He pulls his shoulders back and for a moment I detect a tinge of jealousy. "Sorry to intrude," he says. "I need to visit with you, Liam."

Liam gently scoots me off his lap. "Sure thing, what is it," he asks.

Anthony glances around the small apartment nervously. "Umm, hey man can we talk outside."

"No," I speak up. "No, whatever it is, it's about me. Please don't hide things, it only makes me distrust more. Please," I plead.

Anthony sighs and looks to Liam to answer.

"Addison, it will just take a second. It's fine, nothing for you to worry about I'm sure." Liam stands and heads to the door.

Rushing by him, I stop in front of Anthony searching his strained expression. Something happened. Placing my hand on his chest I push him up against the wall. "Spill it," I say the hellcat in me coming out. "You will not keep things from me."

Anthony looks over the top of my head to Liam and he sighs behind me. "Fine, what is it?"

Anthony pushes me back a step and then takes my hand leading me to the sofa. "Sit," he orders. I obey and scoot down so he can take the seat beside me. "It's Javier, he showed up at the estate this morning. He came with a large number of men. They searched the entire place, took all our files, computers, everything we retrieved from Oliver's and left."

The next thing I know I'm lying on the couch and I'm in a dark tunnel. Liam and Anthony's voices are echoing down the lonely black hole. Hell. I've fallen into Hell. My heart tries to fold in on itself as I gasp for breath. I realize the priest was right. It is not God that is punishing me. It is the Devil himself. He has set his sights on me. He is preparing me for a life with him. No one can save me now, no one, not even God himself.

Chapter Eighteen

Addy

Why is it I move a step forward to just take two back?

"Fuck, Addy. Look at me," Liam says as my eyelids flutter open. "Addison, they are okay. Javier didn't hurt anyone. It's fine, everything is good."

I sit up straight as if someone electrocuted me. "Luis, Anna, Mrs. Cortez?" I gasp struggling to catch my breath. "Dylan? Are you sure they are all okay?"

He runs his hand over the back of my head gently massaging his fingertips through my hair, trying to soothe me. "Everyone is fine."

I cover my mouth, stifling my cries. "You all should've left me. You should have left me at the club."

Anthony joins us on the couch. "No, Addy. We shouldn't have. You are priceless. Besides, this guy…" he points to Liam, "he needs you. You should have seen him before he met you. A complete mess he was." He winks and gives me a warm smile.

Liam snorts. "He is right, but anyhow, we got the laptop fired up and we are going to call them so you can see for yourself. Okay?" He slides his hand over my back gently stroking me. I nod my head at him.

Anthony leans over clicking buttons on the computer so fast, he can't be typing anything but nonsense. But, it lights up and a sound repeats itself over and over until Dylan appears on the screen. The relief on his face when he spots me is visible over his features. "Addy, thank god you are safe." He looks over his shoulder. "Anna, Luis we are connected."

Two more faces pop into the window. I'm so overcome by emotion. Oh my god, I spit at Luis. How could I have done that? These people risked their lives for me. I try to rise from the couch but Liam grips me tightly around the waist.

"Hey guys, are you sure you are all okay?" Liam asks.

They all nod. "They didn't hurt anyone just searched the place and raided my office," Dylan says. "He told me he didn't need my help that he would find Addison on his own. Liam I am so thankful you are such a pain in the ass. You truly are the voice of reason. If you hadn't taken Addy…" he trails off and pulls Anna who has been crying non-stop into his lap. "She, has been worried to death about you, Addy."

"I'm sorry. I'm so very, very sorry. I should've told you. I should have told you!" I jump up and run to the bathroom.

As soon as I lower myself in front of the porcelain bowl everything I just gorged myself on comes purging out. Liam is behind me. He rubs my back as I heave and heave and heave until there is nothing left inside of me except guilt. When I'm done I grab the toothbrush from my suitcase and brush until my gums ache. He leans against the doorframe watching with his arms folded across his chest.

Saving Addy

"What did he do to you?" he asks after I dry my mouth off.

I stand there. I want to tell him everything and yet I don't. What will he think of me? I try to shove past him, but he doesn't budge. Instead, he closes the door behind him, lifts me off my feet and sets me on the counter. He takes my face in both of his hands forcing me to look at him. "What did he do to you?" he repeats.

He is so beautiful. His eyes hold me and once again the safety net is extended. Today I grasp it for dear life, I can't do this alone anymore. I need him. I must have his light, otherwise the devil is going to take me down. I reach out and trace the scratch over his cheek. "It's a long story, Liam."

"And? I've got all the time in the world." He stares deep into my eyes. He leans in past my wall and lightly brushes his lips over mine. My head swims, he is so warm. An unfamiliar tingle dances over every nerve in my body making my stomach clench.

When he pulls away I feel the loss. I need him. I wish there was a realm where nothing existed but he and I. He wants answers and I must give them to him. Somehow I know that he'll be careful with my secrets. I thought Brian would take care of them too, but he didn't understand how. Will Liam?

I drag my eyes from his and stare at his chest. He doesn't move. He keeps his arms braced on either side of me on the counter. He will not let me go until I tell him. They risked everything for me, I have to explain it to him.

"I stole from Javier when I was sixteen," I whisper it so quietly I don't know if he can even hear me. "My uncle borrowed money from him. Javier made me pick it up and told me that if he didn't repay it he would

131

take me as payment. I realized my uncle could never pay the loan, so I left Mexico with the cash and never looked back. Well, not until I stupidly returned to run an immunization clinic and his men spotted me."

Liam places his forehead against mine breathing what sounds like a sigh of relief. "Thank you, Addy. Thank you for trusting me."

"That's not all," I grimace as my story is about to get uglier.

"Go ahead." He kisses my temple and bends down capturing my eyes with his. "Tell me everything. Place it at my feet."

"When they found me, I ran, stupidly right into the hands of Brian. I didn't know who he was. I thought he was saving me but, I learned how wrong I was." I take a deep breath quickly wiping at the tears cascading down my cheeks. "When Oliver decided I was no longer useful to him, he sold me. He sold me to Javier. I had been waiting for him to come so he could deliver me to Javier's doorstep but then Dylan came…" I let my words trail off.

Liam stands upright releasing his grip on the counter. He turns away from me and places his hands on his head. "You thought we were taking you to him after we rescued you? Javier was the new master you were talking about?"

"Yes."

He slowly spins to face me. "You are mine, Addy."

"You are mine," he growls, and I notice the darkness lurk behind his eyes.

He is claiming me.

He will never let me go.

His claim frightens me, but it does something else, my stomach tightens, my pulse races. I need to be his. I knock through my haphazard wall and slide to the floor at his feet. Wrapping myself around his leg I cling to him. He doesn't stop me. He just runs his fingers through my hair. I close my eyes. He is my master, my light, my home. Not because he demands it, because I want it.

Liam

Javier Galindo is a dead man. I glance down at Addy wrapped around my leg. She has been wandering in a world where everything has been against her. All she has ever done is try to do her best, she worked hard so she could help others, and this is what she got back? Men, evil fucks have been tossing her about like a damn rag doll and that ends now.

I'll help her get what she deserves. She is the strongest person I've met. It's just going to be the two of us for a while. Time is what she needs. I'll have Anthony stay while I get everything in place. Once she is feeling better, then we will figure out the next step.

Her large doe eyes peek up at me. I know she is expecting me to correct her for kneeling at my feet. I'm not. From here on out we do what Liam and Addy need. No one is going to tell us where we go from here. "Addy, I will go out and talk to the others about everything you shared with me. Do you want to join me, or would you like to rest?"

She sighs and rubs her face over my pant leg, like a kitten seeking comfort. "I will go back out. I need to apologize to your dad for spitting at him."

I grab her hand and slide her up the length of my body. "Addy, I need you to promise me something."

133

She lifts her eyes to mine and asks, "what is it?"

"I need you to promise me that from here on out you keep no secrets from me and that you remain completely honest on how you are feeling. If I ever make you uncomfortable, please let me know right away. You can tell me anything." I run a finger along her jaw.

"I promise." She doesn't pull from me, she maintains eye contact and allows me to explore the line of her face, the curve of her neck.

"Tonight, I would like you to show me your scars. Can you do that for me, Addy?"

She drags her eyes away from mine to stare at the floor. "They are ugly, why would you want to see them?"

Tugging gently on her hair I force her gaze back to me. "Because I want to see you. I want to know everything about you. I want to know your pain, your pleasure, your fears. I want you to bare your soul."

"I did that with Brian, I let him in, and he abandoned me," she whispers.

The beast huffs, Brian, fuck Brian. He was a pussy. I quickly tuck my feelings on him away. "I am not Brian. You made me a promise and I will make one too. I promise you, Addy, I will never abandon you. I'll always do what I think is right for you."

She kicks at that imaginary rock on the ground with her toe, the gears in her mind churning. I need her to trust me, *please trust me, Addy.*

"Okay." She stares into my eyes. I realize that I am asking more than I deserve, more than she is probably ready to give but she needs to be strong. Javier is looking for her and when the time comes to face him, she will need to be a warrior not the broken pixie she thinks she is.

Chapter Nineteen

Addy

Oddly, I have felt a sense of relief all day. The fact that I am not in Mexico is probably a contributing factor, but I think it is because I've let Liam in. It was naïve of me to assume I could allow Brian in and that he would help me. Sure, I know that I was rescued because of him and I will forever be grateful for that, but he could never save me the way that Liam can.

My dad's voice has been whispering to me all day. I've made the right decision. Liam will crawl inside me and mend my broken parts. He will. I understand thoughts like this would seem illogical to most. But, he will bring back the magic and the light.

I have to admit since Anthony left for the evening and it is the two of us, I am nervous. He wants to see my scars. I haven't been ashamed of them until now. When you spend months upon months naked and on display for all it takes away a normal sense of modesty. Oliver always appreciated my scars. Liam won't see them the same way, he'll see me as damaged, flawed. He is different from those men. What will he think of his angel after he sees the tangled mess of lines across my back?

"What are you thinking about?" he asks pulling me out of my head.

He takes the seat next to me on the sofa, setting a mug of steaming tea in front of me.

I shrug my shoulders at him, suddenly shy. He has changed since coming here. Without Dylan around I can tell that Liam is more relaxed and confident about the decisions he is making with me. At the estate everyone seemed to doubt his intentions. They are good so that doesn't frighten me. But he is a formidable opponent and I am sure he will push me to the edge of my boundaries.

"Remember our conversation earlier," he warns.

And so, it begins. Taking a deep breath, I jump in headfirst. He is going to drag me into the deepest waters. I can only hope I don't let go of the net. "I'm nervous about showing you my scars."

"I know." He rubs his hand over my back lightly but doesn't offer me an out. "Finish your tea, then we will head to bed."

With shaky hands I pull the mug to my lips. The liquid warms me, and I focus on his gentle touch which is still foreign. Oliver had been the only one who ever offered me gentle. He never harmed me, not once. He always ordered others to do it. He would bring men with him, they would hurt me, and Oliver would watch. When it was over they would leave the room and he would wrap me in his arms until my shaking would subside. Then he would take me back to my room until next time. In the beginning I questioned his actions but after a few times, I gave up. He was a man I could just not read. The longer things went on the less I cared to figure out who he was.

Saving Addy

When my cup is empty, I stare into the bottom before setting it down on the coffee table. No going back now. Liam wants to see the darkness I have been living in. Can I do this? I opened myself to Brian am I willing to do it again?

Liam takes my hand and leads me to the bedroom closing the door behind him. The room suddenly feels tiny. He undresses and hops into the bed in nothing but his boxers. If I wasn't so nervous about showing him my scars, I would drool over him. But, my mind is not there. It is teetering on the edge of panic.

"Take your time, Addy."

I stand in front of him for a long minute, willing myself to open pandora's box. There will be no going back after this. I hope he doesn't look at me and change his mind. Brian abandoned me, if Liam does I won't recover, of that I am sure. I grip the bottom of my sweater and drag it over my head. Then I edge to the bed until I am standing next to him. He tugs at my hand urging me to sit down beside him.

My breath is caught in my lungs as I cautiously sit facing away from him. Silently I offer him a glimpse at the torture I endured. A black-and-white picture that will never quite capture the moment. There is no blood, no tears, no vomit to accompany the reality of the marks upon my back. Yet, I sense that he sees it, he feels it, perhaps he even smells it. The warmth of his hand ghosts over my skin, but he does not touch.

"May I?" he whispers into my ear.

"Yes." My shaky intake of breath makes him pause for a moment but soon his warm palm glides over the cool skin on my back.

137

His fingers slide over each raised line on the roadmap of torture. Slowly he traces the lines, sometimes pausing before the trail continues.

"Ugly, huh?" I say as his hand finally drifts away.

He pushes me backward onto the bed, so I am laying down. His face hovers over mine. "Addy, what they did to you was ugly, but you are not."

"If you stay with me, you will constantly see them. You will always think of me as the girl that was tortured and raped." Tears leak out of my eyes, pooling in my ears.

"No, no I won't. I will forever see you as an angel. A pixie angel that fell from the heavens. If you hadn't fallen, then I would have never had the privilege of seeing one for myself."

He turns me over to my stomach and his touch continues, becoming one of worship, of admiration. It is not as gentle as before, it is possessive. He is pulling the evil out and replacing it with something different. "Your scars are like vines in a garden. Think of them as vines that have reached out against all odds and climbed their way up to the light. They are strong, allowing you to pull yourself out of the darkness. They are not lines of weakness, they are strength."

I sob into the pillow at his words. He is changing me. I feel it. He is sucking the poison out as one would do a snake bite. It hurts but yet it heals at the same time. Slowly my muscles relax, and my tears dry. The bed shifts and the room goes dark. When he returns, I curl myself in tightly to his chest. I hope I will sleep without the demons knocking on my unconscious mind. Liam's strong body will be on guard as I dream of gardens and fairies once again.

Liam

One step at a time, I will help her. Tonight, I have a surprise for her. The movers are coming today, my stuff is all packed. It will be the last night in my apartment.

Yesterday was a pivotal point for both of us. She opened a door as I closed one. She threw it wide open. I stepped in and as I did, I heard the one behind me close. Sophia will always hold a place in my heart, but I am ready to move on. She was my teenage crush, a girlfriend I had for only a fleeting moment. I held on even when I knew I needed to let go. But, Sophia led me to Addy.

The world will always take you where you need to be. At the juncture of great heartache, we don't see it, we can't. But, once the clouds clear and the sun comes out you notice that everything has led you in the right direction.

I watch Anthony jog up the steps. I'm trying to control my jealousy over him. He has made a spot for Addy in his heart. I sense that he had hoped for more but when he locked her in my room, the other day I knew it was his way of stepping aside. He is one of my very best friends, I trust him with my life even if he drives me nuts most of the time. He runs at a faster speed than me, which is surprising since he is older than the rest of us. You would never know. He is the epitome of good looks and health.

"Morning," he says with a flair. He heads directly to the pot of coffee. While he pours himself a cup he stares at the door to my bedroom. "Did she sleep well?" he asks nodding towards it.

"Yes, actually she slept the entire night. She is still sleeping."

"Good, so where do we start. You have me for two days, after that I'm heading back to the estate."

"Well, the movers are coming today so if you could take Addy out, keep her busy. Take her sightseeing or whatever. Once the place is cleaned out I'm going to seize the opportunity of the empty space and create a little surprise for her. So, bring her home around six or seven. I should have everything set up by then."

"Sure. I'm the guy everyone can trust with their girl," he says sullenly. This isn't like him.

"Hey, what's going on, Anthony. Does it bother you I have feelings for her?"

"No, I'm…I guess I'm just not enjoying the single life as much as I used to. Maybe I'm having a mid-life crisis," he jokes but I sense the sadness in his voice.

"You will find her someday, and actually I will be excited and terrified to meet her," I tease. "If she turns out to be like you, it'll be quite the treat, cotton candy with a side of whiskey."

He chuckles. "I guess you are right. Someday."

Addy peeks her head out.

"Shit, I'm sorry. Did I wake you?" Anthony says as he hops up to approach her.

"No, I was awake."

"Good, put on something warm. Our first stop is breakfast at the greasiest diner we can find. Liam is letting us out to play."

She looks around him for confirmation of his statement. I nod my head. She hesitates but just for a split second before turning back into the bedroom to do what Anthony asked.

He turns to face me. "What has changed?"

I shrug my shoulders at him.

Chapter Twenty

Addy

I like Anthony. He is fun, and light-hearted. Every woman we passed on the way to the diner stared at him, but he didn't seem to notice. His focus is solely on me. After we fill up on what I am sure was a heart attack on a platter we decide to walk around the area. We need to burn off a few calories and then we can do a little window shopping. We pass one with a large skull stenciled into the glass. I pause, it is scary and beautiful at the same time. Vines climb out of the mouth and then crawl back into an eye socket, breathing life into death.

Anthony watches me carefully. "Remind you of something?" he asks guardedly. I turn to face him and notice the hesitation on his face. He is worried that I've been triggered by the image.

"Yes, actually it does remind me of something." I grab his hand and pull him into the tattoo shop with me. He stumbles in behind. A big burly guy is sitting at the counter, he gives me a look and I can see that he fights the urge to roll his eyes.

I stalk right up to him. "How is your schedule looking for today?" I ask, straightening myself to my full height which is almost half of his.

Saving Addy

He chuckles. "All clear, little lady. What did you have in mind? A tiny bunny perhaps?"

"Cute, but no. I will require your services the rest of the day for what I'm wanting."

He snorts. "Do you have any tattoos?"

"No."

"Well, let me tell you it doesn't tickle." He looks at Anthony and this time he does roll his eyes.

I rip my shirt off over my head and turn my back to him. "It can't hurt worse than this can it?"

When I spin around the man bows slightly towards me. His gaze meets mine and I see he understands. "Let's get started then." He walks to the front of the store turning off his open sign.

Anthony stands silently by me the rest of day, gently holding my hand, every now and then he brushes hair from my eyes. It's almost as if he knows where I am. The pain lulls me and I roam to that dark quiet place inside of myself. It differs from the one behind my wall. This place is special, it can only be unlocked with pain. I've missed it. I smile and close my eyes. I allow myself to float, detaching from my physical body. Anthony is here, he will watch over me while I drift.

When we leave the shop, he finally speaks. "That was beautiful."

Blushing, I lean into him as we walk hand in hand. "The tattoo?"

"I think you understand what I mean."

143

LM Terry

I stop him before we head up the steps to Liam's apartment. "I didn't get the tattoo just so I could go there…you know to that place inside myself. I didn't do it for the pain."

"I recognize that, but you did so with such ease and beauty it did not pass unnoticed by me or the man tattooing you." He tucks a stray lock of hair behind my ear. "Have you missed it?"

"I guess so. I didn't realize how much until today. It draws me into a world I can't explain." Anthony seems to know where I went, where the strike of the needle allowed me to go. What would Liam think?

"Umm, do you think Liam appreciates things like that?" I ask. It's not that I don't feel pain, I do but sometimes it brings me peace. It takes me to this subconscious place that I don't really comprehend. At times I crave it. I didn't expect anyone to understand, I thought I was just broken and sick but today Anthony made it seem like it was okay. He recognized what it was, and he perceived it to be beautiful not strange or demented. Beautiful he said.

He kisses my forehead. "He will understand. Talk to him when you are ready, he will probably be hesitant at first but give him time, he can offer you what you need I have no doubt. What a lucky bastard." He thumps my nose once then pats my bottom. "Off with you, he is waiting."

I trod up the stairs, pausing to look at him as I enter the building. He gives me a nod and then turns and walks away. As I make my way to Liam's apartment I realize that I am alone. I could leave, I could disappear into the city, I could go wherever I choose. Where would that be? After thinking about it for a brief moment my feet move, and they take me precisely where I want to be.

Saving Addy

Liam answers the door in nothing but a pair of low-riding sweats. He leans against the doorframe. "Where's Anthony?"

I clear my throat and struggle to keep my eyes on his face. "Ah, he...well I don't know exactly, he walked me to the steps and then left."

"He just dropped you off...outside?" He crosses his arms over his chest.

My tongue darts out grazing my bottom lip as I gaze at his muscular biceps. "Yes, he, he must've had somewhere else to be."

"Hmph, turn around and close your eyes," he instructs.

"What?"

"You heard me." He spins me and places a blindfold over my eyes.

"Liam?"

"Shh, it's okay. You only have to keep it on for a minute or two." He pulls me back into his chest wrapping his arms around my mid-section. I place my hands out in front of me as we begin to walk. His breath brushes over my ear. "Don't worry, angel, I won't let you bump into or trip on anything."

He kicks the door after he pushes us into the apartment. I jump at the sound of it slamming shut.

"I missed you today. I only had the company of the movers. I've been patiently waiting for Anthony to return you to me," he purrs.

My stomach clenches tightly, the warmth of his breath on my neck and the scratch of his beard against my cheek is doing something. I'm excited, excited to see what he will show me, excited to see his sexy body again.

Sexy? Oh yes, sexy and at the moment he is mine. After months of nothing but sensory deprivation and fear, this is nice.

"Sit down," he instructs.

Carefully I crouch and the smooth, soft touch of satin is under me. A smile breaks over my face. Liam must notice because he gently traces my lips with his finger. "You are not scared?" he asks.

"No, I'm excited," I clap my hands, I can't help it. This reminds me of the little surprises my dad always left hiding for me.

He laughs. "Okay then, are you ready?"

I nod my head feverishly, then he reaches behind me to loosen the blindfold. As it slips away, I blink a few times, my heart constricts so tight I don't know if it will ever beat again. Tears form like icicles on my lashes as my eyes glide around the room. It has been completely transformed….to a garden…a garden at night. Thousands of tiny, twinkling lights grace the ceiling giving it the illusion of a clear evening sky with stars blanketing the earth. There are pots surrounding us, vessels of beautiful flowers in every color of the rainbow. In the corners are vining plants climbing towards the heavens.

My eyes roam to Liam, he is sitting across from me. We are perched on sleeping bags and between us sets a faux fire pit. It warms me as I stare over it watching the light cast shadows over Liam's features. A sob escapes my lips and I cover my mouth. "Liam…"

He opens his arms and I crawl to him, climbing into his lap. "Shhh, baby. It's okay."

"This is amazing, you did this all for me?"

146

"Yes, all for you. I would like to give you a real garden someday but for tonight we will have to pretend." He kisses my temple as we watch the flames dance in front of us. "Well, I have to admit the fire pit was for myself." He laughs before continuing. "You remind me of campfires and starry nights. So that is for me."

"I love it. I absolutely love it!" Shifting I rub my hands over his beard, then lean in and brush my lips across his. He holds perfectly still. When I pull back, I see the spark I ignited, and it's not a reflection of the flames behind us. "I have a surprise for you too."

"You do?" He sounds surprised, surprised by my words by my kiss.

"Yes, close your eyes." My hand brushes downward over his eyes. After they are closed, I stare at him for a moment. How did I get so lucky to find this man? I want to stay with him forever.

 Scooting off his lap I stand and undress, my hands shake as I unhook my bra and slide my panties off. Am I just showing him my new ink or am I offering myself to him? I bite my lip hard. Think, Addy, if he sees you naked it will stir his desires, he is a man after all. He wants to understand. He told me so yesterday. He said he wanted to see me, my pain, my pleasure…everything. I want him to.

I take a deep breath and turn so that my back is facing him. "Okay," I say shakily.

The moment he opens his eyes I know. I sense them on me. I feel them roam over every vine, every flower now gracing my backside. He stands. He is silent, the warmth of him so near it sets my freshly inked skin on fire. The sensation of having him stand so close behind me while I am undressed sends me to a euphoric state, I lift my face to the twinkling lights above. This is the place where I begin to heal, here in this tiny little apartment. My mind fills with everything surrounding me, it pushes the memories of the dark lonely cell at the club to the very corner of my skull. It shoves them into a trunk slamming it shut.

"Addy, it…" his voice is strangled, words trying to form, but he is struggling to say exactly what he wants. "It is the loveliest thing I have ever seen. You have to be the most courageous, strong, woman I have ever met. You don't belong here with me in this place. You belong in a castle in the clouds, you are a mythical stunning creature that no mortal should be allowed to ever look upon. Only other winged beings should be privileged enough to lay eyes on you. And, yet, you are here…here with me."

No one has ever said anything like that to me before and I didn't just hear it, I felt it. His words caressed, made love to me, they worshiped me, I'll never leave this man. Never. I will go wherever he goes, I'll do whatever he does, I belong to him. Slowly I spin as tears streak down my cheeks.

The intake of his breath as I face him, sends a bolt of excitement to a place I thought was dead. "Addy, you don't have to. I didn't do all this so you would…" his words trail off. I reach out and take his hand placing it at the base of my throat, allowing his fingers to wrap around my neck, to possess me. I am not afraid. I am giving myself to him.

He keeps a loose grasp as he closes the space between us moving until our bodies are flush, where there is no border between our souls. His grip tightens and he pulls me, so we are nose to nose. "I don't want to hurt you," he whispers.

"You can't, it's not possible. The only way to slay me would be if you were to walk away." My breath prickles over his lips. I watch as he parts them. My heartbeat trips as he leans in and devours me. Our kisses become greedy, hungry. How long I had waited for the magic to return.

In one evening, this magician has turned my cell into a castle and the broken pixie into a fairytale princess.

He drags himself away from me, leaving me panting and shaky. My trembling fingers glide over my swollen lips. "We can't do this, not tonight, you are not ready," he says breathing heavily.

I groan and reach for him. He takes a step back. "Please, Liam, please give me something." I've never experienced pleasure from being with a man. He can give that to me, I know he can. He wants me too, the bulge in his pants betrays his act of self-discipline.

He hesitates but then retrieves the blindfold and covers my eyes once again. "Addison, if you are uncomfortable with anything I do, you will tell me?"

"Yes," I whisper. My heart is hammering in my chest. Literally I am blindly trusting him. If he gives me this, I will give him everything, he'll own me, and I've never wanted anything more.

"I mean it, Addy, I know you have not been given the choice of how someone touches you. You do now, if you want to stop we stop, if you want to slow down we slow down. I will not take you tonight, but I will give you pleasure if that is what you want."

"I trust you."

He gently urges me to lie down on the floor, the cool silk of the blankets caresses my back and I sigh as I ease into position. "How are you feeling," Liam says above me.

"Excited....umm, maybe a little scared."

"It's okay, I will stop if you ask me to. What exactly are you frightened of? Is it the blindfold? I can remove it."

"No, it's…" I huff with embarrassment.

"Tell me otherwise we aren't going to do this," he scolds.

"I've never, well I haven't felt pleasure…only pain. I'm afraid I won't be able to," I admit so quietly that he has to lean in to hear me.

"If what you say is true and you trust me, you will. I promise." His lips brush over mine and he slides his body down beside me. He leans forward his lips glide down my chin, over my neck then his hand finds my breast. I arch into it. It is warm and inviting. His calloused fingers grip a little tighter and his thumb rolls over my nipple.

He goes slow, giving me plenty of time to adjust to the sensation of his touch. He whispers wonderful things, letting me hear the comforting rumble of his voice. His words start out sweet and as his hand roams lower over my torso, they go from clean to dirty. He tells me what he is going to do to me, and it creates an inferno between my legs.

"Do you like this, Addy? Do you enjoy my hands on you? My mouth?" His mouth covers my breast and his tongue teases over my nipple.

I can't answer him, but I moan and writhe under his ministrations. Everywhere he touches tiny bolts of electricity penetrate each nerve waking up my entire system. He gently tugs at my leg and drapes it over his thigh. His lips find mine again as he coaxes little mewling sounds from me. His palm glides down to my naval and I lift my hips encouraging him.

Then his hand dips between my legs. I gasp into his mouth. He stills and whispers into my ear, his breath hot, "You okay, angel?"

"Yesssss," I hiss then moan as his fingers delve farther finding a magical button. "Oh god," I groan as I arch off the floor. I knew he was a magician. They swirl in tiny circles and I find the longer he does this the deeper I fall into myself. "Don't stop please don't stop," I beg.

He groans when I say his name and slides a finger inside of me, his thumb resumes the pressure over that wonderful place that only he knows about. The gentle way in which he worships me turns slightly rougher and my muscles tighten, my legs tremble. What is happening, shit, I'm going to lose control. He must be watching me very closely because he eases his touch and slows down allowing me to catch my breath.

"Don't be scared, Addy, you are so close, baby. Allow me to take you somewhere you've never been. Let go." He presses his body tightly to mine and runs his free hand over the top of my head, his nails gently caressing my scalp. He drops his head to mine, kissing me languidly and then he curls his finger inside me and mercilessly pushes until I explode. My entire body trembles and I groan out his name loud enough for the entire complex to hear. His magical touch releases my chained soul and I soar until slowly I float down to earth.

"Oh my god," I breathe out. "I didn't know, I didn't know." I roll my head back and forth. My throat constricts as I choke back my tears.

He removes the blindfold and stares so deeply into my eyes I am sure he is in tune with all I am feeling and thinking. "That was incredibly beautiful and an experience I will never forget," he moans.

My face flushes, I'm slightly embarrassed. After everything that has been done to me in my life, I've never let someone have such control over me. Every time a man touched me I hid behind my wall. I did not allow myself to feel anything.

The tears flow, and I grip that safety net tighter than I ever have. He holds me tight to him as the darkness spills from my body. I am healing, my soul and mind finally realize I am safe and protected. Liam doesn't speak he just continues to hold me.

Liam

What an amazing woman. How she fell into my arms is also amazing. The terror, the heartache that brought us to this moment in my apartment in D.C., it is extraordinary actually. "Hey you okay, angel?"

"Yes, thank you, Liam. Thank you for showing me the magic again. This is all so incredible." She motions to our fictitious garden as she snuggles into me rubbing her face over my chest.

"The night is not over yet. We haven't even had supper." I uncurl her from me and head to the kitchen for surprise number two.

When I come back into the living room, she looks sad. "What's wrong?"

"I...umm, I didn't. Don't you want me to please you?" Her eyes drop to the floor.

I set the tray I am carrying down and sit beside her cupping her check. "You did please me, Addy. You put your trust in me and that pleases me. I want you to be one hundred percent ready and I know that now is not the time. Don't assume it is because I don't want to, I do. But, not right now. Okay? We will both know when the time is right."

She nods her head then her eyes roam to the tray I set down beside us and I see her excitement return. "Is that what I think it is?" She claps her hands like an excited child.

"Well, if you think it is hot dogs and smores then yes. Since the movers took everything, I had to get creative," I say winking at her.

"This is perfect, I have a sweet tooth and oh how I've missed the gooey chocolaty taste of a good smore."

Handing her a roasting stick I inquire about her day with Anthony.

"We ate breakfast and then spent the rest of the time at the tattoo shop," she answers. She takes the stick and holds it over the flames of the little kerosene container.

"I can't believe you did that all in one shot, you must have a high pain tolerance?"

"Umm, yes something like that. When we passed the shop, your words came to me and I couldn't think of a better way to spend the day. Now, when I look at my back in the mirror, I will have different memories."

"Well, it is beautiful, Addy." I hate to ruin the mood, but I should visit with her about what happens from here. I rest my arms on my knees and take a deep breath. She might not want to stay with me, and I will have to live with that. The choice must be hers. "I need to talk to you about what our next step is. Anna has offered her cabin in Colorado to us until we figure out where to go from there. Would you want to come with me? If not, I understand, and I will make sure you get to wherever it is you would like to go."

Addy pops a bite of her hotdog in her mouth and stares into the flames for a moment. "I am where I want to be...with you. So, if you are going to Colorado then that is where I'm meant to be."

"You're positive?" I ask grabbing her chin so I can see into her eyes.

"Surer than I've ever been about anything." She blinks several times attempting to hide her tears.

"Honesty from here on out. Okay?"

She nods her head.

I crack open two root beers and hand her one. "How about a toast to us, to new beginnings and more magic to come?"

She giggles as we clink our bottles together. "This is honestly the best night I have had in many, many years, Liam. Thank you, now pass me one of those Hershey bars."

I give her a candy bar and then help her with a marshmallow on her stick. "So, I thought we would drive to Colorado and do a little sightseeing along the way. But, if that will be too much for your back I can book us a flight."

"No! I love road trips. I am so excited!"

"Excellent, then it is settled. We leave in the morning after we say goodbye to Anthony. It feels good to finish up my life here in D.C., I didn't belong here, I should've packed this place up months ago."

"Why were you here? For work?" she asks as she licks melted chocolate off of her fingers.

"Yes, I worked for the FBI. But, recently I quit and went back to working with Dylan and Anna." I lean over to help her with the mess her smore is making. My eyes catch hers as I suck her finger into my mouth slowly licking the sticky, gooey candy.

She clears her throat trying to hide her face as she blushes. She is so damn cute. I don't know how anyone could have ever hurt her. "These are much messier than I remember," she says.

Laughing, I release her hand. "It wouldn't taste as good if they weren't messy. All things messy are usually tasty, you know smores, ribs and ice cream cones."

She smiles at me. "You are right, I never thought of it that way." She laughs. "We should find as many messy things to eat as we can on our road trip."

"Deal, you don't need to talk me into it. But, now we should get some sleep."

"I'm so excited how will I never be able to sleep." She stands helping me clean up our supper mess.

After I put the salve the tattoo artist gave her on her new ink we settle into our sleeping bags. I drag hers as close to mine as possible draping my arm over her. "Goodnight, sweet Addy," I whisper.

"Goodnight, Liam." She smiles and scoots as tight to me as she can. "Thank you for another night under the stars," she murmurs as her eyelids grow heavy and she drifts off before I can even respond.

I smile to myself, so much for her having a hard time sleeping. I'm glad, she deserves to sleep in peace. Tomorrow is the beginning of a new adventure.

Chapter Twenty-One

Addy

I am sad that we are saying goodbye to Anthony today. I will miss him. We are meeting him for breakfast at the same diner he and I went to yesterday. Liam ran across the street quick to the mini mart to pick up a few things for our road trip. Butterflies are flying around in my tummy at the thought of our adventure. I'm so unbelievable excited. I have a lot of cataloging to do, just in case Javier does find me I want to store away as much as I can. My stomach drops at the notion, I hope I never see him again.

"Addy?" a familiar voice says above me.

"Father Landon, what are you doing here?" I question, then realize that was not a proper greeting. "Please, please join me. I'm sorry, I'm so surprised to see you here."

He looks around the diner as he slides into the booth and sits across from me. "I suppose I have a quick minute. I'm in town for a convention. I am also surprised to see you here. Are you alone?" He scans the room again.

"No, Liam and Anthony will accompany me soon."

"Ah, I understand, very good. Will you all be in the city long? Perhaps we could get together for dinner some evening?" he asks.

"Oh, that would be lovely, but Liam and I are headed to Anna's cabin in Colorado today."

"Colorado, a beautiful state. Is Anthony going as well?" he inquires, and I notice he is not looking at me as he speaks. He is focused on the entrance.

"No, he is flying back to the estate," I reply wondering why Father Landon seems so interested in our plans. He didn't even ask me how I was doing. Maybe I am reading too much into this.

"It was nice seeing you again, Addy. I better be going, or I'll be late for my seminar."

"Oh, are you sure, the others will be here any minute. Are you positive you can't join us for breakfast?"

"Thank you, Addison, but I must go." He winks and then turns walking out of the diner.

Did he wink at me? What was that all about? I don't have time to ponder the encounter as Liam and Anthony enter together. They are both laughing. I am glad. I hoped that I would not cause a rift in their friendship. They've both been a little jealous over me.

"Addison, you look amazing today," Anthony coos. "I think the cold air has done you good. Me on the other hand not so much. I need to get back to warmer temperatures. But, I hear you and Liam are only heading into a colder climate if that is possible." He shivers overdramatically.

Anthony makes me laugh. Oh, I'll miss him. We order and then stuff ourselves until none of us can take another bite.

"I'll bring the car around while you two say goodbye," Liam says.

Anthony stands and they give each other a quick bro hug and then he slides into the spot beside me that Liam just vacated. "I will miss you, Addison Davis, but we'll see each other soon?" he questions tipping his head at me.

"I hope so, but I am afraid you'll have to come visit me in the states. I don't think I will ever return to Mexico."

He sticks out his bottom lip in an exaggerated pout. "Life has a way of changing even the best of plans. So, you could change your mind. You were a wonderful addition there." He taps the end of my nose and then leans over giving me a tender kiss on the lips.

My face flushes under his attention. "I'm going to miss you too, Anthony. Thank you for everything. If it wasn't for you, I would be running around butt naked and it is a bit too cold for that." I chuckle, then lean over and kiss him on the cheek.

"Until we meet again," he stands and holds his arm out for me to take. He walks me out to the car opening the door for me. He closes it once I'm settled inside without another word. I give him a tiny wave as we drive off.

"You will see him again," Liam says reading my mind.

"I'm sure you are right," I say sullenly. Pulling away from the diner made me realize that I miss them all, everyone at the estate...even Dylan.

He reaches behind my seat and I hear a sack rustle. When he pulls his hand back, he hands me something. I take it and giggle. "For some reason these reminded me of you," he says.

I laugh harder. "You are a brave, brave man." He bought me pixie sticks. I haven't had one of these paper tubes filled with nothing but pure flavored sugar since I was a child. "You know I will bounce off the walls, if I indulge in these."

"I know, but I figured it could make an interesting trip," he says laughing.

Liam

It took a week to finally reach Denver. Addy's enthusiasm is contagious, so I indulged her spontaneous side and we stopped at every attraction along the way. She even wanted to visit the world's largest ball of twine. Nothing got us too far off the beaten path and if I am honest with myself I've enjoyed the trip.

I've spent my life working and searching for Sophia. Addy has forced me to slow down and smell the roses so to speak. One day she made me stop along the side of the road because she noticed a field of deer grazing. We sat there for almost an hour. She observed the animals, and I watched her. I've never seen someone in awe of everything around them. She is an incredible soul. I am so glad to have met her.

"Are we there yet?" she says bouncing in her seat.

"I'm going to cut you off of the pixie sticks," I scold. "We will be there soon just a few more hours."

"It is good to see mountains again. It reminds me of Utah."

159

"Do you miss it?"

"No, not really. It seems like a lifetime ago, almost as if it wasn't my life but one I watched in a movie. I went to school in Salt Lake City. It is beautiful there, but I don't miss it. The only things I miss are my dad and work. I enjoyed working."

"You'll get back to it, Addy, I don't doubt that one bit. Anna's cabin is wonderful, and it will give you a place to rest and figure out what you want." I take her hand in mine and press tiny kisses on each of her knuckles not taking my eyes off the road.

"So, you've been up here?" she asks.

"Yes, for a few days last summer. It was a bitch to get to then, I'm hoping we don't have any problems now with all the snow. That is why I rented this four-wheel drive."

She laughs. "You don't seem too excited to be going to a snowy get-a-away."

"Like I said, the white stuff is pretty, but I hate the cold."

She smiles and snuggles down in her seat. "I will keep you warm," she purrs.

I glance at her. Is she flirting with me? She giggles. Yes, that is exactly what she is doing. My dick twitches in my pants. Fuck, I've been sleeping next to her all week and have been able to hold myself in check. But, if she keeps this up…stop…not possible…I need to wait until she is ready. She'll tell me, won't she? How will I know?

After a few more hours we finally make our way to the gate leading back up to Anna's cabin. The driveway has been cleared. "Anna is someone who gets things done, let me tell you. She sent me a text this morning saying she had the cabin stocked and the heat turned up for us. She pays a local gentleman to keep an eye on the place for her."

"It is so far away from civilization," Addy says in awe as the cabin comes into view. When I stop in front of the house, she faces me. "Thank you for bringing me here. It is wonderful."

We both get out and lug our suitcases up to the porch. She swivels around taking in the landscape as I kick the mat to locate the key. When I open the door, warmth filters out towards us. "It's getting late. Let's unpack and see what we can find to eat."

She follows me in and her eyes dart to the high ceiling. The cabin is beautiful, a true work of art, the craftsmanship is extraordinary. "We'll take the master bedroom upstairs," I tell her as we kick our boots off by the front door.

"We must call Anna tonight. I have to thank her. This is amazing," she says as she runs her hand over a large wood beam running up to the ceiling.

"Yes, she will want to know that we made it. I love it here, I'm happy we have the opportunity to enjoy it and this time I have a lovely companion." She flushes at my compliment. "Follow me."

We make our way up the stairs and she squeals in delight as she rushes around the room. I busy myself hanging clothes in the closet but notice that she has gotten quiet and hasn't come back out of the bathroom. I set the stuff down in my hands.

"Addy?" She is frozen in front of the mirror. Her eyes dart to mine and then she crumbles to the floor. "What is it, sweetheart?"

I sit down on the cold tile and wrap her into my arms.

"I don't deserve all this, Liam," she whispers.

"Addy, we have been through this. What you didn't deserve was a room with nothing but a thin mattress and a blanket. What you deserve is the world. You are a good person. You need to quit blaming yourself, just because you took that money from Javier does not make you a bad individual. You were saving yourself. You had no choice. None."

"I'm sorry I didn't mean to ruin our arrival. It overwhelmed me suddenly, the realization I am really here and not even a month ago my life was so different." She wipes her eyes and sits to face me. She places her hands on both sides of my neck, stroking her thumbs over my skin. I keep as still as I can, giving her time to explore my body. She leans in and offers me a feather lite kiss on my lips. Then she dips her head and trails down the side of my throat then back up the other side. When she reaches my mouth again she whispers over it, "thank you for being so patient with me, Liam. You are the only person I've been able to trust since my dad." She drops her face, and I feel her tears seep into my t-shirt.

I run my fingers through her hair as she cries on my shoulder. Again, I should've been more aware of how she might feel coming here. She spent years held captive, healing doesn't happen overnight. "Hey, baby, lets finish unpacking later. Why don't we go make that call to Anna?"

She sits up and nods in agreement.

We head downstairs and I set the computer up so we can video chat with Dylan and Anna. As it rings them I browse the cupboards. Christ, Anna must have thought we would be here for months with the amount of food she had stocked. Addy squeals behind me, I laugh, evidently they answered. I sit down beside her as the connection completes.

Saving Addy

"You guys made it," Anna says.

"It is beautiful, Anna, thank you so much for letting us stay here." Addy can hardly sit still her excitement has returned.

I brush her hair off her shoulder, my eyes will never get enough of her. I turn back to the screen. "Anna, really the cupboards are exploding. We will never eat all of this food."

She laughs. "You can never be too prepared. Plus, I wanted to make sure you had plenty of variety." She winks at me. I know she wanted to make sure Addy had as many choices as she could offer.

"How is my dad?" I ask.

"He will be here in a minute. I sent him a text saying we were online with you." Dylan says. "Hey man, while the girls are chit chatting could you call me on my cell?"

Addy immediately turns to me with a worried look on her face.

"It's just business, Addy. Stop, I can see your worry from a thousand miles away," Dylan scolds.

"Yes s…Dylan." She drops her eyes to her lap.

I nudge her forcing her to glance up at me. "I'll be right back. You and Anna can have time for girl talk or whatever it is you call it."

She smiles but I can see that she is not convinced. Everything makes her suspicious and you can't blame her. She has been programmed to expect the worst. "Okay."

As I leave the breakfast bar, she asks Anna if Anthony made it back safely. She is always worrying about others.

It only takes one ring for Dylan to answer. "Hey, sorry but I needed to talk to you. I've been trying to come up with a solution to the Javier problem. I sent a courier to him with a check for a hundred grand and a letter telling him I was paying off Addy's debt to him. He sent it back as confetti with a note saying if we cared anything about her I would return her to her family."

"Fuck him! Does he think she hasn't told us what the fuck happened? He is not her fucking family!"

"I know, I know. Calm down, she'll hear you. I thought if it was about recouping his money, it could end peacefully, but I see now it will not be so easy."

"It's possible he won't come looking for her if she stays in the states. He didn't search for her while she was in school in Utah."

"I don't know, Liam. He seems pretty determined this time."

"Fuck."

"Anyhow, I wanted to let you know that I tried."

"Thanks, man. I'll figure out something. We could set her up with a new identity. She needs some time before I push her to think about things like that."

"I agree, you should be safe at the cabin. Get those cameras synced up to your computer to keep an eye on things. No one knows you are there except, Anthony, Luis, Anna and me. We are keeping it quiet. We aren't naïve, I'm sure he has eyes and ears here on the estate. I swear when he came the day after you left he knew she had been here."

"I'll get everything set up. Thanks Dylan, our victory over Oliver was short lived. I'm so sick of these fuckers."

"Me too, me too. Oh, and I have something on a happier note I wanted to talk to you about. Um… Anna and I are expecting."

"Expecting what?"

Dylan laughs. "Expecting what? Are you serious? A baby you dumb fuck."

The phone slips from my hand. I pick it up clumsily. "Sorry, a baby! Like a real baby?"

"No, a fake one. It's okay you should've seen the look on my face when Anna told me." His voice cracks, the emotion noticeable even over the phone. Damn, Dylan with a baby, I never would have imagined.

"Congratulations man. Really, I am happy for you both." My mind wanders to the broken girl sitting out in the kitchen. I've never thought about having a family…until now. I shake my head. We are a long way from anything like that.

"I've been keeping her away from anything that has to do with the business. I don't want her stressing. We have known since we got back from saving Addy, but we wanted to wait until she hit the three-month mark to tell everyone."

"Wow, a baby. That is exciting."

"Anyhow, Anna and I want you to be the godfather, so you better have your ass back here in six months."

"Oh, Dylan, I am honored but I don't know if I am the person for the job."

"Of course, you are, you are like a brother to Anna and me. So, shut up and accept the responsibility. I didn't get a choice and neither do you." He laughs and then hangs up.

That fucker, he always thinks he has to have the last word. I make my way back to Addy. She is giggling as Anna holds up the tiniest little shirt that says *daddy's mini me*. "Oh, Anna, I am so excited for you both."

I slide up behind and wrap my arms around her. She turns and gives me a quick peck on the cheek. "Congratulations, Anna," I say.

"Thank you, Liam," she says looking down and rubbing her belly.

My father pops into the screen. "I guess you heard the good news," he says.

"Yes, very exciting. How are you doing dad?"

"Good, thanks to Addy being so insistent about me seeing my doctor I am feeling more like myself again." He smiles kindly towards her.

"Okay, well I hate to break up this little call, but Addy and I are starving. We just got here, so she hasn't had much time to check the place out."

"You will call us again tomorrow?" he says giving us both a look of that wasn't a suggestion but an order.

"Yes, dad. Goodnight, talk to you all soon."

Chapter Twenty-Two

Addy

I wake, stretching like a cat. Crap, I jump off the bed, landing with a thump before I realize where I am. I glance around as I rub my hip. I've got to quit doing that but when I wake up my first thought is always get the floor and kneel. Will that ever change? I'm glad Liam wasn't in here to see me act like a fool. Oh, my god something smells good. I quickly dress so I can go in search of him and whatever it is he is cooking.

It is peculiar waking up, getting dressed and having the freedom to do what I want. Strange, wonderful and if I admit it to myself a bit scary. At the estate I had a lot to keep my mind busy but here it will just be him and me. I don't want to spend all my time in my head, that is all I've been able to do for the last year. Living is what I crave, I peek out the window before heading downstairs. Who knew having a window to look out of would be such a novelty?

It's snowing! Big wonderful, fluffy flakes! I run down the stairs jumping the final two. Liam's laugh rumbles across the room. "It's snowing!" I exclaim.

"I see that," he says as he points to a chair at the breakfast bar. "I suppose you will demand I go out in that shit."

"Shit," I say feigning offense. "Absolutely, we will go out in this *shit*."

He laughs again throwing his head back. "Can't I watch from the window?"

"No, we are going to make a snowman."

"A snowman?"

"Yes, have you ever heard of them? Button eyes, carrot nose…yadda yadda."

He winks as he sets a plate stacked high with pancakes in front of me. "I know what a snowman is, I've never made one."

"What? Never made a snowman? Oh, Liam, you've missed out on something special. Well, it is settled. Snowman first and then we can do anything you want." As I finish my sentence I worry about what it is, he might choose to do. He must detect my anxiety. He is so sweet he eases my fear right away.

"Hmm, after you force me to go out in the cold I think I would like to come inside, curl up with some cocoa and watch a good movie."

"Oh, that sounds as wonderful as my idea!" I say excitedly shoving a bite of food in my mouth. I close my eyes to savor every detail.

He shakes his head and sits down in the seat next to me. "Addy, I am going to ask you something and I hope you won't take it personally, I'm curious, have you always been like this?"

I swallow and reach for my glass. "Like what?"

"Excited, you find joy in each little thing. Is this your normal personality or…" He lets his words trail off and I can sense his regret at asking the question.

I think about it for a second. "I guess I've always enjoyed life. When I was young, my mom spent much of her time in bed. I was constantly begging her to come outside and see the different type of flowers my dad planted. Sometimes I would ask if she wanted to check out my new tricks with the jump rope. Rarely would she agree, most of the time she wouldn't do more than open one eye at me. I remember a day when it was raining, and I hoped she would come sit with me on the front porch. She told me it was a stupid thing to do. Why would we watch it rain, Addy? You are supposed to stay inside when it rains, she scolded me. It was then I realized that everyone doesn't regard the world the same way."

"I'm sorry," he says leaning over to rub my back.

"It's okay, Liam. She was a drug addict. She didn't experience the same childhood I did. She didn't have someone like my dad to teach her to see the positive in life while still recognizing the bad." I pause for a moment and decide that now is as good a time as any to tell him about my connection to Javier. "My mother worked for Javier. She was a drug mule. It was how she fed her addiction. When my father met her, he tried his best to help but she couldn't break the cycle, it always called her back. She left when I was seven and a few years later we learned she died of an overdose."

"Oh, Addy, I'm so sorry, I lost my mom too. I never knew her, she passed away giving birth to me. I carried a lot of guilt over it, but my dad helped me through."

"Sounds like we are both pretty lucky to have had such wonderful fathers. Luis is so nice. I still feel terrible for spitting at him."

When I say anything about spitting on his dad he always finds it funny. I don't find it amusing in any way whatsoever, it goes against everything I was taught.

"I'm sorry I laugh whenever you mention it. I would've loved to spit at him a few times during my teenage years," he admits

"Liam! You wouldn't have!"

"No, you're right, he would have whopped my ass."

I giggle and realize how amazing it is to hold a normal conversation over breakfast with someone. I let my gaze settle on him. "This is nice," I say motioning my fork between us. "Talking, it is nice."

"It is, but you are about to ruin it by making me go out in the artic."

"You're not getting out of it no matter how much you complain," I demand as I get up to clear the dishes. "Why don't you get ready? I'll clean up."

He grumbles and makes his way towards the stairs. He pauses at the bottom, and winks. He is joking. I think he might even be excited for me to teach him my mad snowmaking skills. As I start the water in the sink, I look out the window imagining an ordinary life, one where I'm doing the dishes taking care of my spouse. Wait. No. Addy, you need to keep a level head, while all this is nice you know it will more than likely be short lived.

Liam clears his throat behind me. I turn around and double over laughing at the site of him. "Really?" All I can see is his eyes, he has so many layers of clothes on if he falls over there is no way he is getting back up.

"I told you I don't like the cold." He waddles over to the door and I watch with an amused smile on my face as he struggles to put his boots on.

"Well, good luck with that. I'll dress and meet you out there," I say giggling as I trudge upstairs.

When I get outside, I search for him. I can't find him anywhere. Unexpectedly he jumps out from the corner of the house and tosses a snowball, hitting me on the side of my head. "Oh, you are in so much trouble." I chase him down and easily catch him. His bulky winter gear has slowed him down. He turns to face me putting his hands up in surrender.

"I surrender, I surrender," he says. I stalk up to him and with one quick shove to his chest he falls backwards.

Laughing I tell him to move his arms and legs. "While you're down there you can make a snow angel."

"A snow angel?" he asks struggling to sit up.

"Here I will show you." I lay down beside him demonstrating the movements. He stands up and towers over me.

"God, you are beautiful."

I squint up at him. "Liam, you were supposed to do one too," I pout.

"Nobody makes a better angel than you," he says. He reaches down offering me his hand and pulls me to my feet. We both swivel to look at my masterpiece, laughing.

"Okay, first thing we need to do is get the ball rolling. Literally." I scoop up a handful of snow and shape it into a small ball. Out the corner of my eye I see Liam back up. "I'm not going to throw it at you silly. It is for our snowman." I bend over and roll it around on the ground as it gets bigger and bigger.

"Huh, so that is how it's done." He mimics me and before we know it we have a large snowman.

"He is nearly as tall as you are," I joke jogging up to the porch, I grab the bowl I filled with snowman parts. "So, I couldn't find buttons, but we have peppermint candies and lucky for us carrots. Liam grabs the carrot from me and bites a big chunk off. "Hey," I scold ripping it from his hands. He winks at me and for a moment I'm lost in his eyes. I blink a few times trying to pull myself out of them.

"We need arms," I announce after the face is complete. We search around the property and I notice a pile of bricks gathered along the side of one of the buildings. It strikes me as I stare at them, I haven't hidden behind my wall for over a week. I peek over at Liam as he scours through the brush. He holds up two sticks tipping his head questioning whether they will work. I make my way over to him but glance over my shoulder once more at the pile wondering if I really need my wall anymore.

"Will these suffice?"

"They are perfect," I tell him. After we finish, he makes me pose by the snowman and he snaps a picture on his phone. "I should check on a few things out here, why don't you start some hot chocolate."

"Sounds good, thank you for indulging me today."

He nods and turns to jog down the driveway. I wonder what it is he is checking on, maybe he is worried we forgot to close the gate. When I get to the porch, I stare at our snowman. How did I get here? How did I go from a slave to a girl building a snowman in the middle of Colorado with a handsome guy? I'm happy. Happy. I place my hand out and smile as the snowflakes fall on my glove. The magic is back.

Liam

Being with Addy is refreshing. How she does it I don't know. She makes everything fun. Today was the most peaceful day I have had in a long time. But, before I become too lost with her here I need to make sure the security cameras are all working. They all look good, I'm not terribly worried that Javier will locate us. No one knows we are here but my dad, Anthony, Anna and Dylan.

Inside I find Addy curled up in a blanket, a fire in the fireplace and two mugs of cocoa. Man, I could get used to this.

"Hurry your hot chocolate is getting cold," she teases.

Quickly I strip out of all of my winter gear and then jump on the couch beside her. "I bet you are nice and warm under there and my hands are oh so frozen." I tug at the blanket sliding underneath. She squeals and backs up trying to move away from me.

Somehow I end up on top of her staring down into her eyes, slowly I slide my palms under her sweater. "Mm, yes, you are warm." I say seductively.

She giggles pushing at me. "Liam, stop, I was just getting warm." She screams as I connect with her silky, smooth skin. She bucks and laughs so hard it knocks us both to the floor.

The mood suddenly shifts, our laughter dies, and the only sound is our heavy breathing and the crackle of the fireplace. I lean back up against the couch and watch as she slowly rights herself. She crawls into my lap and tucks herself into my shoulder. I reach over to the coffee table and hand her cocoa to her and then take mine. "This is good, Addy, I can't remember the last time I had a cup of hot chocolate."

"Me either," she sighs after taking a sip and rests her head against my chest.

"So, what would you like to watch? There is a selection of DVD's under the tv stand."

"Can we just talk?" she asks hesitantly. "I know that I said it would be your turn to pick but I have had no one to talk to in so long…"

"Hey, don't ever be afraid to ask me anything. Of course, we can talk. Actually, I would prefer that to watching a movie."

"Really?"

"Yes, Addy. I want to learn everything about you." I set my mug down and then take hers from her. I tug her over to the rug in front of the fire and coax her to lie down. I grab the blanket and cover us both up cradling her in my arms.

"This is nice," she sighs.

"It's perfect."

Saving Addy

We talk for hours and before we realize it the cabin has grown dark, the only light the amber glow of the flames. She tells me about her life before and I tell her about mine. We share embarrassing moments, struggles, heartaches…everything. The only thing we avoid discussing is what happened to her after she fell into Oliver's hands.

"Shit, we passed the whole day away talking," I tease. "Addy, I don't think I've felt so comfortable with anyone….ever."

She pushes me onto my back and crawls on top of me, her hair spills down around her face and shoulders. She is the most beautiful creature I've seen. "Me, too. It's like I've known you forever, Liam." She leans down and kisses me. "Do you remember the first day we met?"

"Yes, when you stepped out of the car, my heart stopped and then I watched you as you stared into the sunset. It was breathtaking."

She blushes and dips her head, so her hair covers her face. I brush it back and pull it over her shoulder. "Don't be embarrassed, you were prettier than any sunset."

She peeks up at me. "I hadn't seen the sky in so long," she whispers. "It was a beautiful sunset but, when I turned, and you were there." She stops and shakes her head. "Hm, you were there and your eyes…when I looked into your eyes the weight of the world drifted away. I was safe…my brain had a hard time with it but my heart, I think my heart has always known."

I sit with her still straddling me and grab the back of her head pulling her close. Lightly I brush my lips over her mouth then trail down her neck. Her hips move ever so slightly but enough that my cock has definitely taken notice. When I pull away to meet her eyes, I see how flushed she is. "Not yet, baby," I groan.

"Liam, I will not break. I trust you," she whispers.

"I didn't bring you here to take advantage of you, Addy. I brought you here to give you time to reflect…to heal."

"You made me feel so good when we were in D.C. I want that again…I want to make you feel good too. I have never felt this way…never. Please?"

"Soon, baby, it's just not the right time." It takes everything in me to gently push her off my lap and stand. "Let's get something to eat and then we can continue talking upstairs." She looks sad. I hope she is not assuming I don't want her.

"Is it because you think I'm dirty?" she asks.

My heart falls out of my chest and splats on the ground sending blood rushing everywhere. "What? No, Addy." I drop to my knees in front of her. "No, I want to be with you more than anything." God, I am a complete idiot.

"It's okay if you do. It is how I see myself."

"Addy, you are beautiful. Not once have I thought that. But, you thinking about yourself that way breaks my heart. That right there is why we should wait. I want you to be one hundred percent sure you want to be with me. You need to come to me with no hesitation, on your terms…with confidence."

"You know how I survived?" She curls herself into a little ball, hugging her legs to her chest. My throat constricts, she reminds me of Anna. I was the one to find her after she was raped, I wasn't sure she would ever recover, but she did. Will Addy?

Saving Addy

"Tell me." I sit in front of her giving her my undying attention. As much as I hate for our discussion to have turned dark, it is necessary. If she doesn't get it out, it will poison her soul.

"I built a wall inside my mind, a brick wall. Carefully, I tucked all of my memories behind it. Hours I spent envisioning each brick and then when the men would come I would hide. It helped block out what was happening to me, where I was. I have waisted so much time there…until you brought me to the states with you. I haven't used it since I woke up in your apartment." She places her head on knees. I watch as her tiny body trembles.

"Addy, don't hide your tears from me, you don't have to cry in silence."

"Oliver had them punish me for being too loud. Sometimes, I would forget, and I would cry out. It didn't take me long to learn. I just wanted it to end." She peeks at me. "I just wanted it to end. No matter how I pleaded with my eyes, I couldn't make them stop. All I could do was hide and the only place I had was behind my wall."

"I understand, sweetheart, I'm so sorry." I wrap her up in the blanket and pull her into my arms.

"I'm sorry I made it seem like I didn't want you, angel. I've never desired anyone as much as I do you, but we will wait for as long as you need."

"How will I know?"

"When you no longer need your wall."

Chapter Twenty-Three

Addy

I've been having daily video chats with Luis and each day I am stronger. Liam and I have spent the days easily together, he is so sweet. Lately I've caught myself in my head, not behind my wall, no not there, my mind has mostly been in the gutter. Part of me wishes he would let off the sweetness. Yesterday he was chopping wood for the fireplace and I was perched by the window drooling over him. He has the bad boy look going for him, I wish he would allow that side of him out to play. The one I catch staring at me sometimes, but he quickly tucks him away and the charming Liam returns. My thoughts ran rampant while I watched him and before I knew what was happening my hand had made its path down the front of my pants. I finished the day, hiding my face from him, a permanent blush had set up residency in my cheeks.

Sometimes I think he realizes what he does to me. The way he looks at me, brushes up against me. Not only has he kept the fireplace sufficiently stoked, he has managed to keep my crotch stoked as well. Is it time? He said I would know. He knows more about me than anyone, I've been completely open with him. But, I would be lying if I said I wasn't terrified. I am, I trust him, but I've torn so much of my wall down. What happens if we start and I get scared, I will have nowhere to hide. I guess that was his point to waiting. He needs me to be present. He doesn't want me to hide from him. He wants my wall totally pulled down.

What is all the commotion downstairs? I close the laptop and peek down from the top step. I find Liam dragging a tree into the cabin. What the heck? "What are you doing?" I ask, trotting slowly down the stairs.

He tugs hard one more time, and the tree slides all the way inside. He straightens and grins at me ear to ear. "What does it look like, silly?"

"Well a tree, but…" It dawns on me, Christmas. I've been so wrapped up I hadn't even considered what month it was.

He watches me intently and sees I am slowly putting two and two together. "I thought we could decorate it today. Christmas is only a week away."

"Oh, Liam, you should go home. You don't have to stay with me, I will be okay. God, I'm so self-absorbed, you need to be with your family for the holidays."

He holds up his hand to stop me. "Actually, my dad and Mrs. Cortez are flying in to spend the new year with us. So, we can celebrate with them when they arrive. I don't know about you but I'm looking forward to a nice quiet holiday with you." He winks and goes right back to struggling with the tree.

"Here let me help you." I laugh. A tree, I haven't celebrated Christmas since my father passed, that is probably one reason it didn't even occur to me how close the holiday was.

"Hm, I guess we will have to improvise. I didn't think about it, but we don't have a tree stand or any decorations," he says in exasperation, throwing his hands up in defeat.

I laugh again. "Oh, Liam, my how you underestimate this pixie's creativity. How about you figure out how to support it and I'll take care of the decorations?"

I give him a quick peck on the cheek before my treasure hunt begins. I search the cabin, every now and then I stop and watch him fight with the tree. *I must have done something right for God to bless me with such an amazing man.* I pause at the thought; the inner dialog is so foreign it takes my breath away. I am lucky. I am blessed, Liam is the best gift I've ever received. He senses my eyes on him and turns to me with a concerned expression.

"What is wrong, Addy?" he rushes over.

"Nothing, absolutely nothing."

He drags his finger under my eye and holds it up for my inspection. "What do you call this?"

I giggle. "I call that a happy tear."

He wraps his arms around me. "You sure that is what it is?" He tips his head questioning me.

"I'm positive," I say with confidence. It's time, this man has been with me for several weeks, alone, in the middle of nowhere and not once has he even tried to take advantage of me. He is mine, I'm never letting him go. Never.

"Okay then." He hesitantly backs away still eyeballing me. "So, I will assume you like the tree?"

"Yes, it's wonderful. Is it ready?"

He laughs. "I make no guarantees it will remain standing until Christmas, that is why it is nowhere near the fire."

"No, that is good thinking. Here, you can help me with the decorations." I grab his hand and drag him to the table, and we set to work for several hours.

"I feel like I'm back in grade school," he grumbles.

"Hey, you were the one who drug the tree in. This is the best I can do," I tell him.

"No, this is perfect. I'm just not as crafty as you are." He holds up his paper snowflake creation showing me it is square.

"That is my favorite!" I exclaim. "It's original, anyway." I giggle.

"Fuck," Liam yells for the umpteenth time. He sucks on his injured finger.

"Let me finish." I laugh taking the string of popcorn from him.

"Walla! I think this should be enough." We gather our paper and popcorn treasures and set to work on the tree.

After we've finished we stand and admire our masterpiece. He presses into my back wrapping his arms around me. He whispers in my ear, "thank you, Addy."

His words startle me, and I turn to face him. "What for?"

"For making me feel young at heart again and happy. You've made my world a better place."

Liam

I've decided to wait until my father gets here to talk to her about the next step. We have some decisions to make. I know she does not want to return to Mexico, and I understand why. Javier is a dangerous man, and he has eyes everywhere. I'm willing to live in the states, I like it here, but it changes things for me. Leaving the FBI and going to work with Dylan was a big decision for me. I still want to continue on that path, I will just have to figure something out with the others. I can't force her go back. I don't want her living in fear. She has done enough of that.

I chuckle as I listen to her and Anna video chatting. This has become a routine for them. She has a session with my dad and then Anna hops on and the discussion immediately turns to the baby. Addy is helping her with tips on easing morning sickness and she comforts her by letting her know that everything she is experiencing is all a normal part of pregnancy. Addy is one of those individuals you would never realize from first meeting how smart she really is. Her happy-go-lucky attitude and one foot in the fantasy world probably prevents people from seeing her passion for serving others. She is amazing. She needs to get back to her career soon. She has so much to offer.

I hear Dylan and get up to say hello to him, but he asks Addy if he could speak to her alone. Her voice trembles slightly but she agrees and glances at me nervously as she carries the laptop into the bedroom. Hmm, I wonder what that is about? Surely he wouldn't discuss any news of Javier with her.

Chapter Twenty-Four

Addy

"Hey, Addy, can I talk with you in private?" Dylan asks as I'm video chatting with Anna.

"Uh, yeah, sure. Let me move to another room." I peek over at Liam, he shrugs his shoulders, but he is curious about what Dylan wants to speak with me about.

After I settle on the bed upstairs, I stare into the screen, Dylan appears to be nervous. "Okay, it's just me," I tell him.

When he is deep in thought his brows furrow and he is the most intimidating person I've see. When he finally speaks I jump slightly. "It's a medical question, well sort of, no it definitely is," he says.

Hmm, Dylan at a loss for words? "Go ahead, as a professional you have my utmost attention and of course I will keep everything private."

"It's Anna. She wants to…well she wants to have sex and I don't mean like, umm well vanilla stuff. Do you follow what I am trying to say?"

He is worried about hurting her, I really judged him wrong when I first met him. "I understand. It is fine as long as she is comfortable, and she is not having any complications such as spotting or anything like that. Um, for the more non-vanilla stuff, if you are careful and it makes her happy then it should be fine as well. You will not hurt her or the baby Dylan. Anna knows her body and her limits, she wouldn't ask you for something that would harm either of them."

His shoulders relax and I hear him let out a long breath. "Okay, I've been telling her no, but then she assumes I don't want her. She asked me if I was still attracted to her the other day. She thinks she is getting fat."

I smile warmly at him and try to encourage him. "She is going through a lot of hormonal changes and sometimes those override our rational thoughts. I'm sure you are doing your best. All you can do is love her and offer her all of the support you can. Communication is the key." As I'm speaking I realize I relate to this situation. I've been feeling like Liam doesn't want me and maybe just maybe he has been feeling like Dylan, he is afraid of hurting me.

"Thank you, Addy, this was something I couldn't talk about with Mark or Anna's regular doctor. This makes me feel better." He smiles and rubs at his chest. This has really been weighing on him.

"Hey, I have a question for you too. You remember the night I…um…well I heard you and Anna?"

"Yes," he says sheepishly.

"Hm, is Liam into that? You know the stuff you and Anna like?" Oh my god I can't believe I just asked Dylan that, shit.

Saving Addy

"Addy, I…I can't lie to you, but I also don't want you to be afraid of him. He has experimented but you've been with him long enough you can see that he is very disciplined, and he wouldn't ask that of you. He knows how much you have been through. He would never expect…"

I hold up my hand to stop him and laugh nervously. "No, I'm not scared Dylan. I, oh I don't know," I say exasperated.

"What is it, Addy? Why did you ask me that, has something happened between you two?"

"No, it's, you are right he is very disciplined, a complete gentleman. But, I kinda want him to, well to just deal with me like a normal woman. A woman he wants, someone he gets lost in and doesn't treat as if I were a porcelain doll. I want to experience his fire, his passion, I'm not scared of him, Dylan."

He raises an eyebrow and sighs. "Oh, I understand now. Sounds like you know what you want. Does he?"

"Whenever I try he always stops me and tells me he doesn't think I'm ready. He has been correct to an extent but, now, now I need something more from him."

"Addy, you already answered your question in the advice you gave to me. Communication is the key."

"You are right," my cheeks flush as I realize this is the deepest conversation Dylan, and I have had. I guess we might become friends yet. "Thank you."

"No, thank you. Anna loves your daily conversations. Maybe someday you can come back and work here on the estate. Mark will be leaving us soon. He is planning on moving closer to his family."

I shrug my shoulders at him. It is a nice thought, but I'll never return to Mexico. Never. But, now he put the idea in my head my chest aches that I can never even entertain the notion. I loved it there, well until the smell of cigar smoke drifted around the house to the where I was sitting.

When I get back downstairs Liam is waiting for me. "What was that about?"

"Nothing," I reply.

"Hmph, what did he want?"

He has been torturing himself I can tell. Worry lines are etched over his brows. "Liam, he had some medical questions, nothing I can share but I promise you that everything is good. He is fine, Anna is fine, and your dad is fine."

He breathes a sigh of relief, but his apprehension isn't abolished. "So, did it have something to do with Javier?"

"No. You should talk to him yourself. I'm sure he could use a friend right now. Anna is in full baby mode and it's making him a little stir crazy." I smile trying my best to ease his fear. "I'm going to go for a short walk so why don't you call him now?"

"I'll go with you," he states heading to the door to gear up.

"Ah, no. I'm a big girl, Liam, I can walk all by myself. I won't go far, I'll stay in the clearing, promise."

He kicks his boot back off leaning against the wall. "You sure? I don't mind, really."

"I'm sure, I just need some fresh air."

Saving Addy

Liam

I'm not going to call Dylan. He will think I'm being nosy. Addy is a big girl she is correct, she can have conversations with others, and I have no right to ask what they are about. Anyhow it's Christmas Eve and I want this evening to be special. So, I'll keep my mind busy with supper. Anna helped me with a little surprise for Addy. She mailed me a package and luckily the delivery man made it up here through all the snow. Prime rib, wine, cheesecake and chocolates. She also sent a present for her with instructions I was not to open it or peek and if I did, she would kick my ass.

I considered getting Addy a gift, but I didn't want her to feel bad about not having anything for me. Her being here with me is gift enough but she wouldn't see it that way. So, I did the next best thing. I retrieved something that was already hers, so it's not from me, I'm just the one who had it sent here. When it came I was tempted to open it, but I stopped myself, she will show me if she wants to.

Actually, her going for a walk is perfect. It gives me a few minutes to get everything set up. Addy said she hadn't celebrated a Christmas since her dad was alive. I can't imagine what her last few have been like. I will make this one the best I can. I love her and I want her to have the world. My thoughts abruptly stop. Do I love her? I don't know but what I do recognize is that I would give her anything, down to my final breath.

"It's snowing again!" she exclaims throwing the door open wide letting a burst of frigid air and wind into the cabin.

Glancing up from the stove my heart stills. Her face is flushed from the cold and her hair is wet from the falling snow. When I say I can see her wings, I'm not lying. She is remarkable. Anthony told me I am a lucky bastard and I agree with him. I'm an incredibly lucky bastard. She is mine, all mine. God, I yearn to go over to her and strip her down, make love to her with my eyes then…fuck…stop. Check yourself Liam, you're giving her a nice sweet Christmas not an x rated one. Crap, I may need to go take an icy shower before supper.

"What are you cooking?" she asks as she saunters over with a…um…a devilish grin on her face?

"It's a surprise so no peeking, go upstairs and get ready for dinner. I left a present for you on the bed." She looks surprised and is about to argue that I shouldn't have but I stop her. I know her better than she knows herself. "It's not from me it's from Anna and before you ask no, I don't know what it is."

She laughs excitedly. "Okay but first…" she leans close pretending to want a kiss, but she slides her palms under my sweatshirt.

"Fuck, Addy, your hands are freezing!" I yell, trying to dodge her.

"Oh, yes, yes they are, and you are so nice and warm." She chases me to the living room and falls on top of me onto the couch. We laugh so hard my ribs ache.

"You are being ornery this afternoon," I scold, and slap her on the ass.

Shit…why did I hit her…

"Mmm," she groans, her hips jerk, and she grinds herself on my thigh. She glances up at me batting her eyelashes and runs her tongue along her teeth. "I have been a bit naughty today," she teases then slides off of me and heads upstairs.

What the fuck was that? I glance down at my hard as a rock dick. I toss my head back onto the cushion staring at the ceiling. I wonder how much longer I can control myself around her. In the beginning I saw Addy as an angel, I still do but lately my mind runs away with the image. It strays from the sweet category to a more well how should I say, a more Victoria Secret one.

Cold shower it is. What the hell did she and Dylan talk about? She seems, different, I don't know, more confident? Shit, I jump up, somehow that little two-minute encounter made me completely forget that I was cooking.

Chapter Twenty-Five

Addy

*M*erry *Christmas Addy,*

Hopefully Liam was a good boy and didn't peek at this package. It is for you but in the end it will be for him. All of our long talks have meant so much to me, I think we are healing together. An unfortunate sisterhood but none the less I am so thankful to have saved you. I consider you my best friend. It is nice to finally have a girl to talk to.

Anyhow, in the box you will find a dress. This is not just an ordinary dress it is a magical dress. One I wore myself once. It will make Liam go crazy, and he will not be able to control himself. It will look beautiful on you, especially with your new tattoo. I can't wait to video chat with you on Christmas, for a little how should I put it…girl gossip. I love you, Addy, and I hope you have a wonderful Christmas with Liam.

Love Always and Forever,

Anna

Opening the lid on the box I cautiously peer inside. I pull out the dress sliding it through my fingers. It is so silky soft and wow, what an amazing color. I bet Anna was drop dead gorgeous in the thing. It is the same color as her eyes. As I walk over to the mirror, I hold it up to myself. Won't Liam find it a little weird I'm dressing up for dinner here at the cabin?

I smile at my reflection and think about it. Between the dress and the gift, he won't be able to resist. I need him, it's not just a figure of speech either. I really, really need him. When he sits or sleeps next to me, my body aches for him. His lack of touch is physically hurting me. I need his hands on me.

After my shower I put on my robe. I don't want him to see the dress yet. Not until we are ready for dinner. I hid it in the far corner of the closet. When I exit the bathroom, he is sitting on the bed in nothing but his boxers. "Oh, hi."

"Hi," he says seductively. "I'm disappointed. I'm too late to join you."

I'm not sure how to reply, this is what I wanted, wasn't it? "It's all yours." I give him a tiny smile and blush.

Once he closes the door, I let out the breath I had been holding. Every nerve in my body is tingling with anxiety. Scared, excited, happy, all my emotions are skipping through my system and I am almost in overload. It is time, tonight Liam will make me his.

Searching around I find some old newspaper and wrap my gift for him. As I slide it under the tree, I spot a box under there already. I glance at the steps and gently slide it towards me. It is in a shipping box and is addressed to Liam. He said we wouldn't gift each other, my present isn't a real gift, that turd better not have bought me anything. For a moment I think about not giving him mine. No, it is perfect he will understand the minute he unwraps it….I hope. I push it back where it was.

"Addison, what are doing?"

Busted. "I was putting something under the tree." Liam walks over and stares down at me. His eyes roam to where my newspaper wrapped gift lies.

"Addy?"

"It's nothing really, Liam. Just a small token, you'll see."

He sighs and then his focus is directed to the kitchen. "Supper is almost done, why don't you get ready and I will finish up."

He is dressed nicely in black jeans and a blue button-down shirt the same color as his eyes. I guess my dress won't be too over the top. He took the time to look nice. "Whatever it is it smells amazing," I say rising from the floor.

He turns and flashes me a bright smile. "Go on and get dressed, you will see. Anna helped me with a little Christmas Eve surprise dinner."

I pause at the bottom of the steps and grin to myself. "Anna helped me with a surprise too."

He stops and glances up at me. I wink at him and saunter upstairs.

The room still smells like his cologne and my stomach tightens. I grab the dress and slide it on. Tears threaten to spill out the corner of my eyes and I focus on swallowing the lump in my throat. It is absolutely beautiful. I spin around. It has an open back. I stare at the vines and small flowers climbing along me. You can't even see the years of torture there, thanks to Liam I only see my strength and it is now etched into the pores of my skin. As I am taking one last look in the mirror, I hear Liam yell up from below. "Supper is ready, angel."

I head downstairs and pause at the bottom of the step suddenly very shy. This feels almost like a real date. It's been years since I've felt this way. Liam turns and drops the glass in his hand. We both stare at each other for a long minute. "Addy," he breathes.

I bite my bottom lip and start up the steps. This is too much, I feel ridiculous. He rushes forward and pulls me back down wrapping his arms tightly around my waist. "You are beautiful, is this the surprise that Anna sent?" he says softly.

"Yes, I will go change. It is just you and I. It is silly."

"No." He leans away slightly and while holding me with one arm still at my waist the other snakes up my spine drawing lines over the vines there. His touch sends goosebumps to break out over my skin. "Fuck, Addy. You are incredibly sexy. You could only wear this here if you wore it anywhere else you would attract every man in the vicinity." He brushes my hair aside and places light kisses along my shoulder blades. "And, you are mine," he growls.

Oh my god, his warm mouth on me is…oh god…I don't want him to stop.

He moans and spins me to face him. He tips my chin and when his gaze settles on me I am lost, drifting in the weightlessness they provide. "You and Anna are naughty, naughty girls aren't you?"

I grin up at him. "She said it was magic dress."

"Oh, I don't think it's the dress that holds the magic." He leans forward and kisses me with such passion I fight to remain standing. He pulls me tight and his hand runs up through my hair and grips the back of my head pushing me closer to him if that is possible.

193

When we break apart, I stare up at him. I want him to take me now. He wants to take me now. I sense it in the way he looks at me hungry, like a man half-starved. "Do you want me to go change," I ask hesitantly.

"No. I can control myself, magic dress or no. Come let's eat, Anna has been busy it seems. We have prime rib and..." he stops and runs his tongue over his top lip, making me almost groan out loud, "and...other delectable deserts."

I chuckle nervously. "We will have to thank her."

"Yes, yes, we will." He tips his head and his eyes roam over my entire body.

He pulls a chair out for me and pushes it in gently once I am seated. He kisses my head before setting down beside me. My nerves are quelled for the moment as my stomach growls at the feast before me. "Oh my gosh, this is all for us."

"She sent enough for five people." He laughs and the heat is put on simmer for the time being.

Liam is attentive the entire meal. When he brings the cheesecake out, he insists on feeding it to me from his fork. I giggle when he brushes a crumb from my bottom lip. "You realize I do know how to feed myself."

"I know but I love it when your tongue darts out and your eyes close. When you pull it off my fork it captivates me." He says hypnotically.

I'm so wound up from the tension of being alone with him for several weeks I may self-combust. If he doesn't give in tonight, I will die. By the time he finishes feeding me I am all but panting with my legs tightly squeezed together.

He rises and cleans off the table. His eyes are on me while he works. I want to help him, but I'm wound so tight, I can't seem to get my bearings.

"I can get this, angel, are you okay?"

"Yes," I whisper.

He smiles at me and continues to clear the dishes. "Did you enjoy the meal?"

"Yes."

He laughs lightly and walks around behind me dragging his hand along my shoulders until he reaches the opposite side of the table and returns to his task, his eyes never leaving me. "You are quiet suddenly."

"Hmm, I'm fine. The food was wonderful, thank you." My pulse is racing, Liam is the sexiest man I have ever laid eyes on and every ounce of his attention is on me. He has hardly touched me but between the feather lite touch and the seduction of his voice I am worried that I will lose control of myself.

He chuckles as he loads the dishwasher, I'm glued to my seat. I'm not sure what to do, does he think I'm ready? He acts like he might be a little more willing tonight.

He stares at me for a long moment before coming back out from the kitchen. I see he is questioning how far he will take this. Before he can say anything I jump out of my chair. "I have a gift for you." I grab his hand and drag him to the couch. He sits down eyeing me suspiciously. I bend over to retrieve the present for him.

He has tormented me throughout dinner, maybe I should repay the tease. I drop to my knees pretending to reach way under the tree and lift my ass high. I know that the dress is tight, and he is probably getting quite the show. Did I just hear him groan? I smile to myself and twist to catch his reaction. "Here it is!" I hold it up. He sits forward trying to tame the bulge that has grown in his pants.

I perch on the edge of the couch beside him and hand him the present.

"I like the newspaper wrapping," he laughs. "Shit, it's heavy. You didn't have to give me anything. I am just happy to be here with you." He brushes a lock of my hair behind my ear.

Nervously I chew on my bottom lip not taking my eyes off of him. Will he understand? He slowly peels the paper back, then stops and stares as he sees what it is. "Addy," he whispers.

My eyes drop to my hands. This was dumb, you are stupid, Addy. A knot forms in my throat. His large hand covers mine and I peek up at him...he understands. "I took it down."

He sets the brick in his lap on the coffee table in front of us and turns to face me cupping his hand over my cheek. I lean into it. "Addy, are you sure?"

I shake my head. "My wall is gone, but I don't want you to treat me differently, Liam."

"What do you mean?"

"I want you treat me like any other girl."

"But, you aren't any other girl. You are my angel," he says brushing his lips over mine.

Saving Addy

"I don't want you to treat me like I will break. I want you to do things to me you would normally… well things that you would do to any other woman."

"Addy, I…" he leans back running his hand through his hair.

"Never mind." I kick my heals off and run upstairs to the bathroom and lock the door behind me. What was I thinking? He will never treat me like an ordinary girl. No one will, I'm stupid little Addy, a girl who was a slave, who was used, beaten…and broken.

Liam knocks on the door. "Addy, open the door."

I ignore him. He bangs louder. "Addy, *please*."

He hits the door so hard that it shakes on the hinges. I crawl back and stare at it. "Addy, fucking open this door. I'm not asking, do it now!" he roars.

That's more like it I think. He isn't being nice. I stand and swing it open. He is panting, looking like he was about to break the door down. "That, Liam. That is what I want. I want you to stop treating me as if I were a porcelain doll."

He grabs me and kisses me so hard his teeth graze over my lips. He pushes me backwards until the back of my legs hit the bed and then he gently shoves me onto the mattress. He towers over me and the internal struggle plays over his features. "Close your eyes," he orders.

I swallow hard but obey. The bed shifts and he slides up alongside my body. His breath is hot over my ear. "I will tell you everything that I am going to do to you tonight, Addy."

I tremble but not out of fear, no not that it is…anticipation. I nod my head slightly.

"First, I'm going to undress you, and I will enjoy watching that dress slipping off of your body. Then my eyes are going to make love to you, Addy. I will study every square inch of you at my leisure. They will drink you in and my mouth…" he pauses and his tongue snakes up along neck. I roll my head to the side giving him more access and the rumble of his laugh vibrates down my entire body. "Do you like my mouth on you, Addy?"

"Yes," my voice trembles as my need for him increases.

"I'm glad, very glad to hear that because I will taste every part of you. Then I'm going to explore you with my hands, I will run them everywhere. Your body belongs to me, doesn't it?" His hand glides down my arm and he captures my wrist pressing his finger firmly over my beating pulse.

"Oh, god, yes. It exists for you…only you."

"You will give yourself to me tonight won't you?"

My tongue darts out to wet my lips. "Yes, sir."

He pauses for a minute at my words and then he grinds his erection against the outside of my thigh. "Fuck, Addy, you are making me so hard, see what you do to me? Do you know what I will do after I touch you?"

I'm so tightly wound that whatever it is I am going to explode on contact. This is the most erotic moment I have ever had, and he has done nothing but whisper in my ear. He needs to know what I want, Dylan said to tell him.

"You will take me hard and make me yours?" I moan.

He growls and rolls me over to my stomach. The zipper on my dress releases, the cool air rushes over my bottom. "Did Anna send you this as well?" He snaps my thong and I squeak at the sting it provides.

I wiggle my ass, trying to get him to touch me there again. "Yes, sir."

"Remind me to thank her later, it seems this was a gift for me."

"No, sir, it is for me. She knows how bad I want you."

"Oh, she does, hmm, have you been swapping stories with Anna? Have you been having naughty thoughts about me you shouldn't be sharing with others?"

Is he angry? He kisses my ass cheek. No, he is definitely not angry. "Yes, sir."

He spanks me lightly and then resumes running his tongue over the area. I groan and lift my hips off the bed. He sits on his heals and yanks the dress off of me. "Addy, are your eyes still closed."

"Yes, sir."

"You may open them." He flips me over and when my gaze meets his, we can no longer control ourselves.

I sit up and unbutton his shirt as he leans around to release the clasp on my bra. "I want you, Liam, I *need* you."

He kisses me hungrily as I push the shirt off of his shoulders. My hands shake as I reach for his belt. He reaches down and helps me. "Addy, we should slow down."

"No," I say desperately.

He leans back and then climbs off the bed shoving his boxers and jeans to the floor. I crawl up higher dropping my knees open slightly, his eyes drop and then he buries his head between them. I fall backwards sighing loudly. "Oh yes, yes!"

He groans, and the vibration sends me over the brink. I come so hard that the world around me goes black. Before I regain my senses, I realize I am standing on the edge of the cliff once again and then gently he shoves me over. I cry out and fist the sheets under me. "Oh god," I moan.

He crawls up me not taking his eyes off of mine as I struggle to recover my vision. Then he plunges into me in one swift motion and we both sigh loudly. He stills, buried deep inside me. This…this is right. This is so right, nothing has ever been so right, so perfect. He gazes deep into my eyes. "You are mine, Addison, you know that I can never let you go now."

I'm at a loss for words, I nod as hot tears run down the side of my face. He brushes them away settling his weight fully on top of me. "I want to be yours," I say softy.

"Don't look away," he orders, and his hips grind against me rocking upwards and I lose my ability to speak, to move. He has found a place somewhere deep inside of me that leaves me helpless and only he has the key to release me. He pulls back and then pushes forward again hitting that spot. It almost hurts, almost. It is such a strange sensation. His thrusts get more insistent.

I watch him watching me, I can see his hunger, his possession, he will keep me…forever and I have never craved anything more. He tilts his hips and I can't control it any longer. I drag my nails across his back and arch off the bed. He drives into me relentlessly, filling me completely. When he pushes my legs up to my chest, he takes me further into the abyss. He leans up, towering over me and his abdominal muscles tighten as he descends into me. He is so damn sexy it is intoxicating.

He is like a Greek god hovering above me. He is worshipping me, giving me his strength, his essence. A warm tingle runs up from my toes and I press my head into the pillow and scream out his name. He groans as he hears it fall from my lips and he thrusts one final time before collapsing on top of me.

"Addy, angel?"

"Thank you," I whisper then my emotions release, and a torrent of tears begins. Tonight, was amazing, it was the first time I experienced something other than pain and humiliation. The only time I wasn't sitting on the other side of my wall praying for it to be over soon.

"Oh, baby, it's okay. Let it all out, I love you, angel."

Liam holds me the rest of the night, whispering words of love and placing gentle kisses on me.

Liam

I wake up with a start, shit, Addy is gone. I trip over the sheet and my own two feet, falling out of bed but then I hear giggling. Quietly I perch at the top of the steps and listen to Anna and Addy. They are both laughing. It's not gentlemanly to eavesdrop but I need to know that Addy is okay with what happened last night. I must admit that was a first for me, I've never had a girl cry for hours after making love to me. She seemed happy but yet sad.

"It was wonderful, thank you for the dress it worked," Addy says.

Anna laughs. "I'm so thrilled for the both of you. It's nice to hear that you two are getting along so well."

"I feel a little stupid, afterwards I cried. He was so sweet. He didn't make me talk…he just held me."

"Oh, Addy, I understand completely. The first time after… it's a milestone, it is a sign you are healing. I'm sure he was concerned. It has to be hard for the guy too. It's not easy being with someone after they have been hurt so badly."

"I didn't think about that. Do you think I pushed him too fast? Now, I feel bad, I didn't even consider his feelings."

"Addison, Liam doesn't do anything he doesn't want to, trust me. So, tell me, how was it?"

They both laugh and then Dylan scolds them. "Girls are you two gossiping about things you shouldn't be?"

They just giggle more. I'm happy that Addy isn't so afraid of Dylan anymore. He is my best friend, and she is my girl, so I want them to get along.

"Dylan, Merry Christmas! Thank you so much for your advice the other day, it…helped." Addy giggles again.

She talked to Dylan? Wow, she really is trusting him. I guess I should reveal myself, I shouldn't be eavesdropping. I'm glad to hear that Addy is okay and from the sound of it she enjoyed herself last night.

I grab a pair of sweats and head downstairs. Fuck. She is sitting at the table in nothing but one of my t-shirts.

"Liam!" She jumps up rushing towards me and throws herself in my arms. "Merry Christmas! I made you breakfast," she says after giving me a quick kiss. "Dylan and Anna have been video chatting with me while I've been waiting for you to get up."

I plop down in the chair she was just sitting in. It is warm from her bottom. I stare at her enticing back side as she bends over to get my meal out of the oven. Oh fuck, she has no panties on, and I can see that delicious spot where her butt and thighs collide. *Merry Christmas to me.*

The rumble of Dylan's laugh reminds me we are not alone. I turn to him and he cocks an eyebrow at me. "Late night?" he asks.

I shake my head ignoring him. "Merry Christmas you two." Anna blushes, and I am reminded of her role in last night. "Anna, I think I should thank you for the gift you sent to Addy and me, it was…ah…it was very nice."

She busts a gut laughing. "Liam, stop, you will make me pee my pants. You know having this baby on my bladder does that."

I chuckle, I love Anna, I'm so happy she and Dylan are together. "I was talking about the meal," I tease.

"Oh." Her face turns red and then she realizes I am teasing, and her features soften.

"The dress was nice too."

Dylan smirks and pulls Anna closer to him. "Anna, what did you do?"

"Nothing, I may have sent Addy my dress."

Dylan smiles seductively at her. "*The* dress," he says.

"Yes," she whispers.

Dylan looks at me. "Hey man, we can talk later…I have things I need to attend to."

Anna squeaks in delight and gets up and dashes out of view of the camera.

I laugh as the screen goes black.

"What was that all about?" Addy asks as she sets my breakfast in front of me. She slides in the chair next to me curling her legs up to her chest.

I resist the urge to let me eyes roam over her bare legs. "Dylan and Anna are feisty this morning, he loves to chase her."

"Oh," she says her eyes getting large as her understanding settles in.

"How are you feeling today?"

"Good…no actually I'm great." She gives me a shy smile.

"I was a little worried that maybe we should have waited, or that I hurt you."

"No, you didn't hurt me…it was perfect. I'm sorry I cried after." She stops and chews on her bottom lip. "It was the best experience I have ever had, Liam."

I lean over to kiss her. "I'm glad, that makes me happy."

"I'll let you eat. I'll go get dressed."

"Nope," I pull her into my lap, and she yelps in surprise. "I enjoy seeing you in my shirt, it is as sexy as the dress."

"But, it's Christmas. I can't run around half dressed."

"Why not? It's just you and me, angel."

She snuggles up under my chin. "Okay." She smiles against my neck.

"I didn't get a chance to give you your present last night."

She sits up. "Liam, you said we weren't gifting each other."

"You gave me a present." I tap her nose, reminding her.

"A brick, that is hardly a gift."

"It was the best gift I've ever been given," I say sincerely. It is, her tearing her wall down to be with me, it was the best thing she could have ever given. "Besides, mine isn't a real gift either. You will see."

She bounces excitedly on my lap and I groan. "Oh," she exclaims then drops her head, shyly.

I chuckle and pull her in close and bite her neck gently. "See what you do to me?"

She turns herself around to straddle me and rubs herself over the length of my cock. My hands reach out to unbutton her shirt. Her breasts are so beautiful, hmm, I palm both of them and lean in placing light kisses on the underside of each. She sighs loudly and leans her head back gripping the chair tightly.

When she rights herself, she reaches down and pulls my cock out stroking it up and down slowly. Her eyes meet mine and she smiles. She looks proud of herself and I quickly push thoughts away of how all of this must be for her. I focus on treating her like I would in any other situation, forgetting her past. She stands on her tiptoes and then lowers herself down letting her head fall to my shoulder. Fuck, she feels so good.

I grab her hips tightly guiding her up and down on my throbbing cock. Shit, I could get used to this. Her moans grow louder prompting me pull her down harder and faster. I run my hand up her stomach, between her breasts until I reach her neck, she drags herself away from my shoulder and stares into my eyes. I can almost see herself opening to me, giving everything to me. My grip tightens over her throat and her eyes roll back into her head and she comes hard. Her muscles tighten around me and I can't hold on any longer, I release myself to my own pleasure. I drag her by the neck to my face and kiss her groaning her name into her mouth.

Her face falls to my shoulder, the only sound in the cabin is our harsh breathing and the beating of our hearts. When she sits up, her eyes are slightly glazed, she grins and then looks down to where we are still joined. "Is it always going to be this good?" she asks.

"No," I breathe. "It will be better."

She smiles bright at my words and nods. She grabs my hand and places it over her heart, it beats strong. "You have healed my heart, Liam."

I take her other hand and place it over mine. She stares at my chest her hand rising and falling as I try to catch my breath. "You have healed mine as well, Addy." I dip my head to capture her eyes and she smiles. "I think I'm falling in love with you," I admit to her.

"I'm glad," she says as a tear slips down her cheek. "Because I can never leave you Liam."

"I know," I whisper.

Chapter Twenty-Six

Liam

After breakfast Addy and I went upstairs to shower but instead we spent the whole day making love. We made it eventually. After we dragged ourselves out of bed, off the floor, then out of the bathtub but hey we finally made it. When the hot water ran out, we found ourselves back in reality.

"I don't think I've ever had a better Christmas," I tease her.

She laughs. "Me either."

The computer starts buzzing and Addy walks over and clicks it on while I head to the kitchen to get us a snack.

"Oh, thank god, Addy," my dad says.

I abandon the search for snacks and go to stand behind her. He sounds worried.

"Hi, Luis," she says shyly.

"Why haven't you two been picking up? We have been calling you for hours, Dylan was about ready to send the team out."

Addy covers her mouth and drops her head. The embarrassment radiates off of her. I pull her up and then sit in the chair and drag her back into my lap. She struggles to get me to release her, but I don't let go. I will not allow her to feel any shame over what we have been doing.

"I apologize, dad. We have been…busy."

My dad's eyes widen, and it is his turn to be embarrassed. "Oh, oh I see. I'm sorry, son. We, we were worried. Addy, I'm sorry I didn't mean to upset you."

"I'm not upset," she says softly, then a little grin appears on her face.

"I'm glad. So, I can see you two have been having a wonderful Christmas."

"Yes, yes, we have." I hug her tightly.

"Good, well I'll tell the others to call off the troops, you have been located." He laughs. "I will let you both get back to…" he looks down and then up at us, "to whatever it is you have been doing."

"It's okay, we were getting kinda hungry," I tease. Oh, this is rich seeing my old man at a loss for words.

He gives me that dad look and then tells us he and Mrs. Cortez will arrive in Denver two days before New Year's Day.

"I am so excited to see you both," Addy exclaims clapping her hands.

My dad laughs and looks at her lovingly. "We are anxious to see you too. Addy, please don't neglect to call me tomorrow so we can continue our sessions."

"I won't forget, I promise," she says crossing her hand over her heart. "Did you have a good Christmas, Luis?"

"Yes, Mrs. Cortez made a feast after we had church services with Father Paul."

"Is Father Landon not back from his conference yet?"

My dad looks confused by her question.

"Conference? Father Landon was transferred to another parish."

"Oh, I saw him in D.C., and he said he was there for a conference."

"You saw Father Landon? When?" My father asks sitting a little taller in his seat.

"I ran into him the day we were leaving. He was at the diner we were having breakfast at."

"I didn't see him there," I say. Something isn't right, my dad seems nervous that she met him. Why?

"Oh, he left just before you and Anthony walked in. I asked him to stay but he was in a hurry to get to a seminar."

"Addy, did you tell Father Landon where you were going?" my dad asks, and his question puts me on high alert. Dylan said they thought Javier might be being fed information from someone on the inside.

"I may have mentioned it. He was in a such a rush I don't recall."

"Well kids, I must take care of a few things. Liam please watch your phone in case Dylan, or I need to reach you. I will talk to you tomorrow, Addy, Merry Christmas," he says and then the computer goes dark.

"I feel bad for worrying everyone." She turns to face me.

"I don't." I laugh and flip her off my lap then drag her to the couch. "If I don't give you your present it won't happen till tomorrow and I want you to have it today."

She watches me nervously as I retrieve the package from under the tree. She slowly drags the tape off of the top and then stops, looking at me hesitantly. "It's not going to make me cry is it?"

I shrug my shoulders. "I honestly don't know, Addy." I place my hand over hers. "It is your belongings. Most of your stuff had been dissolved but these are your personal items, they have been stored by the investigators assigned to your case. I had them shipped to me earlier this week. I did not look inside."

She drums her fingers on top of the box. She is fearful of the memories that will be released. Finally, she opens it and pulls the cardboard back, peeking in. She quickly looks up at me, then throws herself at me. "Oh, Liam!" she cries. Whatever it is has made her very happy.

She pulls out a tiny figurine of a pixie fairy. She wraps her palm around it pulling it to her chest, tears filling her eyes. "My dad gave me this…it is the only one I was able to keep." She opens her hand looking at it again before handing it to me.

I smile at the cute little trinket. I wish her father was alive, I would thank him for making her into the wonderful, fun-loving woman she is. As I roll the pixie in my palm, I make a promise to her dad that I will love her the way she deserves to be loved. I'll do everything in my power to keep her safe.

When I glance up, she is watching me. She smiles as if she had been listening to my thoughts then she delves back into the box. She pulls out her wallet and tosses it on the table. She covers her mouth as she stares into the package. "My photos," she looks up and beams at me as tears run silently down her cheeks.

I brush them away and then pull her into my chest placing my chin on her shoulder so she can show them to me. "Oh, look this is my dad and I in Africa." She laughs and cries at the same time. "He was there to work, but we went on a safari, he was afraid of the giraffes. It took a lot of convincing to get him to take this picture."

I stare at the man in the picture standing stiffly next to a giraffe, the young girl beside him is grinning widely. Oh, my sweet Addy. I squeeze her. How often I had wondered what she was like before her abduction. How did she come out with her personality still intact? I don't know but I'm glad for it. Photo after photo she shows me all of their adventures.

"Wow, you have travelled a lot."

"Yes, he showed me the world," she says sadly. "I miss him."

"It's okay to miss him, Addy, I am so happy you are sharing these with me. I feel like I'm getting to know you and your dad a little better."

She smiles over her shoulder at me. Then she comes to another one and chokes on a sob. "It's...it's our garden." She draws her finger over it. She is sitting in the middle of a pretty flower garden squinting up at the sun.

211

"This is the last photo my dad ever took, I was sixteen, he passed away a week after this was taken."

"You were a beautiful young woman, he captured you well. This picture radiates how happy you were."

"I can't go back," she whispers.

I realize she doesn't mean to the time in the photo or even to the place...she means Mexico.

"I understand, Addy."

"But, your family is there, your work..." her words trail off.

"Addy, we'll figure it all out, I would never ask you to go anywhere you don't feel comfortable going. I'm not leaving you. It will be fine. Let's not think about it right now. When my dad comes in a few days, we will discuss it but for now, we are focusing on getting to know each other. I think we are doing a good job of that."

She curls into me still holding the photograph to her chest. "Thank you, Liam, this has been the best Christmas I've had since my dad passed. Thank you for sharing me with him today."

"I love you, Addison."

"I love you too, Liam." She closes her eyes and minutes later she drifts to sleep in my arms. I gently tug the photo out of her hand and stare at it for a long time allowing my worry to return. My father seemed concerned about Addy spotting Father Landon in D.C. Surely a priest would not be a mole, would he?

Addy

"Do Dylan and Liam seem a bit distracted?" I ask Anna.

"No more than usual. To be honest, I think Liam is just working with Dylan on how he can work from the states. He doesn't want to leave you. I wish you could come home. I miss having you here."

I sigh, home, it felt like home, but I feel at home here with Liam too. He is my home. "I wish that was a possibility, but Javier would find me. It would also put you all at risk and I can't do that."

"I understand how you feel, really I do. It will all work out. Don't worry, the guys will figure something out."

"Yes, I am sure you are right. Hey, I'll let you go. I think I'll get some fresh air."

"Talk to you tomorrow?"

"Of course, I love our daily talks. See you then." The screen goes dark and I stare at it for a long moment.

Liam went outside a while ago, he said he wanted to check on things. He was going to start the vehicle and let it run for a while since it's been sitting. We are supposed to pick Luis and Mrs. Cortez up in two days. I'm excited to see them, I had wondered why Mrs. Cortez was coming along, Liam informed me she and his dad had been dating since his health scare. He seems thrilled about it and it couldn't have happened at a better time. Liam's attention has been on me, so it is nice Luis has had someone to watch after him. Plus, they make the cutest couple.

As I am heading out the door he comes back inside. "Going somewhere?"

213

I laugh. "Yes, I'm going to sit on the porch for a bit to get some fresh air."

"Okay, angel. The sun is setting and it's damn cold, don't stay out too long."

"I won't, I just need a few minutes to breathe in the mountain air."

He kisses my cheek and heads to the kitchen. "I will check my emails and then hop in the shower. Think about what you want for dinner."

I nod and head outside. God, it is beautiful here. I perch on the porch swing and close my eyes gently pushing myself. This is one of the most peaceful places I have ever visited. How did I get so lucky to find Liam? Brrr, he is right it is cold tonight. The wind whistles through the trees making an eerie sound and I pull my jacket a little closer around me. I should go back inside. Liam will want to start supper. We have been cooking meals together each night. It is one of my favorite things to do with him.

When I get in, the sound of the shower taunts me. I think about going up but my tummy growls if I go up there it will definitely delay our meal. While the thought is enticing, we will have time for that after. Supper first, dessert later. I smile to myself thinking about another night of passion to come with Liam. As I pass the computer I see he forgot to shut it off. I lean over the table to power it down but notice what is on the screen. It is filled with little boxes of video feeds. They appear to be from around the property.

I sit down in front of it. An uneasy feeling settles over me. Liam must think there is a need to have all these cameras. Did he put these in, or have they always been here? I don't know why but it makes me nervous. I'm about to click out to call Anna and ask her about them but I notice a dark car pull up by the gate. I watch in shock as someone gets out and walks back to his trunk retrieving a pair of bolt cutters. Another man gets out….the flick of a flame in the dusk sends me bolting upright and my chair crashing loudly behind me.

Liam comes running down the stairs. "Addy, are you okay."

My eyes flit to his and he must see the terror in them because he runs to me pulling his phone out of his pocket. "Addy, I need you to listen to me. This is very important."

My hand is over my mouth trying to stifle the scream that wants to rip from my throat, but I nod at him.

He pulls me to the side of the stairs and pushes on a small panel that opens. "Addy, I want you to hide in here. Take my phone, tell Dylan that Javier has found us. Do not come out. Whatever you hear, do not come out. Stay here until Dylan tells you it is safe. Do you understand?"

"Liam, you have to hide with me," I whisper.

"No, Addy. There is only room for you. I will deal with Javier. Promise me, Addy, promise you will not come out no matter what," he says with urgency.

I nod and climb inside the dark hole in the wall.

Liam hands me his cell. "Addy, it is ringing Dylan now. Listen to him, angel. Don't come out." He pushes the panel shut and I listen as he runs through the house. Is he hiding my things, hoping Javier will think he is here alone? Oh god, how did he find me? I tremble and hug my knees tightly to my chest, listening to him stomp around.

"Hey, man what's up?" Dylan says.

"Dylan?" I squeak, trying to control my trembling.

"Addy? What is it? Are you okay?"

Dylan's breath picks up and it sounds like he is rushing somewhere. "He…. he's here," I whisper and then I cry. He is here. Oh my god, I can't go back to that life, I just can't.

"Addy, where is Liam?" Dylan is calm suddenly.

"He…he is in the living room. I saw Javier at the gate on the camera. I think Liam is hiding my things, so he won't know that I am here. He made me hide under the stairs and told me to remain here until you tell me I can go out."

"Okay, Addy. Stay on the line with me. I'm going to get help so you will hear me talking to my men, but I am here for you, okay? I will not leave you, sweetheart."

"I'm scared, Dylan," I choke out.

"I know, just breathe, focus on your breathing and stay right where you are."

The crash of the front door sends my heart soaring to my throat. Liam yells, "what the fuck!"

"Where is she?"

"Oh, god, Dylan, he is inside," I whisper.

"Stay where you're at, Addy, it's okay," Dylan tries to soothe me through the receiver. He barks orders to people around him and I try to focus on that.

"I know she is here with you," Javier yells. "Come out, come out wherever you are," he shouts in singsong voice.

My trembling intensifies and my teeth chatter. I shove my fist in my mouth trying to keep from crying out.

"Addy, you are doing good, sweetheart, stay with me."

"He is calling for me, Dylan," I say as quietly as I can.

"Stay, Addy. You have to stay there."

I listen to the heavy footsteps banging through the house and things crashing as his men search for me. He is going to find me. He knows I'm here.

"Nothing boss," a man's voice booms near where I am hiding making me jump.

"Oh, she is here. I can smell her, send a few guys to check the outbuildings."

The scent of his cigar permeates through the crack in the panel filling my nose, I shiver violently at the familiar odor.

"So, how have you been enjoying my little slave Mr. Sharp? I paid a fortune for her. I hope all the hard work that Mr. Wright put into her training has not been undone. It looks like you may have been spoiling her."

"Fuck you. I don't know what you are talking about."

Javier laughs loudly. "Oh, I think you know exactly what I'm saying. Did she tell you how she stole from me and then ran away, right into Oliver's hands?" He laughs harder. "Not a very bright girl, but she is easy on the eyes is she not?"

I hear a loud crack and then Liam groans. He hit him. He hit Liam. "Dylan, he is hurting him," I whisper.

"Addy, I need you stay where you are no matter what you hear," Dylan warns.

The beating intensifies and Liam's grunts become louder. "Dylan," my voice cracks.

"Cover your ears, sweetheart," Dylan says calmly.

"She's not outside boss," a man bellows.

"Oh, Addison, I know you are hiding from me. Come out and I will leave your little boyfriend alone."

"Dylan, I have to go."

"No, Addy, don't. It's okay, just listen to the sound of my voice," Dylan soothes.

Liam cries out and then there is a loud crash. I shove my fist into my mouth again, Javier is hurting him badly.

"Addison, it looks like your boyfriend can sure take more than your uncle ever could. I will have to up the ante maybe I should start removing body parts."

"Dylan, I have to go out there. Please try to get here quickly, Liam is hurt and….tell him I love him."

Saving Addy

"Addy! No! You have to stay where you are!" Dylan says urgently.

I hang up the cell and take a deep breath. I love Liam, I cannot sit here and let Javier hurt him. I push on the panel gently and it pops open. I drag myself out.

Javier is glaring down over Liam. He is tied to a chair, one eye swollen shut and blood everywhere. My sob prompts Javier to stand to his full height and slowly turn to face me. His eyes meet mine and instantly I fall to my knees and lower my head to the floor.

"Addy, no," Liam moans and Javier hits him again.

He moves close and touches my hair lightly. "Up," he says menacingly. Once I am upright, he crouches in front of me grabbing my chin harshly forcing me to look at him. I choke back a cough as the smoke from his cigar burns my eyes and nose. "Well, hello, Addison. It is so nice that you could join us. Your boyfriend was fun to play with but I'm guessing that he is not nearly as entertaining as you are."

I'm trembling in his hand, blinking hard as tears run down my face. "Remember the last time we were together?"

When I don't answer he squeezes my cheeks in warning. "Yes, master."

"Well, that was nothing compared to what will happen tonight."

"Take me and leave her be," Liam pleads behind him.

Javier laughs. "Why would I do that? I am not into men." His eyes sparkle in delight as he stares into mine. He wants to hurt me. I see the wheels turning at all the cruel things he is thinking of doing to me.

"I can help you break into the business. With Oliver gone, you know that someone will rise and take his place and that person could be you…with my assistance."

"No," I whisper as I process what Liam is saying.

Javier grins as Liam's words register with him. He cocks an eyebrow. The thought intrigues him. He releases me and stands drawing a chair over to sit in front of Liam. "Go on, I am a man who likes to wheel and deal. Let's hear your offer."

"I worked for the FBI for the past four years and before that I worked for Manuel Velasquez. I've learned many things about the industry," Liam says with an air of indifference.

If I hadn't spent so much time with Liam, I would be afraid of him. His whole personality changed the minute I came out of hiding. He will do anything to protect me…even if it puts other young women at risk. Oh, no, what have I done? But, I had to come out, Javier would have killed him, and I couldn't let that happen…even if that means I return to the life of a slave.

Javier smirks at me over his shoulder. "Wow, Addison, you have really moved up in the world. Snagged yourself an agent, I'm impressed." He turns back to Liam.

"So, here is the deal. You come and work for me. You will live at my estate until we learn to trust each other, and I'll let her go…that is *after* tonight. I'm not leaving until I enjoy what I paid so much for."

"No. I will come work for you, but we leave now," Liam states through gritted teeth.

Javier shakes his head and my stomach drops. "I don't think you are really in the position to make too many demands Mr. Sharp. My deal or I walk out of here now. I wouldn't delay your answer. My cock is begging me to drag her out of here by the hair and to leave you behind to cry for her."

My heart plummets, I can't watch them finalize the arrangement…Liam will agree. He is going to leave me. He sees no other choice. I want to scream at them both.

"Deal," Liam says with finality.

"No!" I stand up and rush to Liam falling to my knees in front of him. "You can't, Liam, no, you can't do this. You can't do this, he will hurt too many people, just let him take me." Liam closes his eyes, blocking me out.

Javier grabs me by the back of my hair and drags me towards him. "Let the fun begin, we don't have much time," he sneers at me.

He unzips his pants and forces my mouth down hard onto his cock. "Oh fuck, yes. I missed this mouth. Damn, I may have made a mistake with this new agreement."

I choke and tears spring to my eyes, my teeth graze him. I was not prepared for any of this.

He backhands me, his ring slicing my cheek. Blood trickles down onto the carpet. "Watch your fucking teeth!" He growls and Liam grunts loudly behind me.

No. Not in front of Liam. He cannot make me do this in front of him. He shoves my head down hard, chocking me again. I can't breathe, I tug back hard. Unable to control my gag reflex I vomit down my shirt and onto his black shinny boots.

"You fucking sick bitch!" Javier howls.

He shoves me towards one of his men. "Get her in the shower, I will be there in a minute."

Liam pleads for me, begging him to stop. Javier hits him before yelling at someone to clean his shoes.

The man pushes me into the shower and turns it on. "Strip," he orders.

Oh, god, this is not happening. No. This. Is. Not. Happening.

"Now!"

I undress and wash myself quickly. When I look up Javier is glaring at me. "I guess your training has waned." He grabs me and drags me out. I glance down the hallway and see Liam still tied to the chair. He appears to be unconscious.

Javier pulls me into one of the bedrooms and forces me to kneel in front of him. "What an unexpected turn of events, Addison. I have to say I am a bit disheartened you won't be going home with me but, you understand don't you? Your boyfriend's deal was just too favorable to pass up. Your uncle will be so disappointed he didn't get to see you. He has been such a good boy, working for my competition so I stay ahead of the game. Well enough chit chat…shall we begin?"

And so, it does….

only this time there is no wall to hide behind.

After what seems like days. Javier drags my beaten, bloody body back out to the living room, and he throws me at Liam's feet.

Saving Addy

"Say goodbye to your boyfriend."

I peek up and Liam is staring at me. The look on his face will haunt me forever, I have never seen someone more sorrowful in all of my life.

He whispers, "I'm so sorry, angel."

Scooting forward I lay my head in his lap. "You can't leave me," I weep.

"Ah, isn't that sweet. Let's go," Javier orders.

A man pulls me off Liam and another unties him. As soon as he is untied he grabs the blanket off a chair and drapes it over me. "Out." Javier demands.

They drag us both out, not even giving me time to dress or put on shoes. The snow stings the bottom of my feet.

"What are you doing? You said you would let her be, leave her here!" Liam shouts.

Javier stops and turns before getting into his vehicle, he chuckles. "I am," he says ominously and then he turns to get into the car. He pauses before tucking his head in. "Light her up, boys."

I watch in horror as his men go into the cabin with gallons of gasoline. When they come back outside one of them stands on the porch, lights a cigar and tosses it inside.

The doorway and windows turn orange. I spin around as the outbuildings all go up at the same time and our SUV. My eyes meet Liam's and then one of the men pushes him into the backseat of a car.

Liam screams, "stop, you can't leave her here! She will freeze! Addy, Addy, listen, angel, stay by the fire as long as you can. Addy, listen to me, it will be okay just stay by the fire, don't wander off." The man shoves him hard one last time and then shuts the door.

I watch as the four black vehicles drive away.

The roar of the fire is the only thing to keep me company now.

I'm in hell. This is it. Hell has finally consumed me. I spin in terror as Anna's beautiful cabin burns.

The fire is hot, and a puddle slowly forms beneath my feet. My eyes shift to our snowman morphing beside me and my heart sinks. I glance around, nothing but melting snow, fire and the dark forest surrounding me. I sit down as close as I can to the burning building and tuck the blanket under me as tight as I can. Someone will come won't they?

I watch the fire burn and as I sit there something changes in me. My dad's pixie broke a long time ago, back in my cell. That seems like forever ago. Then I became an angel, Liam's angel. But, now I feel them both dying. My body hurts, my mind hurts…my heart hurts. I have to let them go….I can't be them any longer.

I stare up at the moon as the flames dance before my face.

I'm not sad,

no, I'm not even scared anymore,

no, Javier made sure of that,

no, what am I?

Saving Addy

I am…I am pissed

I am fucking pissed that is what I am!

My eyes close and I envision Liam's angel drift up to the heavens carrying the broken pixie in her arms, back to where they belong.

Goodbye sweet Addy….

When my eyes open again, I stare into the fire and cry out, a sound that would frighten even the strongest of men. I laugh out loud like a crazy inmate in an asylum…the only things that can hear me are the creatures of the night.

As my re-birth begins my new wings sprout. I make a vow…Javier Galindo is a dead man and I will be the one to draw the last breath from his body.

The pixie, the angel. Gone.

A phoenix has been born from the flames this night and she will get her revenge. The devil's disciple, Father Landon, is right…I don't deserve this, and neither does Liam.

The flames seem to understand, they whisper their words of encouragement.

Javier Galindo will pay for what he has done.

Chapter Twenty-Seven

Addy

I will not die. No, I've got plans. I scour around and stumble across the pile of bricks throwing as many as I can into the remaining fire. I need to stay warm until Dylan arrives, he will, of this I have no doubt. The only question is how I play this when he does. He won't let me out of his site. Liam and Dylan have a bond, he knows that Liam loves me, and he'll try to keep me safe.

Shoving the warm bricks under my blanket I watch as the stars hide themselves in the new morning light. No one can see the phoenix, no, not yet. I smile thinking of seeing my dear uncle again. He is somewhat to blame for all of this, but Javier uses people's addictions to his advantage. My uncle was partially a victim, I understand this. Javier used my mom's addiction to get her to haul his drugs into the states and he used my uncle's addiction to gambling to get to me. Last night he used Liam's love for me so he could build an empire in the world of human trafficking. Well, that is not happening, no, I'll make sure of that.

I'll take Javier's pain. It is nothing actually. He forgot where I have been the past several years. I have learned a few things along the way. Things that might not have been of use to me with the men there but in Javier's world, I think they will be very, very useful.

Liam and the others worked so hard to take down Oliver. I am not going to allow Javier to rise and assume the position. I recognize his weakness now. I don't know why I didn't see it before. Fear, fear of pain kept me blind to them I guess. But, I am not ignorant any longer.

Liam will never forgive me for this, he won't. But, I love him, and I can't let him work for Javier to save me. He wouldn't be able to live with himself if he learned his actions led to others being hurt. He couldn't see that last night in his worry for me. He is such a good man. I've been to hell, what is a little more time there. No other woman will go through what I went through just to spare my hide. I've already lost Liam either way.

Ah, the cavalry is coming. The sound of the beginning and the end. Blades cut through the quiet of the dawn. I hope you are ready Javier Galindo.

"Addy, baby. We are here, it is all going to be okay," Dylan's voice rains down upon me.

"Sweetheart, where is Liam?" Anthony asks as he scoops me up rushing me back to the helicopter.

He lifts me up into Mark's arms. I try to speak but, I can't. I'm so cold my teeth chatter, you can't break your teeth from something like this can you?

"Addy, where is Liam?" Dylan repeats leaning in helping Mark strap me in. They are dumping more blankets on me.

Suddenly I am so tired, so very tired. I need medical attention. I'm barely hanging on. I survived the night for Liam. I endured for him. They need to know where he is, or they will waste precious time looking for him out here. "Mexico."

Dylan holds my face in both of his hands, he is so close I can feel the heat of his breath on my skin. So warm, he is so warm. "Addy, I need you to focus. Where is he?"

"Mexico. Javier," I struggle to get the words out as I slip away to another world, a dark one.

Liam

I can't concentrate on anything else but my fear for Addy. He left her outside, in the middle of nowhere, with nothing but a blanket. If that wasn't awful enough he beat her so bad that there is no way she'll survive out there for long. Did she even reach Dylan? Did he answer the call? I'm sure that when they don't hear from us they will send someone but, how long would that take? Please god, please let her be okay.

How will I find out? Damn I should have protected her better, first Sophia and now Addy. I am a worthless piece of shit. I thought I was saving her, but I doomed her by making that deal. I am a prisoner and she is...

"Show Mr. Sharp to his new quarters," Javier says. He is enjoying my internal struggle. Evidently I am not being effective at keeping my emotions masked.

"You put her out of her misery, you realize there is no chance of her surviving out there, or in the world. Look at this way we gave her what she wanted," he chides leaning back in his chair.

"What the fuck do you mean?" I shouldn't take the bait but when it comes to Addy, I need to know everything about her, even if it is something I may not want to hear.

"The day I purchased her from Wright, she begged me to kill her. Obviously I didn't, but…" he shrugs his shoulders. "Mr. Sharp, girls like her don't survive long in this world. She lived in a fantasy land. She wasn't very smart. Young women such as her are naïve, they are easy prey and when they are used up, they are discarded. You should know this, I'm sure you understand how they are targeted? No?"

"I'd like to go to my room."

He laughs. "Don't worry boy, we'll toughen you up. You'll learn our ways and soon we will have our pick of women… won't we?"

Chapter Twenty-Eight

Addy

W as I dreaming? I glance around the beautiful room, sunlight streaming through the arc window. When I try to sit up it reminds that no, it was no dream. My eyes dart over to the chair beside my bed. Anthony is sleeping soundly in it. I must have passed out. Thank god they brought me back to Mexico. Fuck, I feel like I've been hit by a bus.

After a brief examination of my body, I see that Javier did quite a number on me. Dammit, it will take me a few days to heal up before I can call my uncle. Everything, everything in my life has moved me to this moment.

"Addy, you are awake," Anthony rushes towards me but slows his movement as he reaches the bed. He sits on the edge and places his hand lightly over the top of mine.

He will expect some sort of emotion out of me. I've only tried to stop tears not start them. Let the old Addy out, just for a few days and then you can put her away until it's over. I push a small tear out the corner of my eye and he pulls me gently into his arms.

"Oh, sweetheart, I am so sorry. You are safe now," he whispers into my hair. "Are you hurting? Mark will want to see you. He will give you something for the pain."

I try to speak but cough instead. He quickly pushes me off his lap and goes into the bathroom coming out with a glass of water. After a few large gulps, my voice returns. "I'm okay, Anthony, please no medication."

He nods his head sadly. "I'll be right back, Addy, I will get Mark."

After he leaves I push the blankets farther down hoping that I have all of my toes, oh thank god. I was so worried that I would get frostbite. My mind churns, yes, I remember I sat by the fire. I put the bricks in the flames and tucked them in the blanket. I flop back on the bed and close my eyes. I need to focus on healing and convincing everyone to let me go to stay with my uncle. I was never good at acting. My participation in the school play involved costumes and makeup. Well, Addy, you better convince them, or you will be sneaking out the window.

Anna comes rushing into my room throwing herself on my bed, Dylan following quickly. "Oh, Addy, I am so glad you are awake. I'm so sorry."

I try to sit up and she takes my hands pulling me up gently. "I am okay. I'm so sorry about your cabin and…Liam."

She hugs me closely, rocking me. Dylan sits down behind her and reaches around rubbing his hand over the back of my head. My throat catches at his touch and suddenly I don't have to fake the tears.

How did I get so close to these people in the short time I have known them? How did I fall in love? My chest squeezes. The loss of Liam hits me hard. He is gone. He left me. My head knows he was trying to protect me but my heart hurts. I miss him.

231

Mark comes in, Anna and Dylan move to other side of the bed perching on the edge so he can check me over now I am awake.

"How are you feeling, Addy?" he asks sitting beside me and fluffing pillows so I can recline.

"I'm okay. I'm fine," I say on a shaky breath.

"You were really beat up and hypothermia had set in when they found you. You are lucky to be alive," he says brushing my hair out of my face and tucking it behind my ear.

The gesture reminds me of Liam. I choke back a sob. I don't know what to say. I remember what happened to me. I don't need them to tell me. They are all trying to help but I wish they would all just let me be.

"Anthony told me you don't want anything for the pain, but, Addy, your body will heal faster if you are not in pain. You know this. I will only give you what you need, and we'll watch over you. You are safe."

Luis and Anthony stop in the doorway hesitantly. I look away from them. Luis lost his son because of me. The guilt slowly creeps up my spine and I fight the urge to run. "I would like to be alone, I'm tired. Please." I roll to my side and turn my face into the pillow, I cannot face Luis, I can't.

The bed shifts as they leave but I sense I am not alone. Everyone left but him.

"Addison, my son is the most honorable man I know. Whatever he did, he did because he felt he had no other choice. You and I both realize that there was no way to have stopped him, Liam does what Liam wants to do."

When I don't say anything, he continues. "Please don't feel guilty, none of this is your fault. I just…I just need to know what happened, Addison, please tell me what happened. I need to know for my sanity."

I take a deep breath and roll over to face him. He slowly climbs on the bed. He reclines beside me on the pillows and pulls me into his chest. I whisper, "he made a deal with Javier. He offered his knowledge of the business and in exchange they let me go."

Luis remains quiet as I relay the rest of the story, lightly stroking my hair the entire time. I tell him everything…well everything except what happened after they left. I cannot tell anyone what I am.

"Thank you, Addison," he says tugging my hair gently until I look up at him. "We will figure this out. Liam has a plan I am sure. He is a smart boy."

I nod at him and close my eyes. There is no way he has a plan, he wasn't thinking, well he was, about me but after that there was no plan. I know this and Luis knows it too. "I'm going to talk to the others, and I will send Mark back in. He is right, don't suffer unnecessarily. Get some rest and we will visit more tomorrow."

I nod as he slides out of the bed. "Luis, I love him."

"I know you do, sweetheart, and I hope you recognize he loves you too. This will all work out," he says, but, I can see the worry on his face.

Mark comes in and does a quick exam. He helps me to the bathroom, dopes me up and then he is gone. As I drift, I imagine myself preening my new feathers. I have to be ready to face Javier. Time for me to use those talents he so kindly paid for. Smiling, I fall into a deep sleep.

At some point I wake up and move to the bench seat. Liam and I are still under the same moon at least. Oh god my heart aches to be with him. This pain is worse than anything my body has experienced. How dare Javier take Liam away from me? I'm tired of people taking things away from me.

And then there is the matter of Father Landon. What am I going to do about him? He told Javier where I was. He was the only one who could have done so. Is he even a priest? Can I kill a priest? Seems a little taboo. Javier probably has something over him, and he is a victim too.

"What are you doing up, hon?" I turn to see Anna leaning against the door frame.

"Couldn't sleep."

She waves her hand for me to go to her. "Come, lay with me in my room, the baby has been kicking me all night and Dylan is up working late."

I follow her and crawl into the middle of the bed beside her. She grabs my hand and places it over her swollen belly. "Can you feel it?"

I place my head on her tummy as well and smile against the soft cotton of her t-shirt. "I do. Oh, wow, you have a taekwondo expert in there." I giggle, the baby growing inside of her is so lucky to have a mother like Anna.

She runs her fingers through my hair as I rub her belly. When her hand stills I glance up to see that she is sleeping. The little one seems to be fast asleep too. As I'm trying to untangle her from my hair Dylan comes in and crawls up behind me to help.

He laughs quietly. "What was going on here?"

"The baby was keeping her up and I couldn't sleep either, so she invited me down here. I was just getting ready to go back to my room but as you can see she has me trapped."

Once he gets me untangled I move to crawl off the bed, but he stops me. "Stay please. I don't want you to have to be alone. She won't care you stayed."

I hesitate, he makes no indication he will leave if I stay. The thought of going to my room is not appealing, I can't quiet my mind there but, here it is peaceful. I slide back up beside Anna and curl myself into her again. Dylan shuts the light off and then he is behind me. His large arm settles over me, his hand resting on Anna's stomach. Warmth, protection, friends, the only thing missing is Liam.

"You are still his angel, Addy. He will return to you, you will see," Dylan whispers.

I close my eyes and dream. I am flying, I fly until I come to a giant bean stalk. I reach out and grab it. The wind whistles in my ear. I'm up high above Javier's estate, I can see the guards at their posts, they look like little toy soldiers from here. My focus moves upwards, the stalk disappears in big white fluffy clouds.

I climb and climb until I reach a garden. The flowers here are larger than any I have ever seen, and they glow. I sense someone as my hand lightly brushes over every color of the rainbow, the petals so soft they tickle my fingertips. Then I hear a voice on the wind.

"I've been watching you."

I spin but nobody is there. The voice is recognizable, one I haven't heard in so long. Brian.

"You will sacrifice yourself for him. The same as I did for you."

Where is it coming from? I wander through the garden until I come to an outdoor labyrinth.

"You are doing the right thing. You can't let them turn him into a monster like they did me."

I try to speak but it's as if I have no voice here. Am I only meant to listen?

"You are strong, you are beautiful, and you are worthy of love, little Addy."

Brian always called me his little Addy. I have missed him. Curiosity rushes me forward while fear pulls me back. I want to tell him so many things. I want to tell him thank you for saving me, for sacrificing himself so that Anna could save me. But, at the same time I want to scream at him. I want to hit and kick him for not saving me sooner, for not loving me longer or maybe for not saving himself.

I trip on a vine crossing the path and fall flat onto my face. But, the voice speaks again prompting me to rise and continue on.

"I told Anna once you were quiet, little Addy. I may have been wrong. You are a spitfire."

Suddenly I find myself at the center of the maze and there lying on the ground is a sword. The one I envisioned laying at Brian's feet the day I surrendered to him, the day I submitted. Oh, how much has happened since then.

"Take it, I'm giving it back. I thought you were surrendering. I think that is why I fell in love with you. But, no you did not surrender little spitfire you were only surviving. Pick up your sword and go fight for your man. You will win…I have no doubt."

Saving Addy

I wake with a start, falling to the floor with a thud. Anna rushes to me. "Addy, Addy, are you okay? You were dreaming."

"He gave me back my sword," I say on a shaky breath. Shit, I am still in their room. Dylan is gone and she is dressed and appears to have been awake for some time.

"Who?" she asks perching on the side of the bed staring at me.

Before his name falls off my tongue I stop myself. I realize how crazy I will sound. It was just a dream. I don't want to scare her. He was a frightening man. I could see past that. Anna saw it briefly, but I know how terrified she was of him. I decide it best to keep it to myself.

I raise my hands above my head and stretch. I laugh and tell her no one. She looks at me with concern but drops the subject. "The others went down to breakfast, if you are up to it why don't you join them? I can't stomach all the smells down there, so I stay here with my toast and tea."

She heads towards the bathroom, but I stop her and give her a quick hug. "Thank you, Anna, you are the best friend I've ever had."

"I love you, Addy, now I have to go before my bladder bursts." She laughs and I release her reluctantly.

I will miss her. When she closes the door, I pick up her cell and google search for my uncle's phone number. Amazingly it is there, it has not changed. I quickly dial him.

"Hola," the familiar voice answers.

"Uncle?" I force out on a long drawn out breath.

"Addison? Addison, oh my god! Javier told me you were dead. Addison!"

"Can you please come get me?" I sob.

"Where are you, mija?" he says, I detect the concern and relief in his tone.

I rattle off where I am, and he tells me he will be here soon. Before, I hang up I make him promise to not tell anyone. "Javier doesn't want me anymore," I explain.

"I know, I know, Addison. He told me what transpired. I am so sorry, mija, this is all my fault," he cries softly on the other end.

"It is okay, I understand. Please, just come get me. I have to go now."

I delete the call from the log and then head down to my suite. There is much to do this morning.

After I shower, I pack some of the clothes Anthony gifted me the first time I was here. Everything was left in my room as it was. No suitcase so I grab a trash bag and careful fold all the items placing them neatly inside. Just as I am about finished Anthony steps in.

He halts in the doorway taking in my actions. "What are you doing, Addy?"

"My uncle is coming to pick me up," I reply keeping my eyes lowered to my task.

"What? Addy, I don't understand," he runs his hand over his head watching me and I see he is uncertain of what to do.

"Javier doesn't want me anymore. I can go home. I want to go home," I state flatly.

He grabs my hand, pulls me down to the dining room and orders me to sit. "Stay here, while I get the others."

Mrs. Cortez comes bustling in and stops abruptly when she sees me. "Oh mija!" She rushes towards me kissing me on the cheek. "You need to eat." She fills a plate for me.

The rumble of voices draws our attention to the doorway. Dylan steps in and tilts his head at me. Shit. He is not happy, not in the slightest.

Luis, Anthony and Mark all follow behind. My nerves tingle. They don't want me to leave, question is will they *let* me. "Addison, what is going on?" Dylan says grunting as he lowers himself into the chair next to mine.

"I called my uncle from Anna's phone. He is coming to pick me up," I say to my plate of food.

"That is not a good idea, Addy," Luis argues from across the table.

"He is already on his way. I appreciate all of you, really I do. Javier is not a threat to me anymore and I would like to go home." I bite my lip hard to keep myself from crying.

Dylan sighs. "Addy, we can't keep you here but please reconsider. From what you have told us your uncle is part of the reason you ended up in this situation."

"It will be fine. He is a good man, really. Poor choices have plagued him, but he won't hurt me."

Dylan slides a cell phone over to me. "Take this. I want you to call me when you arrive, and I want the address of where you are staying before you pull out of the driveway."

I nod and peek up at him. "Thank you." I giggle. "Dad," I add.

"Addison, I mean it. If I could keep you here I would, this is a bad idea. But, if you insist then you will call me when you get there, and Luis will come visit you once a week to continue your sessions with him. Don't think you can run away from us, Addy. You are part of our family now," he says. For a moment I want to call my uncle and tell him I've changed my mind.

My eyes skip over the men at the table. One is missing, and he is the most important piece of my world. Liam whispers from every corner in this place, my heart aches here. Besides, I have a plan. And, if it works...Liam will be back here with his family by the end of the week. Dylan says I am a part of this family but not as much as Liam is.

I shake my head and we continue our meal in silence. When I finish and rise from the table Dylan grabs my hand stopping me from walking out. "Addy, I am going to figure something out. I'll get him out of there, I promise you."

"I know you will. I am sure he'll be home before we know it." I offer him a tiny smile and then pull my hand out of his to head back to my room.

Chapter Twenty-Nine

Addy

"Thank you for coming, uncle," I say scanning the scenery outside my window.

"Addison, I was so relieved to hear your voice. I am so sorry…for everything," he says taking my hand in his not removing his eyes from the road.

"I love you and I do not blame you for anything that has happened. But…"

"But, what, Addy?" he asks nervously.

Closing my eyes, I draw a deep breath. I roll my head from side to side. "We are not heading home yet. I want you to take me to Javier's competition, Raphael Gonzalez." I reach up and pull the ponytail band out of my hair and shake it allowing the strands fall around my shoulders.

"What? Addison, what is going on?"

"Javier told me you were working for him as a mole. He said you were feeding him information about his strongest competitor. Gonzalez. Correct?"

"Addison, yes, but I cannot take you there. What are you doing?"

"What I am doing is getting my revenge and you my dear uncle will help me. If you don't...well...I'm not going to give you a choice, let's put it that way." I turn to him my eyes ablaze.

"Addy, you will get yourself killed. I will do anything for you but if you think you can outsmart Javier...you can't."

"I already have. Take me to Gonzalez, I need ten minutes of his time and that is all that I will ask of you, besides a place to stay for a few days. Oh, and keep quiet about my sudden rise from the dead. I want to surprise Javier myself with that news."

My uncle looks at me, he is frightened. I hate to scare him. But, I must have complete cooperation. "When do you wish to see him?"

"No time like the present." I smile sweetly at him.

He nods and turns off the freeway changing our destination. I lay my head back on the headrest, phase one accomplished.

My uncle pulls up outside of a luxurious home surrounded by twelve-foot-high fencing. He punches a code near the gate, and it rises. As we walk up to the door, a man greets us with a smile. "Leo, Mr. Gonzalez does not have you on the schedule today, did I miss something?"

"Um, my, my niece would like to speak to him if he is available," Leo says uncertainly looking at me with pleading eyes hoping I will change my mind.

Part of me feels bad for using him but the larger part wants to save Liam. Unfortunately, my uncle will have to be uncomfortable for a short time.

"Okay, well, let me go see if he has a moment to spare." The man walks away casually, smirking, he thinks there is no possibility we are getting in.

Crap, I was sure my uncle could get me in, what if I was wrong? If I don't gain an audience with Gonzalez my plan is sunk. Actually, without him there is no plan. The guy comes back with a look of surprise. "He has a few minutes to spare. Please, right this way." He points to a chair by the front door instructing Leo to stay there, then turns down the hallway.

He leads me to a spacious living area. It has a warm feel to it. Large glass doors off the room catch my attention. I see a tall man in grey dress pants and a white button up toss a football to a younger version of himself. I take a seat on the sofa and glance around quickly. There are family pictures on every surface.

My mind races through what I know about this guy. I've heard that he is a family man and from the looks of it that would be a correct assumption. He takes care of his community, donating millions back into it. Javier would never do this…unless it benefited him in some direct way. He is also known for keeping the peace. His organization does not provoke fear, people mostly love him.

He tosses the ball to the boy one last time and then his eyes meet mine through the glass. He speaks to the young man and then strides inside. "Hola, Leo's niece," he says taking my hand as I stand to greet him. He places a featherlight kiss on top before releasing me. "May I offer you something to drink?"

"No thank you, I am fine. I do not want to take up too much of your time, Mr. Gonzalez. Thank you for agreeing to speak with me."

"It piqued my interest when Samuel announced your arrival. Leo had mentioned he only had one niece, and recently he told me you had passed away." He cocks a brow at me as he pours himself a drink then takes the seat across from me. "You appear very much alive. You were kidnapped while you were running a vaccination clinic, no?"

My eyes get large as Gonzalez relays the information about myself. Did my uncle really talk about me that often with this man? "Um, yes, that is correct."

"Leo told me that Javier Galindo was to blame for your death." He takes a sip peering over the top of his glass at me.

I swallow hard. Guilt creeps into my cheeks as I think about the ugly things I said in the car. He told this man about Javier and I get the feeling that Gonzalez is much smarter than Javier has given him credit for. I also realize that my uncle might be a better man than I had given him credit for.

"Leo is here, why is he not joining us?" he asks.

"I…well…I didn't realize that you knew…" my voice fades.

"You didn't know I was aware Javier was using Leo to get information out of me," he smirks but, seems pleasantly surprised by my honesty.

"No, I was not aware. I apologize. I guess I won't need to throw my uncle under the bus now." I offer a timid smile.

Mr. Gonzalez laughs hard at my statement and then sets his glass down in front of him. "So, do you have a name other than niece?"

244

"Addison Davis," I reply nervously biting my lip. Everything seems to be going well but men still make me nervous, especially powerful ones like the one sitting before me.

"Addison, it is a pleasure to meet you. And, please call me Raphael, Mr. Gonzalez makes me feel old. What can I do for you?"

Anxiously I sit up straighter in my seat twisting my hands together in my lap. "I want to kill Javier."

Raphael leans forward in his seat. "Addy," he says sadly. "I'm not sure what torture Javier has bestowed on you, but he is unreachable. I cannot help you execute him. I do not have the manpower, nor can anyone get close enough to assassinate him."

"I can. He is not unreachable. I can kill him. I will kill him. I need you to take out his men. Mr. hmm, Raphael, if you have a few minutes I would like to share my idea with you. Then you can decide if you wish to help me or not."

"Go on. I'll listen but, I'm sorry to inform you, Addison, that I must tell your uncle if I think your proposal will folly. Leo has worried over you since the day I met him, he loves you very much. I also, do not want to see you get hurt, I have a daughter close to your age," he speaks fatherly.

"I understand but, I hope you'll recognize that my plan will work."

"Let's hear this grand scheme of yours."

"I will offer myself to Javier, he will accept me into his household of that I do not doubt. Then once he is trusting me, I'll tell him about an upcoming auction. One in which he will be interested in attending to begin his journey into the human trafficking world. The auction is held the same time each month, and it happens to be on the same day that his regular shipments go out. He'll take his most loyal with him to Columbia for the auction and he will send a handful to handle the shipment. The rest will remain at the estate."

Raphael raises his eyebrows. "Addison, I see where you are going with this, but I still do not have enough men to cover all three areas."

"Do you happen to recognize the name Anna Velasquez?"

"Yes, her father's business is well known for the work they do. I applaud them, they've rescued many young women, a few from my community." His brows come together with a genuine look of concern. "I was not aware that Javier was looking to expand into that world, that is disturbing."

"He is and I want to stop him. I need you to call Anna's fiancé Dylan Lorenz and render their services. Tell them that you've learned of the auction and you have also determined Javier Galindo will be in attendance." His interest is piqued, all that is left is to reel him in slowly.

"If you know these people why do you not tell them yourself?"

"They rescued me, they will not allow me to put myself in danger and I need to get close to Javier. He thinks I'm stupid, he will let his guard down and when we are at the auction, I'll take him out."

"What if they decline?"

"They won't, they will accept the job."

"Okay, so I call them, they take out Javier's men at the auction. My men take out the ones at the drop site and at the estate. And you eliminate the man himself? Am I correct in your thinking?"

"Yes."

"And, just how are you going to do it? He is a smart adversary, Addison. You are but a slip of a girl, I do not think you can overpower him," he says.

I have him hooked on everything except for how I will kill Javier. "Well, there is one more thing I need your help obtaining."

I finish relaying my plan and wrap it up in as neat a package as I can. The bright red bow on top is Javier, dead. "This will work, it has to. If it doesn't, he'll only grow more deadly. Someone needs to stop him," I plead.

"Okay, Leo's niece. We'll give it a go. You are correct, Javier has progressively gotten more dangerous over the years. I would be lying if I told you I had not tried to assassinate him myself on more than one occasion. This is the best plan I've had laid before me. You realize you will be risking your life?"

"Javier stole everything from me, he took someone I love away from me. Now, he wants to take other girls from their loved ones, and I cannot let that happen. This has to end, one way or another, this has to end."

He nods and rises. "Four weeks until we see if your plan will succeed. I'll have what you need for the job delivered to your uncles in two days, that work?"

"Yes, thank you," I say shaking his hand.

"God speed, Addison. I'll pray for you, and for the young women you will save should we succeed."

Dylan

"She didn't go to Leo's did she?" I ask the minute I pick up.

"How the fuck did you know?" Anthony asks.

"Well, for one she hasn't called me yet. Two, I could tell she was up to something." God dammit, why did I let her leave? I should get her. "Where did she go?"

"Raphael Gonzalez's, they were only there for an hour and now they are on the move again."

"What the fuck was she doing at Gonzalez's? What does this girl have up her sleeve?"

"I don't know but she looks different," Anthony sighs.

"What do you mean she looks different? She just left."

"She is holding herself peculiar. Wait. They are stopping, I'll call you in a few."

Dammit! Anna is furious that I let Addy leave. Liam would be furious too if he found out. What was I supposed to do? I can't very well tie her up against her will. What could she be up to? I'll keep Anthony on her. Maybe after a few days Luis can go visit her and convince her to return to us.

My phone buzzes. "Hello?"

"Mr. Lorenz?"

"Speaking."

"This is Raphael Gonzalez. I would like to speak to you about a job."

What. In. The. Fuck?

After a very interesting conversation my phone buzzes again. Anthony.

"Um, Dylan, I think we have a fucking problem," Anthony says, his tone dripping with concern.

"Uh, yeah, I got a call from Gonzalez. He wants to hire us for a job. Awfully coincidental don't you think since Addy just left his home?"

"Shit. Well, she has been shopping, and she told me she hates shopping. But, that is not the kicker…it's what she bought. One box of expensive Cuban cigars and a fucking dress that would make every man and woman for that matter stop dead in their tracks." Anthony says, his voice dripping with worry for Addy.

"I'm on the way. Don't let her out of your site." What the fuck is she doing?

As I'm driving to Addy's uncle's house, a call comes through from her.

"Hi, Dylan. I wanted to tell you that I made it to my uncles. Sorry I didn't call sooner, but we stopped for a bite to eat and then I needed to pick up a few things from the store," she says. There is not one hint of a lie in her words. Anthony is right something has changed.

"So, you are home now?"

"Yes, thank you for being so understanding, Dylan. I will call you tomorrow, we are getting ready to settle down for the evening, maybe watch a movie or something. Tell Anna and the others I miss them already but that I am happy to be home." This time I catch the lie, I heard it when her voice caught at the word home. She's not home, and she realizes it, she knows where her home is, and it is not with her uncle.

"Okay, Addy. Glad you made it safe. Goodnight, talk to you tomorrow."

Ten minutes later I'm beating on her uncle's door with Anthony by my side.

"What? What are you doing here?" She answers so surprised she looks like she is about to fall over.

I shove my way inside pushing her aside. Her uncle's eyes are as wide as saucers. "Gentleman what is this about?"

"We need to talk to Addison. Alone," I say so menacingly the pip squeak flees to another room.

When he closes the door behind him, I point to the couch. "Sit."

"No," she says defiantly.

"Addy, I said sit," I glare at her trying my best to put the fear of god in her. She is up to something, something that is more than likely going to get her killed. I can't let that happen. Liam would never forgive me.

"What are you doing here?" she asks crossing her arms across her chest.

"Well, let's start with the fact that a Mr. Gonzalez called me about a job. Do you know anything about that?"

"I don't even know who that is."

I laugh, who is this little person in front of me? What the hell happened to her in the course of the day. "Go get your things. You are coming back to the estate," I say leaving her no room for argument.

Her eyes fill with tears and Anthony takes a step to comfort her, but I stop him. "Now," I roar, and she skitters away.

We wait and when she doesn't return I check on her. That little shit! I'm greeted to an open window, the phone I gave her lying on the bed and no Addy. Fuck!

Chapter Thirty

Addy

M r. Gonzalez was kind enough to allow me to stay at one of his hotels. He told me that Dylan had questioned him about me. He said he stuck to the script and said he did not know what he was talking about. We all understand very well what is going on but what choice does Dylan have but to take the job and wait to see what I'll do next.

Now, I need to work on getting into Javier's without Anthony or Dylan seeing me, I am sure they've been watching closely for me to appear and they will stop me before I can get in. I'm sure they have a good idea I am trying to help Liam.

I bet I am a site walking into the church in a dress like this. Everyone I've passed has stopped dead in their tracks, question is will it work on Javier? I stalk into the tiny chapel and walk straight to the confessional booth. When the window opens between my little box and the priest's it immediately slams back shut.

I chuckle. "Oh, Father Landon," I whisper. "Surely you are not surprised to see me are you?"

The window slowly slides open and I can make out his dark form through the decorative wood. "Javier told me you had died," he says disbelievingly.

"I did."

He doesn't say anything, and I laugh again as I wait for him to decide if he is crazy or not.

"What do you want?" he grits out.

"I need a ride to Javier's," I reply sweetly.

"If you go there, he'll let you in, you don't need me."

"Oh, but I do need you. Dylan and Anthony are staked out at his place, they will stop me, and you see I can't be stopped. You realize why don't you?"

"Addison, I am so sorry, I didn't mean for…" his voice trails.

"You meant to. But, don't worry, I am sure he has something on you. That is how he works but…you owe me, and you will let me hitch a ride. While you are there, you could pray last rites over him…that is without him knowing of course. Tell me Father Landon, do you think Javier has any chance of making it into Heaven?"

"Addison, you are playing a dangerous game," he whispers.

I laugh so loud it echoes through the vaulted ceilings of the entire church. "What does he have on you? Do you like little boys?" I hiss.

"I have a daughter. She is two, he…he threatened her and her mother."

His head drops and the still thawed out part of my heart reaches out to him for a moment. This is not who I am. So far I've stomped on my uncle and now on Father Landon…all of us are victims. But, it is not the time to contemplate who I am hurting. Javier must die.

"Give me the ride, I'll tell him I asked you to get me in because I want to be with him. He will think I am crawling back, poor defenseless, stupid Addy. I will not let him know that you allowed me in to kill him. But, when the deed is done, and you are no longer beholden to him….you will quit this charade." I make a spinning motion with my finger. "And, you'll raise your daughter. Show her some good, show her that there is good because the world will eventually show her ugly. When it does maybe the positive you showed her will allow her to hold on."

The window slides shut, and he comes around and opens the door to my little room. He takes one look at me and shakes his head sadly. "I'm sorry, I'm so sorry," he says honestly.

"No, time for that, I have a date with the devil." I follow him to his car.

I didn't see if anyone was outside Javier's. I was lying down in the backseat. Father Landon was just the trick to get in. Nobody questions a priest…I sure didn't.

When we arrive at the front door, he turns. "I must go, Addy," he says nervously. I nod and focus my attention to the man standing guard at Javier's. He looks at me and licks his lips, I don't think he even noticed that I had arrived with the priest.

"Got an appointment little lady?" His eyes roam over the length of my body, stopping briefly at my breasts spilling out of the red dress.

"Just tell him Addy is here to see him," I say batting my eyelashes.

"Um, yeah, okay. Wait here," he says, he looks over his shoulder at me once more before disappearing into the house.

I tap my toe on the ground, kicking my imaginary rock. Time to change, I feel a bit like wonder woman, a quick spin and I'm someone different. A different Addy for a different opponent.

The guard comes back, a glimmer in his eye. He has figured out who I am I can tell. Javier must be intrigued to hear that I am at his door, especially since he thought I was dead. Why would he think poor, stupid little me would survive?

I lower my head and follow, gaining strength along the way from the sound of my heels clicking on the marble floor. Click, click, tick, tick...soon Javier will be mine. The man leads me to Javier's office instructing me to stand in the middle of the room. "Don't. Move." He runs a hand-held machine over me checking for any devices, when he finds none he instructs me to stay put

I fight the urge to smile. Showtime.

But, what I wasn't expecting was Javier to come with others....and Liam.

Oh. Fuck. Me.

Well, no turning back now. Another heart to stomp. There is no helping it.

I gracefully drop to my knees, set the box of cigars in front of me and slide my hands out, palms down, resting my head on the cold floor.

Silence. I tap down the grin tugging at my lips.

Javier bursts out laughing. "By god this is a damn day I never saw coming. The day Addison Davis comes freely to me on her own."

"Addy, what the fuck are you doing?" Liam moans.

I don't answer. Javier is my master and the only one I'll respond to. I've never submitted to Javier, but once I do, he will be putty in my hand. Why didn't I see it before? Oh yes I remember, I was afraid of him. Not anymore.

Javier's footsteps grow near and then a tug at my hair brings my face and his mere inches apart. The angle he has my neck pulled back makes it hard to take in a breath much less swallow. "Yes, Addy, what the fuck are you doing?" he asks.

My tongue darts out soothing my top lip and I see Javier catch the movement. His gaze slowly moves up to mine. "Master, I've come to offer myself to your properly. I am sorry for my bad behavior when you came for me. I forgot my place."

His eyes narrow. "You are free, remember. I made a new deal."

"I can never be free of you. You are my master. Please don't send me away, I know nothing else. I do not belong in the world anymore...I won't survive," I whisper across his face.

He stares into my eyes and I slowly lay my sword at his feet. His brows twitch ever so slightly...and...he is mine.

"Let me please you, master. I brought you a gift," I plead. As he holds my hair he looks down at the box on the floor then his eyes roam back to me. Distrust flits over his features.

He releases my hair opens the box and takes out a cigar. He twirls it through his fingers and then hands it to me. "Will you please light it for me, baby?" He reaches into his pocket offering me his lighter.

Liam must suspect that I brought the cigars to poison him because he gasps from across the room.

"I've never lit one before," I say nervously.

"It's easy, just hold the flame to the end and suck on it like a cock," he sneers, eyes narrowing.

Hands shaking, I pull it towards my face, stopping in mid-air. "But…"

He reaches over taking it from me and placing it to my lips. "Go on, light it."

Gradually I wrap my lips around the tip and groan quietly. I close my eyes and lean my head back allowing his gaze to roam over my neck. I open them just in time to catch the lust smoldering off of him. I light the nasty thing, draw off it and then slowly blow the smoke over his face. "Did I do it right master?" I ask innocently.

His breath catches. My eyes never leave his even though I hear Liam's silent words, I feel the invisible string that connects us tug at me, calling me towards him. I ignore the pull and continue with my audition and it looks like I may get the part. I hand Javier the cigar leaning into him.

"You understand that I will hurt you," he says squinting down at me.

"Whatever you wish, master," I whisper, trembling just enough to make him think I am still afraid.

He grunts. "Everyone out."

LM Terry

When the door closes he stands. I am giving him everything he has ever wanted. What he had chased but never truly captured. And now here I am. What will he do with me? He spins plopping down in a nearby chair and sighs. "What is the game, Addy?"

Hmm, this is new. I detect a hint of uncertainty, a pinch of low self-esteem and a dash of I cannot figure out what this girl is doing. He almost seems like a confused little boy.

I crawl to him cautiously. He is nervous. He has never had anyone submit to him freely. He is such a pussy. When I get to him I inch up his legs reaching for his belt, whipping it out so fast it flings back smacking my ass. A groan escapes my lips as I rub my hands over the bulge in his pants. "I'm sorry for the last time master, please let me make it up to you."

He is stunned as I lower my mouth over him. His head drives into the chair and he hisses. "Oh god, Addy." He grips the back of my head and I allow him to guide me, to push me, to pull me. Whatever he desires I take, sometimes he holds me so long I think I will pass out from lack of oxygen, but never once do I tug away. I'm submitting and he loves it.

He holds my eyes as he finishes and tucks himself into his pants. I rise, picking up the cigar box and carefully set it on his desk. Then I slip to the floor again, kneeling, awaiting his verdict.

He moves closer and crouches in front of me. "Look at me."

I draw myself up and look directly at him. He holds my gaze for a long moment. "Go tell your boyfriend his services are no longer needed, second door to the right on the third floor."

"Yes, master."

He stands and takes a step back. I quickly rise and exit. No hesitation, he will be watching. There are cameras in every room and hallway in this house I am certain.

This I was not prepared for. Why didn't I think about seeing Liam? You are stupid, Addy. You must break Liam's heart...you probably already have. But, there is no other option. None. When I get to the door, I knock quietly. I peek up and see cameras at each end of the hall. I sense his eyes on me.

Liam opens the door and reaches for me. I take a quick step back. "Javier says he will no longer be needing your services. You are free to leave."

"What the fuck did you do?"

I don't respond struggling to choke back tears. I should turn and walk away. Javier told me to tell him and I did...nothing more, nothing less. But, the string is pulled tight and I find it is harder to break away than I thought.

"Answer me," he says.

My feet shuffle. As I spin to make my retreat he rushes towards me and shoves me hard up against the wall knocking air from lungs. "The cameras," I whisper.

Liam punches a hole in the wall right by my head. I duck slipping past him and run. I run until I bump right into Javier. I'm crying, Liam is so angry...so very angry.

"Little one, it's okay," he holds me to his chest as Liam catches up to us.

"Let her go Javier, we had a fucking deal," Liam spits.

259

"You may leave, you were not offering me anything of value anyhow. I don't think you have it in you to flip sides. Your friends are outside my gate, so you won't have to walk." Javier pulls me along beside him as we turn walking away.

"Addison, I will get you out of here," Liam yells down the hallway behind us.

Javier stops, tips my chin up with his finger to look into my eyes. "Do you wish to leave with him?"

"No master," I whisper.

He smiles and continues down the hall. "Well, then let's get you settled in."

Liam

One of Javier's men shoves me out the front gate. When I right myself I glance around. Dylan and Anthony get out of a car across the street and I storm over to them. When Dylan stands I punch him in the nose.

"What in the fuck, Liam?" Anthony says running around to us.

"Why did you let her do that? Have you both lost your minds?" I shout.

Dylan wipes the blood from his nose with his sleeve. "What the hell are you talking about?"

"Addy, why did you let her come here!" I pull at my hair, what the fuck, what the fuck! I've got to get her out of there.

"Liam, Addy disappeared we've been staked out here waiting for her to appear. We haven't seen her so what are you screaming about and how did you get away from Javier?" Anthony asks calmly.

"She is in there now," I scream pointing to Javier's house.

They both exchange nervous looks. What the hell is going on? Did they not know she went inside?

Dylan sighs. "Get in. I think we all underestimated her. She is a determined little shit. I'll give her that. But, I think I know where we can go to get answers."

I fall to my knees, I can't leave. How can I leave her here? It was a relief when Javier told me she was here. I had prayed that Dylan had gotten to her before she froze to death. But, then when I walked in and saw her....it didn't even look like my Addy and she sure didn't act like her. What has she done?

"Come on brother, there is nothing we can do until we figure out what she is up to," Dylan says sadly and helps me to my feet. When I get up, he hugs me tightly to him. "She is strong, Liam. She will be okay."

As we drive to Raphael Gonzalez's they fill me on everything that has been going on. "She was fine at the estate. She gave no clue she had all this planned. I'm sorry, Liam, I shouldn't have let her go but I thought she wanted to see her uncle. Once we figured out she wasn't acting right we came to get her, but she snuck out her bedroom window."

"She probably hasn't even fully recovered from the beating he gave her at the cabin," I tell them. "That night was the worst of my entire life."

"She was in bad shape when we found her, but she bounced back quickly. We should have recognized something wasn't right," Anthony mumbles.

"Gonzalez wants to hire us for a job in Columbia, he says he has information on an auction there. He also said Javier will be in attendance. I confronted him with the fact Addy had visited him prior to his call to me but he denied it. We'll see if he changes his tune with a personal visit from us." Dylan smiles encouragingly through the rear-view mirror.

When we arrive at the gate it magically opens, it appears Gonzalez was expecting us. His guard pats us down and then escorts us to his office.

"Ah, I thought you would stop by today. Please take a seat," he gestures to the sitting area to side of the room. He watches us as he pours four drinks. After setting the tray of glasses on the table he sits crossing his leg over his knee and settles back in his chair.

"So, you are here about the job?" he asks.

"I think you realize why we are here," I say through clenched teeth. This fucker knows what Addy is up to and it pisses me off. She is in danger and he is acting casual about the whole thing.

"You must be Liam. Did you enjoy your stay at Galindo's?" He swirls the ice around in his glass.

I stand ready to deck this motherfucker, but Dylan places his hand out pushing me back into the couch. "No, disrespect Mr. Gonzalez but this is a serious situation to us. We love Addison and she is in danger. We need to know what is going on," Dylan says trying to diffuse the scene that is about to boil over.

Gonzalez sighs and stares up to the ceiling. "Please accept my apologies, I am having a hard coming to terms with what I've done. I'm afraid that I am partially to blame for your Addison being where she is. I should not have made light of the situation."

262

Dylan nods, waiting for the explanation that will surely come from Gonzalez. "She came to me the other day with a proposal for taking out Javier and his men. I was surprised, it was a good one, she is a very smart girl."

Galindo relay's Addison's plan to us and as he finishes he stands retrieving two envelopes from the desk. "She asked me to give these to you," he says handing them to Dylan.

I'm stunned, speechless. Addison did this for me. Oh god if something happens to her I will never be able to live with myself. I want to kill the man in front of me, how could he let her do this! Dylan puts his hand on my leg.

"Well, I guess we have little choice but to ride this out. We can't do anything that will tip him off, the gears are already in motion. You'll make sure you are successful on your end and we will take care of the auction."

"Yes, I will not fail her on my part," he says. "I know that you are all upset with me. But, Javier needs to be stopped and this girl has had the best plan I've heard for getting the job done."

When we get back to the car Dylan hands me an envelope with my name on it. The other one has nothing on the outside. He opens it, his eyes darting over the page. "If you don't turn this girl over your knee when we get her back then I will," Dylan says handing me the letter.

Dear Friends,

I am sorry that I had to treat you this way. Please know that I appreciate everything you have done for me. But, I need to do this. Don't worry, I've prepared myself for the next three weeks. It can't be any worse than the last few years. Anyhow, please accept my apologies, I'm sorry I have brought so much tragedy into your lives.

I wish you the best of luck on your next mission...you are the true angels...you are the ones who save lost souls.

Love,

Addy

I hand the letter up to Anthony and he reads it then turns towards his window quietly. The gravity of what this girl is doing has settled heavily over us. "Well now what," he asks.

"We prepare for our mission. It is one we cannot fail," Dylan says his eyes flicking to mine in the mirror again.

I nod. Addy has taken away any other option, this is all we can do. Gonzalez is right the plan is good, but it comes at a cost...and the price is Addy's soul. Fuck! I run my finger under the seal of the envelope addressed to me. I hesitate. Can I take more? I draw a deep breath and pull the handwritten letter out.

Liam,

I'm sorry I had to hurt you. You could have never lived with yourself had you helped Javier. This I know with all my heart. You are special. You are like my father. A good man, one of two who saw me for me, who loved me for me. I will always love you, what you gave me in the short time we had together is something that will get me through the rest of my days. But, we can't go back, not after what has happened. I'm sorry that Javier had to show you who I really am, he killed the magic. Whatever happens I consider myself lucky to have had you as mine, if only for a fleeting moment.

Please do not hold back on life, you will find love again,

Addy

She has given up. She is saying goodbye. No, that will not happen. Oh Addy, I will never let you go you silly, silly, girl.

Chapter Thirty-One

Addy

Who knew three weeks would seem like an eternity? Javier hasn't been overly terrible. One day he treats me lovingly, the next he punishes me harshly. I think he is angry that I am making him feel. I've had this effect on men before. There is something about giving yourself to someone that makes them...well, I would say weak, but that is not the right word. Vulnerable, that is what it is, and it sometimes causes him to become irate.

I'm sure there is a reason that Javier is the way he is just the same as Brian and Oliver. But, like Oliver I don't care to figure it out. They are too far gone. I give them what they want and that is it. I have no desire to peek into his head.

He trusts me now. One night while we were lying in his bed and he was tracing the vines on my back I told him about the auction. He took the bait. He is hungry for more power. Men like him always are, they are the only ones who will lower themselves to pick it up. He even offered to take me with him without me having to ask. Having candy on his arm, and a well-trained morsel at that will give him credence with the others.

Saving Addy

"Are you excited to travel with me, little one?" he asks as he unchains me from his torture room.

"Yes, master," I answer wincing as my arms fall like dead weight.

"The world is in our hands, Addy." He wraps me up in a blanket and carries me to his suite. He is back to his gentler side, actually I'm surprised he has one, but I think everyone does, we don't always see it.

"Sleep, little one, and then you need to pack for our trip to Columbia," he says brushing my hair away from my face. "Make sure you bring the red dress."

"Yes, master," I say weakly. As he is about to step out of the room, I sit up on the bed. "Master?"

"Yes, little one?"

"May I pack for you as well?"

He smiles and nods, then turns leaving me to lick my wounds.

A wicked smile crosses my lips and I lay back on his bed. This will be my final night here.

After, I sleep for a short time I get up and pack for our trip. For the last three weeks I have treated him like a damn king, setting his clothes out each day. All to prepare for this moment. All of it done so subtly that he hasn't even noticed how I have wormed my way into his bed, his life...his trust.

Everything is almost ready. I walk by the room where Javier holds his meetings before each week's shipment of drugs go out. The sound of glasses clinking and men laughing assaults my ears. I want to flip the door off as I pass, but I can't, not with all the cameras around.

I step into Javier's office without pause. No hesitation, he has eyes everywhere. I open the box of cigars pulling several out and placing them in the small leather cedar lined humidor that Javier uses while traveling. My hand slides across the bottom of the crate I gifted him, and I smile. I place the final one in the case. Closing it I turn and walk out.

Leaving Mexico didn't have the appeal it has had the last few times. This time the devil is by my side. I'm trying to push down my nerves, my fear. Today I know that there are many others all working on a plan that climbed into the head of a silly girl. Please let no one get hurt. This has to work; it just has to.

Javier walks out of the bathroom of our hotel suite, his eyes landing on mine in the full-length mirror I am standing in front of. "I'll be the envy of every man in the room. With you by my side I will command the attention of the auction."

I smile shyly glancing down to the floor. "Thank you, master," I say softly.

He comes behind me grabbing the sides of my waist tightly. "Look at me," he breathes over my ear, sending a shiver down my spine...not a shiver of delight, no, a shiver of terror. I am dealing with a dangerous man. I have not forgotten that.

My eyes find his. "You have pleased me, Addy. Tonight, I know you will be on your best behavior. I want you to point out anyone you recognize, men that would be advantageous for me to meet. You will be a good girl and do that for me?"

Saving Addy

"Of course, master," I smile at him seductively. He swivels me to face him and bends down plunging his tongue into my mouth. I try my best to reciprocate, struggling with the nausea when I taste the tobacco.

He releases me and slides into his jacket as I walk over and open his travel humidor grabbing three cigars. Javier is meticulous, almost compulsive in his habits. He always keeps three cigars in his pocket, smoking them from left to right. My skill at noticing everything is finally becoming of use. I give him a timid smile as I tuck them in before laying my head on his chest.

"Master?"

"Yes," he says staring down at me.

"I'm scared to go to the auction," I whisper. "You won't sell me will you?"

He laughs and wraps his arms around me. "No, little one, I will not sell you."

I wait for the guilt. It doesn't come.

When we arrive, memories rush back into my mind. The fear is palpable in the large room. While it looks elegant, it reeks terror. I tremble, and Javier grips my hand tighter squinting down at me in warning. Breathe, Addy, breathe. You will not be here long.

Javier has no intention of purchasing any of the girls here tonight. He is only here to make connections. Many men come to our table. They recognize Javier to be a man that fits well in their world and they seem to welcome him with open arms. I keep my head lowered. The young women being brought out one by one is making my stomach turn. Tears sting the corner of my eyes. Javier brushes his hand over my back drawing my attention to him. He reaches in his pocket bringing out the third cigar.

"You are doing well, little one," he clucks. The night has riled him up, his lust is visible. All the girls crying, and screaming has pricked his demon soul. He wants to hurt me. He wants to do despicable, vial things to my body. "We will have fun tonight," he whispers in my ear.

Oh yes, we are going to have fun tonight.

He lights his cigar taking a pull off it. He looks at it briefly before taking a longer draw. He reaches over and throws back the shot of tequila in front of him. My eyes never leave him as I watch him clear his throat. He pulls another drag of my poison into his lungs. His gaze finally lands on mine.

"Are you okay, master?" I ask innocently.

He has been feeling so comfortable he allowed his men to take part in the debauchery playing out around us. His eyes dart desperately seeking one of them out. When he finds no one his eyes land back on me. "What have you done?" his raspy voice barely escapes his lips. He is wheezing and struggling to draw air back in. I smile at him as his hand strikes out gripping me tightly by my neck.

"Thank you for the night at the cabin. After you left I found the key to your black heart....master," I spit.

His grip loosens and his hands quickly go to his own throat. I stare with great interest as his eyes flutter. I know exactly how he feels. I cannot tell you how many times I have been strangled by a man, teetering on that edge of life and death, I recognize it well. I stand and lean over, so we are nose to nose, my breath on his face. "I will see you in hell," I whisper then place a kiss on his forehead before turning and walking away without a second glance.

I grab the bottle of tequila off the table along with his lighter and a paper napkin. As I stalk to the emergency exit, I tuck the napkin into the yellow gold liquid. Before I open the exit setting off the alarms I toss it over my shoulder. It won't burn the place down. But, it will keep everyone distracted while I walk away from the man who has haunted my steps since I was sixteen years old. Besides, I don't need to, the team of men waiting in the wings will take care of the rest.

When I get outside I make my way over to the car that Gonzalez promised would wait for me.

Liam

Chaos erupting is our signal it is go time. I race inside taking out every man I encounter carefully looking for victims along the way. My eyes scour the dimly lit room and I spot Javier....dead in his seat. Where the fuck is Addy? As I near him I see the bright red lipstick adorning his forehead. I toss my head back, fuck. She is gone…

Dylan runs up. "Where is she?" he says panting trying to catch his breath.

"She is gone," my voice cracks and I point to Javier's shocked, frozen face.

"How do you know?" Dylan asks looking at me confused.

"I just know," I say sadly. He killed my angel. She may never be the same. This could have been the final straw.

When we get back to Mexico our first stop is Gonzalez's.

"The plan was a success!" he exclaims greeting us at the door.

Not hardly, I think to myself following him and Dylan into the living room. He pours celebratory drinks before sitting down across from us.

"Why the gloomy faces? We won, we defeated Galindo!" he says holding his glass up tipping it before downing it in one swallow.

"Addy was not there. She was gone, there is no trace of her anywhere," Dylan tells him.

Javier sets his glass down on the table, refilling it. He watches us carefully; his mind is in overdrive. He knows something. "She is safe."

"Where is she?" my hands shake as I try to control my rage.

He sighs and runs his hand down over his face. "I will tell you but, you need to adhere to her wishes. I can see how much you love her, so I won't make you suffer wondering what has become of her."

"She is staying here in my community for the time being. At least until she figures out where she wants to go next. I have men watching her from afar to ensure her safety." He sighs before continuing. "She is an extraordinary girl. I finance a free clinic here and she insisted that she volunteer there as repayment for my assistance. I also have her set up with a local therapist, it was a condition of mine. She needs help. She is at the Sunset Inn. I cannot force you to do anything but please take my advice, she needs…time," he says his tone turning sullen. "Just give her some time. Please."

Dylan leans back on the couch sighing. "Liam, she is safe. Let's just go home."

Can I walk away? Does she really want to be alone? She must, she sure made a lot of plans this man. Why didn't she wait for us in Columbia? Why?

Chapter Thirty-Two

Addy

The last month has moved slowly, as if the world stopped spinning the day I killed Javier. Guilt isn't the contributing factor, no, it's the emptiness. I've been seeing the therapist that Raphael recommended but it's not the same as talking to Luis. In fact, I don't talk much there at all. Raphael and his wife invite me to their home once a week for dinner. It is nice. I love spending time with them and their children but when I leave for the evening the emptiness returns.

Last night Raphael gave me a cell phone. I refused, but he insisted. He is one of those men you don't say no to. "The clinic might need to reach you when you are away from your room," he had said, so I accepted.

Now I sit here staring at it as it rings. It could be the clinic, it could be Raphael, but something tells me it's not. After much contemplation I click the answer button and hold it up to my ear.

"Hello."

"Addy, oh my gosh it is so wonderful to hear your voice," Anna squeals.

Fucking Raphael, I should have known. Mental note to kick his ass when I go to dinner next.

"Hi, Anna," I say glancing around me as I sit on the edge of the fountain in the town square.

"How are you doing?"

"I'm good, working mostly. How are you and the baby doing?" I ask genuinely interested. Anna has been on my mind a lot lately. That and other things.

"We are both well. Dylan and I found out we are having a girl!" she exclaims excitedly.

I laugh, she is so sweet. I am happy for her. "Oh, that is wonderful!"

"I miss you. We all do."

"I miss you too." I can't bring myself to think about anyone else. I swallow the lump down in my throat.

"Raphael said it would be okay I call you. I hope it is…. I was thinking we could have lunch sometime?"

I bite my lip, seeing her will make me miss…him. "It's fine you called. Lunch would be nice. I…I will have to check the schedule at work, I'll let you know."

"Oh, okay," she says, the disappointment wavers in her voice.

My eyes dart around, I can feel someone watching me. Is she here? Was she hoping that I would say yes to lunch and she would surprise me by being here already?

"I'll call, I promise," I suggest as encouragingly as I'm able to.

"Okay, I guess I'll talk to you later. Please call, even it is just to visit we don't have to go to lunch, I miss our talks."

"I will. Bye," I force the words out trying to end this before she hears the emotion in my voice. I tuck myself into a little ball. My talk with Anna made me realize just how much I miss her…them.

"Ahhhhh!" I stand gripping my hair and yell at the fountain. Why can't I forget them?

Dammit, why did I accept the phone. I grab my bag and head to the clinic, at least there I can quiet my mind. I keep my eyes lowered to the ground the entire walk. Curious Addy is gone, I don't care about the flowers, the birds, or anything for that matter. When I get inside the receptionist greets me warmly. "Hi, Addison, you have a patient in room four, we aren't very busy today…just one," she rattles off happily.

"Thank you Tina, sorry I'm a little late I had an unexpected phone call."

"It's okay they haven't been waiting long," she says going back to biting the end of her pen and staring at the book in front of her.

After dropping my bag off in the office, I head to exam room four. I'm reading over the information quickly as I walk in shutting the door. When I glance up at the patient, I stop dead in my tracks.

"Hello, Addison," Luis says standing.

I back up. The door halting my retreat. "What are you doing here?"

He doesn't answer but takes a step towards me. I reach for the doorknob behind me not getting to it before he grabs me and pulls me into his arms. I tremble in his embrace.

"Why are you so frightened?" he asks squeezing me tight.

"I can't do this."

"Do what? Accept a hug?" He leans back smiling down at me.

"Anna and now you, why are you guys doing this to me?"

He takes my hand and walks us over to the two chairs in the room. "Raphael called me. He is worried about you. He says you have not been talking at your therapy sessions."

"I don't have anything to talk about," I say haughtily keeping my eyes on my lap. I can't look at him, he looks too much like…him.

"Hm, I see. We hoped that you would have come to see us at the estate by now. It's been a month, Addy."

"Why would I come to the estate?"

"Why wouldn't you? Do you think something has changed?" He asks gripping my chin and turning my face towards him.

"Everything has changed, Luis, you know this," I whisper closing my eyes.

"No, nothing has changed except your attitude. That and the fact you no longer have to hide. So why are you? What are you hiding from?" He releases my chin since I refuse to open my eyes.

"I'm not hiding, obviously," I swirl my hand in front of my face.

"Maybe Dylan is right?" he says on a long breath, standing to leave.

"What do you mean he is right? Right about what?" What could Dylan know about my situation?

"That you need turned over someone's knee."

Abruptly I gaze up at him. "He wouldn't," I hiss.

Luis raises his eyebrows and shrugs his shoulders. "I don't know, Addison. You are acting like you could benefit from a good spanking. Don't be surprised if he doesn't show up here soon. We will not wait forever for you to come to your senses. We all miss you. We'll never give up on you. You are part of our family. I think you may have forgotten that." He opens the door and closes it behind him.

The rest of the day I fume over my conversation with Luis. Why are they acting like this? I've moved on, why haven't they? Have I moved on? No, not really. I'm just going through the motions. Eat, sleep, work. Clinic, therapy, hotel. My world. Grrrr, at least it's easy, what the fuck do they want from me?

I stomp my way to the square. I sit here until it gets dark each day. Here I watch people and pretend that I am normal. If I go to my room too early, I think too much. I toss my bag on the ground and perch on the fountain's edge and swivel staring up at the angel statue. This is my favorite place in the whole city. The angel stands tall in the middle. Her gown dips into a blue pool of water. Her palm is held out as if she is expecting something to land there…a bird, the hand of her lover, a coin. I squint up at her, the setting sun catching my eye. My heart stops. No!

I stand abruptly and trip over my bag. A gentleman grabs my arm steadying me. "Are you okay, Miss?"

Turning I stare at him, I'm at loss for words and then I nod my head. "Yes, yes, I'm fine thank you."

He releases me, tips his hat and continues on his journey. I glance back to the angel, there is something in her hand. I can't quite make it out, but it looks like a small figurine. I glance around and ponder over whether I should wade through the water to get to it. I chew my bottom lip. Fuck it, I kick off my shoes and roll my pants up high over my knees.

As I step in I turn to see if anyone is watching me, I feel a little silly. I'm a grown woman traipsing through a fountain in the middle of town. No one seems to pay much attention. Everyone is bustling in a hurry to get home to their families. When I get to the statue, I reach up and snag whatever it is and clutch it tightly. I trod as quickly as I can back to the edge.

I sit trying to control the rapid beating of my heart. Slowly I open my palm. My other hand instantly goes to my mouth to stop the squeal that just about erupted. It's a fairy, a baby fairy curled up on her stomach sleeping with her head laying on her cupped hands. Tears sting at the corners of my eyes and my chest aches. I wrap my hand around the beautiful little treasure and hold it to my heart. Only one person in the entire world knows about how my dad used to hide trinkets for me to find. Why are they bombarding me today? Why?

I stash the fairy in my bag, trying not to smile as I do. Perhaps I should call Anna. I sure don't want Dylan....or Liam showing up at my door wanting to punish me for acting like a petulant child. Have I been acting that way? I didn't think so, but…I guess I assumed they would all go on with their lives without me. I didn't realize they had been waiting for me. What *are* they waiting for?

Saving Addy

I grab my cell out of my pocket and stare at the little fairy that I set on the nightstand in my room. Taking a deep breath, I call the number Anna called me from earlier.

"Addy?" Dylan answers worry clear in his tone.

Shit. "Yes, it's me."

"It's good to hear your voice," he says the concern diminishing somewhat.

"I was just calling to tell Anna that I would be free on Friday if she still would like to have lunch."

"She would love that. She has missed you very much. She is asleep, but I will sure let her know and have her call you tomorrow to set up a time and place."

"Okay, thank you," I say softly. I want to ask for Luis's number, I want to ask about *him*....but, the knot in my throat is preventing it.

Dylan laughs. "Addy, are you worried about what Luis said to you? Is that why you called? I would never spank you. I hope you understand this. I said you needed one, on more than one occasion, but it is not my place."

"No, that is not why I called. Hm, I guess I was wondering why everyone ganged up on me today. I never expected to hear from anyone ever again. Then today when the three of them confronted me...well, I called because I didn't realize everyone was waiting and I didn't want to hurt Anna's feelings. Oh, I don't know Dylan," I say tossing myself backwards on my bed exasperated.

"The three of them?"

"Yes, it's just been overwhelming."

"Who besides Luis and Anna contacted you?" he asks.

I chew on my lip glancing at the little figurine on the stand. "Well, I don't know for certain, but I thought Liam left me something. I was mistaken…never mind."

"Have you seen Liam?"

"No. I haven't seen anyone but Luis," I reply as my voice rises. Why is he asking me these questions? He lives with these people does he not know? "Dylan, what are you not telling me about Liam?"

"Haaa, it's just he didn't return with me to the estate after Columbia. He said he needed time to think about things. He is okay, he checks in with Luis once a week, but he won't tell us where he is. We tried to find him but, being Mr. FBI, he is a little stealthy. Hey, I don't want you to worry about him, Addy. You said you thought he left you something? What was it? Why do you think it was him?"

I sit up straight on the bed. Has he been here the entire month…watching me? "Um, it's silly it was just a tiny figurine that was at a fountain I sit at. It could have been left by anyone, maybe a child lost it. Never mind, my mind got away from me. Hey, could you give me Luis's number? I think I would like to start my sessions up with him again."

"Addy, that is great news, I'll text the number to you. Luis and Anna are both going to be thrilled. I'm so glad you called," he says happily. "If…if you see Liam, tell him we miss him too. We miss you both. It's just not the same without you guys."

"Sure, of course. I'll talk to you later, Dylan."

"You bet your damn bottom you will. Addison, I told you that you couldn't run from us, that we are family and I meant that. We gave you space, but it's time, sweetheart…it's time. Sweet dreams, Addy," he says and then the phone goes dead.

I grab the little figurine as I walk to the window. It was Liam I know it was, has he really been near the entire time? Has he been watching over me? I broke his heart going to Javier. I assumed he would never want to see me again after that. My eyes roam across the landscape looking for him, nothing, only dark shadows. My gaze lifts to the moon, the same one that shines over Liam…wherever that may be.

I crawl back into bed and place the little fairy on the pillow next to mine and stare at it as I slowly fall asleep. My heart doesn't feel so empty tonight.

Liam

Something changed in her today. I've been looking over her for the past month, it's broke my heart. She has been in the same repetitive cycle, with no improvement in sight. What was disconcerting was that she had lost her spunk, her natural curiosity and fun-loving spirit. But, then I detected a change, a spark, a glimmer of hope that she wasn't lost.

She sits at the fountain every day. Briefly in the mornings as she drinks her coffee and then again after she leaves the clinic. The evenings she stays until dark encroaches on the city and then she hurries back to the hotel. I've rented a room down the hall from hers. It hasn't been hard to keep myself concealed. She never looks around her much. It has been tragic to watch.

Yesterday she pulled a cell phone out of her bag. She stared at it for a long time before answering. A little glimmer of a smile tugged at her lips but when she got off I could see that she was frustrated, sad, slightly angry.

But, it was something…it was emotion, which she had been void of since coming here. She screamed up at the angel fountain as if willing the winged creature to give her some direction…some comfort. She has someone, she doesn't need a statue. It's time she is reminded of that.

I didn't follow her to the clinic after that. I went on a mission. I have been waiting for this day not sure it would ever come. It is time. Excitement coursed through my veins. She is ready to see the magic again. She has to be.

Nervously I watched as she walked into the square after work. Her mood had definitely not improved, she was upset, angry. When she spotted my hidden treasure, she almost tripped and fell. Luckily a good Samaritan was near and caught her before she hit the pavement.

The look on her face as she stared at the angel was priceless. Slowly the glimmer of curiosity returned, and she waded through the fountain to get to it. It was the most beautiful thing I have ever witnessed. She stood on her tiptoes and thieved the item as quickly as she could. When she opened her palm, I saw the raw emotion spread across her features. She searched for me in the crowd but, I'm not ready to let her see me…yet. She needs a little magic. She needs to feel again and then I will reveal myself to her.

For a moment I worried that it might frighten her. I should have known better, she is strong. As she was hiding the fairy away in her bag, the corner of her mouth tipped into the beginning of a smile and my heart exploded. She is mine. She has always been mine.

I know why she left. I understand. At first I didn't, and I was angry that she didn't wait for us in Columbia. She thinks she has betrayed me, that going to Javier was being unfaithful to me. I would be lying if I said it didn't hurt, it did. But, the creature I saw in the red dress that day wasn't Addy, it was a warrior trying to save the man she loved.

I would do anything for her…anything. And, she will do anything for me…and she did. I know it was probably the hardest thing she has ever done. She risked *her*. She compromised her very soul stepping back into that dark world. I thought her spirit may had been lost to the devil, but it's there. She has just tucked it away for safekeeping, perhaps she wasn't even aware herself that it was still there…until today.

I'm looking forward to seeing her again tomorrow. Hopefully today allowed her to see herself.

She is still her dad's pixie and my angel.

Chapter Thirty-Three

Addy

I am greeted to the little fairy still sleeping on the pillow beside me. I jump up, allowing myself a bit...just a bit of happiness. It could be a coincidence but if it's not, then I will find out soon enough. I reach over and grab the cell phone off the nightstand and dial the number that Dylan sent to me.

"Addy, I am happy that you called," Luis's voice glides into my ear.

I chuckle nervously. "I...I um. I thought we could start our sessions up again. If that is okay, I mean if you have time."

"Yes, of course. I was roused this morning by one squealing, thrilled, pregnant lady. She told me to be watching for your call," he says laughing lightly.

"She is sweet, I love her," I reply hugging myself.

"And, she loves you. What made you change your mind? You were being quite the little brat yesterday."

"Ahh," I say nursing the stab to my pride.

He laughs again. "It's okay we all are sometimes. But, anyhow, why the change of heart?"

"I didn't realize that you all had been waiting. I assumed you all had gone back to your old lives...the ones pre-crazy Addy."

"Dylan told me Liam left you something. Is this true?"

I sigh loudly, of course Dylan would tell him. "It was probably just a coincidence. A child lost their toy at the fountain and I fantasied he left it for me. It was nothing, I didn't realize he has been missing."

"Well, he is not exactly missing. He calls me every Friday, but he doesn't say much. You both needed time, but I am happy that you are finally coming around. Maybe he will too."

"Maybe," I whisper.

We finish up our call making plans for him to come to lunch with Anna tomorrow. I have to admit I am excited to meet them and to talk to Luis. There have been many things bugging me lately, he is good at what he does, and it is easy for me to open up to him. One is my guilt over how I treated my uncle, Father Landon and Liam. I haven't talked about any of that to my new therapist. It isn't the same as talking to Luis.

The day goes as normal but as the end of the workday nears my fingers tingle and my pulse picks up. I'm nervous to go to the square. What if it was just a child's toy? Will I be disappointed? Yes, I will.

I walk slowly. When I get there my heart drops, the angel's hand is empty. You are so damn stupid. Why the fuck would you think Liam would want you back. I toss my bag on the ground and take my perch. I sulk and rest my chin on my fist. I consider calling Luis and cancelling lunch tomorrow.

The bell of a snow cone vendor dings. I glance up watching the elderly woman push her cart. She pauses in front of me, then opens the freezer and walks towards me with a cone. She hands it to me and then turns without a word. She winks at me and then shuffles along. I stare after her until the ding dwindles on the evening air.

The cold drip on my hand forces my eyes to return to the dripping treat. Stuck in the middle of blue ice is another trinket. It is a bracelet charm. A tiny little snowman with a carrot nose. I laugh and cry at the same time. It's him. It is really him! I jump up, my gaze sifts through the crowd, but he is nowhere. I pluck the charm out holding it tightly in my fist and lick furiously at the edge of the cone before I end up wearing it. My mind drifts to our conversations of messy foods, cold, snow, oh how I've missed him.

As I walk away from the square I can't help but be excited for tomorrow. It will be a good day, not only do I get to have lunch with Luis and Anna...Liam is here. Even if I don't see him, he is here.

Liam

I have to admit that this is fun, surprising Addy. This morning I gifted her with a bracelet for her charm. The girls at the coffee shop she visits each day were more than willing to help, they both giggled excitedly as she approached. I watched as one of them handed her the cup with the bracelet carefully wrapped around it. Addy's face lit up and again her eyes searched for me.

Saving Addy

As nice as it is to just follow her my body is craving hers. I've allowed myself to get a little closer and I'm definitely feeling the tug, our souls are connected. They always have been. I felt it the moment she stepped out of the car with Dylan and Anna that first day.

Usually she eats her lunch under a tree outside of the clinic but today she is heading back to the square. I hope she is not going home early. I have another surprise for her. Suddenly, she waves enthusiastically. I glance to where her attention is directed. My dad and Anna are at a little outdoor café.

I tuck myself alongside a building nearby to spy on them. My heart swells knowing she is with my family. Things are finally looking up.

"Thought you might be trolling in the vicinity," a deep voice rumbles. I laugh, this fucker. I turn to find my friend leaning up against the bricks behind me.

"Hmph, I guess I let my guard down." I step closer and wrap my arms around him slapping him hard on the back.

"Let's get a drink," Dylan says, and I follow him, glancing one last time towards the café. I catch Addy and Anna hugging each other tightly.

The bar down the street is bustling with patrons so we decide to sit outside in the beer garden. "So, you've been here the entire month?" he asks, cracking open his bottle and taking a long draw off it.

"Yep, I couldn't leave her, Dylan. Please don't be upset, I've given her space and left her alone." I tap my cap on the table waiting for the lecture to follow.

287

He sighs. "I don't blame you. I would have done the same if it had been Anna. Something tells me you aren't currently leaving her alone." He cocks an eyebrow at me.

I laugh. "She told you?"

"Yes, and no. She hadn't reached out to us. I convinced Raphael to give her a cell phone and Anna called her a couple of days ago. We got tired of waiting." He laughs. "Your dad also paid her a visit at the clinic which didn't go well, she was a little pissed over everyone ganging up on her. We didn't realize that you contacted her the same day."

"Hm, that is why she was so upset. It was the first moment I detected any emotion from her. So, I decided it was time. I left her a little fairy at the fountain in the square. I didn't know how she would react. Her dad used to hide things for her."

"It all makes sense now. She didn't know it was you for sure, but I could tell she had a good inclination it was. Very romantic, Liam." Dylan waves the waitress over and orders us another round. "So, when are you two coming home?"

I rub my hand over my beard. "However long it takes to win her back."

He nods. "She called your dad and asked to start their sessions up again so that is a good sign she is ready to move forward. Raphael said she hadn't been talking to the current therapist. Your little fairy did the trick, Liam, she contacted us after she found it."

"I'm nervous about seeing her. Leaving surprises is easy, fun but I realize that we need to talk at some point. I don't want to scare her off. I was pretty angry the last time I saw her. Punching a hole in the wall by her head was not the brightest thing I've ever done. I hope she is not afraid of me."

"Give it a little more time but don't wait too long. Anna is entering her final trimester and I would like it if you both were home before she delivers. Addy has a calming effect on her, it would be nice if she had her there for the birth."

"I'll see what I can do but I'm not a magician, Dylan. I can't make her take me back."

He laughs and slaps his knee. "You are an idiot sometimes, Liam. Has she been keeping your damn trinkets?"

"Yes."

"Well then, I expect she just might want you don't you think? Otherwise she would've left them or thrown them into the fountain."

"True."

"Christ, man, do what you got to do, try this sweet stuff. But, if she doesn't agree to come home…throw her over your shoulder, shove her in the trunk and get your ass back to the estate. We will go from there."

I laugh at his joke…at least I think it is a joke. "I hope it won't come to that but thanks. It's been good to see you."

Chapter Thirty-Four

Addy

As we finish up Luis agrees to walk me to the clinic so we can talk. Lunch went a little longer than we planned. Anna and I chatted the entire time and Luis barely got a word in. I scoot my chair back to rise and notice a shadow creep across the table. My gaze darts up, Dylan is looming over me.

"Hello, Addy," his deep voice glides over me. It briefly startles me. I'll never forget the first moment I laid eyes on him at the club. I shove the fear down. He is not who I thought he was back then.

"Hi," I say shyly bringing my cheek to my shoulder.

"So, when are you coming home?" he asks not fazed in the slightest by my obvious reaction to him.

"Oh, I don't know if..." I drop my head staring the floor.

His laugh rumbles and he tips my chin forcing my eyes to his. "I'm only teasing. I know you'll come home when you are ready."

Saving Addy

That sounded more like a demand than an offer. Do I want to go back? The thought hasn't occurred to me. Javier is dead there is no reason I couldn't. But, it is Liam's home and I don't know if....

"Let's go, Addison, or you'll be late to work," Luis says saving me from the awkward conversation.

Anna and Dylan both hug me and make me promise that I will call them tomorrow.

Luis and I walk hand in hand to clinic. I tell him about how the guilt has been gnawing at me at how I treated my uncle and Father Landon. He encourages me to reach out to them, offering to go with me to visit them in person.

When we arrive at the clinic, he pauses outside before saying goodbye. "Do you think Liam is here, Addy?"

I shrug my shoulders.

"You have been fiddling with that bracelet all afternoon. Is that another *something* that you found?"

I smile shyly. "Yes," I whisper.

He nods. "Liam loves you. I noticed it the first day you were with us." He pulls my wrist towards him and tips the little charm so he can see what it is. "A snowman?"

My grin gets wider. "We built a snowman together at the cabin." My face falls thinking about how I watched it melt as the flames danced around me.

"He must get it from his mother, she was a hopeless romantic." He smiles raising his eyes to the sky then dropping his gaze to meet mine again. "Addison, I want you to remember that there are many new memories to be made."

I nod and then head up the steps to the clinic. "I'll call tomorrow?"

"Yes, until then." He bows rolling his arm in front of him for flare and turns to walk down the sidewalk.

When I get inside Tina tells me we don't have any patients, so I make my way to the office and sit down going over the day's events. I guess I need to think about where I go from here. Does moving forward include Liam? Should I move back to the estate? The motel is lonely. But, does Liam want me there?

A knock on the door interrupts my thoughts. Raphael stands in the doorway looking at me with a shit-eating grin on his face. He takes the seat across from me never taking his eyes off of me. "So, I hear that you are leaving me, well us." He motions around the room.

"Um, no. I've made no decisions who told you that?" I furrow my eyebrows at him, the phoenix fluffs her feathers.

He nods his head slowly. "Addy, why are you staying here? You have so many people who love you. Don't worry about the clinic, I have someone to cover the shifts. They start tomorrow."

What? Tomorrow, what the fuck? "No, I've made no plans of leaving, please I'm not ready."

"Why?"

"For one I have nowhere to go, second I like it here."

Saving Addy

"You like sleeping in a hotel every night? You enjoy eating alone? Did you not get enough of that during your time with Oliver?"

His words force the air out of my lungs, and I jump up placing my hands firmly on the desk. "Why are you treating me this way?"

"Addison, you need to go home."

"Did Dylan set this up with you?"

"No, it was not him."

Hmph, it was someone but if not Dylan, who? No. It couldn't be. "Liam?"

Raphael stands as he speaks. "It does not matter who it was. Your time here is finished. Please come and visit, do not make yourself a stranger. You are a strong girl, in fact one of the strongest I have ever met. I kept them at bay to give you time, that is what you asked for but, you need to move on." He walks over, kisses me on the cheek and leaves.

I'm speechless, what the fuck just happened? What. Just. Happened? My perfect day is going right down the toilet. I was coming around. I agreed to lunch and to resume my sessions with Luis. Why would Liam do this? That's it, I will tell him, who does he think he is?

I grab my bag and pass by Tina and Raphael. He is leaning on the counter chit chatting with her. I stomp by telling them it was nice knowing them as I storm out letting the door slam shut behind me.

On the step I spot a feather, followed by another, by another. I glance down the sidewalk, a trail of feathers leads all the way down the cement path. I straighten my shoulders. Does he think this is cute? It's not. But, this could be useful, they better lead to him…because I am going to give him a piece of my mind.

The trail of feathers or trail of rage as I am calling it points to the observatory. A big sign says it is closed today for a private party. Hmph, smart, real bright leading me to a damn place that is closed. I notice a man walking towards me from inside, his eyes meet mine and he smiles. He opens the door and greets me. "Ms. Davis?"

"Yes," I stammer.

"Please right this way," he turns abruptly, expecting me to follow him.

So, I do. I shouldn't, but I do.

I'm angry and Liam is trying to woo me...bringing me here to the observatory to the place where day turns to night, he knows I love the night. Why be sweet and an asshole at the same time?

The man leads me into a large dark room. He has a dim light with him so we can see where we are walking. It feels empty, the same empty I have felt for the past month. I notice the stars illuminating the ceiling, they provide little light, actually none at all. He instructs me to wait in the center of the room and then he turns to leave.

I want to argue or perhaps chase after him. Now that I'm faced with the imminent possibility of seeing him...I don't know if I am ready. I see the light from the door as he opens it, his frame stepping outside and then black...except the tiny lights on the dome ceiling. Suddenly I hear a click and even the faux stars disappear. I'm surrounded by nothing but darkness. My heavy breathing and the drum of my heart thumping against my ribcage is the only thing breaking the silence.

Until....

"You told me once you wanted me to treat you like a normal girl. Do you remember?" A gravelly voice says from the dark.

"Oh shit," I yelp grabbing my chest. His voice sent a shiver of fear through me but, also something else.

"Well, do you remember?"

"Yes," I whisper.

"Take off your clothes."

What the…hot breath brushes over the back of my neck. A hand weaves through my hair tugging at the tight bun upon my head, gently yanking it. The loose strands fall around my shoulders. And then his touch is gone but I sense he is near.

"What are you waiting for?" he asks in that seductive tone of his, the one that has visited me in my dreams the past few nights.

Hm, I was going to give him a piece of my mind but the sound of a zipper a few feet from me sends me obeying his orders. I rip my shirt over my head, push my pants down but hesitate…what if someone walks in?

As if reading my mind, he answers my question. "No one will enter. It's just you….and me. Nothing more, nothing less. No distractions, nothing."

I shiver and kick my shoes off. I shove my pants the rest of the way down and clutch my pile of clothes closely to my chest. What am I doing? This is crazy, maybe he is still angry. Will he punish me? He was so sweet the last few days, but this is different, a different side of him. No, that's not true, I saw it at the cabin. I asked for it. I wanted more of it but, why is he giving it to me now? Surely he is afraid that I'll run away. Hands brush mine as he takes my clothes from me. How the fuck does he know where I am, how can he see me?

"Are you frightened?"

"Yes."

"Why?" warmth whispers over my face.

"Are you angry with me?" I ask on a shaky breath.

"No, no, I'm not angry, Addy." His hand glides down my cheek and drops to my throat, gripping it lightly, his thumb brushing back and forth over my sensitive skin. My stomach clenches…that and other areas of my anatomy. "Did you enjoy my gifts?"

"Yes, thank you," I lean forward suddenly feeling like I might fall over. I can't tell what is up, down, sideways, there is nothing to hold on to but the darkness and him. My hands land on his hard-muscular chest and a groan sneaks out from between my lips.

He laughs lightly and the air escaping him ruffles the top of my hair. "I'm glad you liked them. Now no more talking, we are going to get familiar with each other again. Do you understand?"

When I hesitate to answer he bites my earlobe warning me into a reply. "Yes, I understand."

He turns me away from him, his erection pressing into my back. His warm mouth roams over my neck. Oh, fuck this is hot, so damn hot. This is the bad boy Liam, the one I caught glimpses of. He bends me forward instructing me to hold my ankles, and he grips my waist tightly. His fingers glide over my spine, his nails lightly raking over my skin. He smacks my ass. The sound echoing through the empty darkness.

"Shittttt…." I hiss pushing back and rubbing against his naked thigh.

Saving Addy

He smacks the other cheek drawing another expletive from my throat. His hand snakes up my spine grabbing a fistful of my hair pulling my head up harshly and into his chest. He whispers in my ear, "I said no talking."

He pushes me forward again and delves between my legs. His fingers trail along me sending shivers somersaulting across my skin. "You like this don't you, Addy?"

I don't answer. He told me not to speak. I will not disappoint him again. He laughs. "Good girl." Excitement courses through me at his words and I offer a smile to the dark.

Two fingers slide into me, my breath catches in my throat. I'm trying to keep quiet, but he is making it extremely difficult. Back and forth, in and out he lulls me to that wonderful place. Just as I think I am reaching the summit, yes, yes, he tears away from me. Argh, no.

He pulls me to a standing position, turns me to face him and gently but forcefully pushes me down urging me to my knees in front of him. My fear rises, everything until now has been unfamiliar but this, unfortunately this is too familiar. His voice rains down upon me and his fingers glide into my hair tugging me forward. I allow my hands to roam up his muscular thighs, focusing on his voice and his scent. He is mine, this is my Liam. My blond haired, blue eyed Liam. Mine.

I suck him into my mouth gripping the base of him tightly. I tease him with my tongue and his fist tightens in my hair. He moans loudly. Yes, mine all mine. Mine to tease, mine to taste. I killed a man for him…and I would do it all again. Suddenly he pushes me from him, and I totter onto my bottom.

He is on his knees, grabbing my throat to gently lay me on my back. The cold floor takes my breath away. His warm mouth is on me, his tongue darting quickly in all the right spots. Fingers push into me forcefully causing me to arch off the floor like a woman possessed. He is no longer instructing me to keep quiet as I moan and speak in a foreign tongue, one he seems to recognize. His exorcism of my body intensifies until the devil is thrust from my body and I yell out to the darkness that is swallowing my demons.

He pulls me into his lap guiding me to straddle him, the hair on his chest tickling my breasts. He kisses me hard, our tongues greeting each other, becoming reacquainted. A moan rumbles from deep inside him and I swallow it. Mine. He is mine. His cock glides between my wet folds, ah, fuck, yes. I rise high on my knees and his fingers dig hard into my hips. He holds me suspended over him for a long moment. The sound of our harsh breathing resonates through the empty space. Even though the room is draped in darkness, we stare into each other's soul.

He pushes me hard onto him and I throw my head back crying out his name. His head delves between my breasts and his hand roams up my back holding me tight against him. His tongue snakes up, licking, biting, he continues to pound into me as I hold myself still over him. Oh. Fuck. Oh. Fuck. Yes. Yes. White light strikes like a lightening bolt in my skull. My light…he is my light. I fall into him, into his safe arms, into my home.

Not relinquishing his hold on me we stay linked for a long time. My head resting on his shoulder. I want to cry. I want to tell him everything, all that has happened between this moment and the one where Javier ripped us apart. But, I can't find any words…none.

"Let's go home, angel," he whispers into my ear stroking the back of hair, easing me into the idea. I was so angry when I came here, mad that he was making decisions for me. Now, that I'm in his arms I grasp that my anger has dissipated. I will go wherever this man wants me to. Nothing has changed and yet everything has.

Saving Addy

He must accept my silence as an answer, I guess there was really no question in the statement. He pushes me off his lap and hands me my pile of clothes. We dress in the dark and then magically the stars twinkle down upon us once again. I still cannot see him, but the lights at least give me something to focus on other than the darkness.

When he shoves the door, the light blinds me for a brief second. Once outside in the fresh air, I tug at his hand and he stops turning to gaze down at me. I lift my eyes to his and the weightlessness returns. He stares at me running his thumb over my cheek. He smiles, and that little dimple greets me. I nod my head and we continue to his car. When he opens it, I glance in the backseat and see he already has my bags.

We don't speak the entire drive to the estate. He holds my hand and now and then he pulls our hands up to his lips and places tiny kisses on my knuckles. Nervously I watch out the window, this is happening very fast. I'm returning to a place I never thought I would see again. To be with people, I never thought I would be with again.

He lets go of me as we get about twenty minutes away. He pulls his phone out and I listen quietly as he speaks to his Dylan. "We are on our way home, can you let the others know that we need a few days alone?" He glances over at me and I turn from him to watch the world slide by. "Yes, in my room. Okay, thanks, man. See you soon."

He takes my hand again and I stare at our intertwined fingers. When we arrive at the estate, no one comes out to greet us. He parks and grabs our bags. The halls echo with our footsteps. I turn to go towards my suite, but he grips my hand forcefully and tugs me down the hall to his.

He sets the bags down and scoops me up in his arms carrying me over the threshold. When he closes the door, the sound of the bolt resonates through my head. I spin slowly and crumble to the floor a sobbing mess.

He pulls me into his lap, letting me cry. He kisses my tears away and gently rubs his hands over my entire body. "I'm so sorry, I'm so sorry," I sob frantically.

"Shh, you have nothing to be sorry for, angel."

I push his chest hard sitting myself up. "I'm not an angel, Liam. Please don't call me that anymore, I'm not her…he killed whatever you thought you saw, it's gone."

"No, no, it's not, Addy. I've watched you and the last couple of days I see her, she is not gone. You. You are not gone. You have had so much taken from you, don't let them have this too. Yes, you are different. I am different. *We* are different but, it doesn't make us less….it makes us so much more. You are more. You saved me, Addy, I understand why you did what you did. Do you understand why I did what I did at the cabin?"

"Yes," I say pathetically wiping at tears with both of my hands.

"We…" he motions his hand between us. "We are stronger because of what happened, not weaker."

I tuck myself up under his chin and stroke my fingers over his beard, tears still falling from my eyes. "I killed him."

"I know, angel. I know. You did good, you did what you had to."

Liam

After having a beer with Dylan, I knew I had to get us home. I had several days of surprises planned for her, but I couldn't wait. So, I decided on a plan that would connect us much quicker and it worked. I have never been more nervous in my life. Would I scare her? Would she run away? Would she fight me and if she did what would I do? Would I shove her in my trunk against her will like Dylan suggested?

Luckily it went well. She was frightened. Very frightened. But, that invisible connection, that cord that strums between our souls sent out a vibration she couldn't ignore. Hottest sex I've ever had, hottest and to be honest the most meaningful. Our reconnection was more than just sex. It was our apology to each other, an understanding that this is more than her and I can control.

Has she been holding all this in for the last month? Maybe I should have reached out to her sooner, yes, I definitely should have. Raphael had me believing that she needed time. I thought she was truly frightened of me after the incident at Javier's, but I think she has been worried about betraying me. I don't see it that way. I wish she didn't either.

Dylan knocks bringing us a tray for dinner. I open the door for him, and he steps inside. "Mrs. Cortez is not a happy camper you both are not making an appearance. I promised her that if you don't come out within two days, she has my permission to drag you both out by your ears."

He sits down by Addy on the bed much to her chagrin. She tries to scoot away but he places his arm around her and pulls her close to him. I laugh picking up the lids off of the platters he carried in. "Damn, I have missed her cooking. Why don't you let go of my girlfriend and go find your wife?" I peek up to catch Addy's tiny smirk.

He grunts and kisses her forehead releasing her. "I've missed her, Liam. You can't keep her all to yourself you know. She is like a sister to me." He pats her leg and she offers him a shy smile in return. Dylan and I exchange a meaningful glance, one of sadness for the loss of Sophia but of joy for having Addy. It is a powerful cocktail. Life has a funny way of turning out. Just when you think you have no reason to go on a new day begins and sometimes it gives you something you didn't even realize you were missing.

Saving Addy was so much more than we ever expected.

The End

Epilogue

Addy

It's been a little over two months and I don't know if I have ever been happier. Life on the estate is wonderful. There is always something to do and someone to talk to. My captivity had to be a precursor to my existence here. It has made me appreciate everyone and everything.

Dylan comes running down the hall sliding to a stop before me. I laugh and grab his hand dragging him with me. "Just in time, daddy," I say handing him a pair of green scrubs. "Wash your hands and come to the room at the end of the hallway. We are all set up."

Liam is waiting outside the door. He must not have been far behind Dylan. "How is she?"

"Good, make sure he gets washed up." I tip my head towards the room Dylan is changing in. "She is in the last door on the left. In case his brain has already forgotten my instructions."

I give him a quick peck and return to Anna. When I open the door the midwife Anna hired looks up from between her legs. "It won't be long," she says.

Anna stares at me with a distressed look on her face, I walk over and brush her hair out of her face. "He is here, just washing up, hon. It's all going to be okay they made it back from the job in time," I say softly, gazing into my best friend's sapphire eyes.

Dylan opens the door hesitantly. "Come on, get your ass over here," I encourage gruffly.

He walks over to the opposite side of the bed nervously and runs his big hands over her cheeks. "I'm here, baby."

After another grueling hour of screams, grunts, pushing, and cursing Dylan and Anna's bundle of joy makes her appearance. I've witnessed several births in my career, but this was the most beautiful one I have ever seen.

There is something about witnessing your godchild come into the world. I make a promise to the tiny creature right then and there that I will show her as much good, as much magic as I can. Starting with her first gift, the little baby fairy that Liam left for me in the hand of an angel.

I smile at the bundle in my arms. I peek back at mom and dad. Anna is sleeping and Dylan's large body is carefully perched on the edge of the narrow bed beside her holding her tightly. He nods at me and I turn to leave the room to show Liam our new goddaughter.

When I open the door, I find him sitting across the hall on the floor his head in his hands. He jumps up when he sees me. I smile at him. He wraps his arm around me looking over my shoulder at the tiny bundle in my arms. "Isn't she beautiful," I whisper.

"She is the most beautiful thing I've ever seen besides the beautiful angel holding her." He runs his finger over the baby's cheek then over her miniature hand, she opens her fist and grabs hold of him. He laughs lightly. "What is her name?"

I look over my shoulder into his blue, soulful eyes. "Sophia," I whisper.

He smiles at me and drops his gaze back to her. "Hi Sophia," he says in the cutest voice, his dimple making a grand appearance.

My eyes tear. He is the most amazing thing that has ever happened to me and he is mine.

All mine.

~~~

Several months later here we sit in the chapel. Liam and I, the pudgy-faced baby resting in my arms. We watch as Dylan and Anna recite their vows to each other. I pull my hand out from under the blanket and peek at the engagement ring on my finger. Liam proposed in the garden two days ago. We haven't told anyone but Dylan and Anna. He notices me admiring the beautiful stone that is set in a pair of tiny wings and squeezes me tight. He places a kiss on my temple and leans over dropping one on Sophia's head.

My eyes roam the church. So many familiar faces. I reflect to the day I didn't want to enter this building. The feelings of unworthiness had plagued me almost to the point of paralysis. So much has changed since then, I am stronger. No, I think I have always been strong. I've made it through whatever life has thrown at me.

I'm so lucky that these people saved me and not only that, they made me a part of their family. After the service is over Liam takes Sophia from me and I help Anna with her dress. She instructs all the ladies to gather at the bottom of the church steps. She is about to throw the bouquet. To keep appearances, I join the other girls but stand off to the side of the group slightly.

She leans back her sapphire eyes sparkling brightly in the sun and tosses the beautifully wrapped arrangement over her shoulder. It heads right for me, but I dodge just in time. Anthony gracefully reaches out over my head snagging it.

"Why did you duck? You little shit," he says grinning down over the top of me. "You are next in line you know," he teases holding out the flowers for me to take.

I hold my hand up to show him the ring on my finger and his eyes open wide in surprise. Luis and Mrs. Cortez cheer in delight as they watch the exchange.

Liam comes up beside me. "Looks like you are just going to have to keep it, maybe *you* are next, Anthony." He laughs and pushes it back into his chest.

Anthony stammers but holds up the bouquet triumphantly. "About time I get something." He grins. "I guess you never know.

LM Terry

About the Author

LM Terry is the upcoming dark romance novelist of Finding Anna, Saving Addy and Discovering Danielle. She has spent her life in the Midwest, growing up near a public library which helped fuel her love of books. With most of her eight children grown and with the support of her husband, she decided to follow her heart and begin her writing journey. In searching for that happily ever after, her characters have been enticing her to share their sinfully dark, delectable tales. She knows the world is filled with shadows and dark truths and is happy to give these characters the platform they have been begging for. She is currently working on fourth novel Death and Daffodils.

Facebook: https://www.facebook.com/lmterryauthor/

Website: https://www.lmterryauthor.com

Saving Addy

Made in the USA
Monee, IL
10 August 2020

37760219R00187